Small Miracles

OLIVIA ATWATER

Chapter One

It was eight o'clock on a Wednesday morning when the Fallen Angel of Petty Temptations walked into a quaint café on the north end of Church Street. There were lace curtains in the windows, and a collection of ferns hung in between the low pendant lights over the small, round tables. It was the sort of café that attracted writers and thinkers—those who would gladly set up shop for hours at a time—though typically, there were still only a few tables occupied. Today, unlike most Wednesday mornings at eight o'clock, there was a substantial queue curving through the bistro tables. Gadriel had never seen the place actually *busy* before.

Easy to overlook, Gadriel had the appearance one would expect from the Fallen Angel of Petty Temptations—that is, not at all special. Her short hair was a plain shade of brown—neither too light nor too dark—and her eyes were the same boring shade, set into a perfectly unobjectionable face. Her height was on the upper end of average, but she carried herself as if she were much taller, such that she had an awkward, gangly look about her. The awkwardness was only amplified by her out-of-fashion trousers and by the sleeveless argyle knitted vest she wore over a white buttoned shirt. All in all, her fashion sense was not the most appealing… but she was *terribly* comfortable, and that was what mattered.

Gadriel was, in all respects, the sort of woman whom one would call 'very pleasant', but also 'very forgettable'—which might explain why none of the café patrons paid her any attention as she studied the customers one-by-one, searching for the man she was supposed to meet there. When the face that Gadriel sought failed to materialise, however, she sighed to herself and joined the unusually long queue in front of the counter.

At the front of this backed-up queue, there was a man—the handsome, fast-talking, sharp-dressed sort who'd likely sinned his fair share already that morning. Said gentleman was currently paralysed with indecision. He stared at the menu board with a slight wrinkle between his brows, shifting from one foot to the other. Before him, the barista at the counter looked on with a brittle customer service smile. Behind him, a woman in line groaned softly.

This had clearly been going on for some time.

"Hm," said the man in front of the counter. The sound had an unusual weight—a *gravitas*, if you would. It made the gentleman's agony over his morning coffee seem deep and meaningful. And perhaps it was a deep and meaningful decision on some level, given what Gadriel knew of the human soul.

But either way, Gadriel wanted a bloody coffee.

The fallen angel sighed heavily. "Just buy the expensive one, won't you?" she said. "It's only an extra quid, you nitwit."

Instead of shouting it across the café, Gadriel used what she liked to call her *inside voice*, which meant that the words came out more like:

"Just buy the more expensive one, won't you? It's only an extra quid, you nitwit."

No one else reacted to Gadriel's comment—none of them could hear it—but the man at the front of the queue nodded decisively to himself. The trick, Gadriel had found, was to make the words sound like something a mortal might say to themselves in private.

"I think I'll have the chai latte after all," the man at the counter told the barista. As he said the words, a great tension left his shoulders; a recognition that he had conquered one more minor existential dilemma in the due course of his human life.

"With extra whipped cream," Gadriel added. "You might as well."

"Could you do extra whipped cream on that?" the man added quickly.

As the man at the counter finished paying and stepped aside, a tall Black woman in an exceptionally tailored beige suit stepped into line just next to Gadriel. Her black, curling hair was closely cropped, accentuating the dramatic contour of her head and her neck. Her eyes were dark and intense, set above broad lips which curved with ever-present amusement. She was, in many respects, all of the things which Gadriel was not—that is, she was impeccably dressed, strikingly beautiful, and nearly impossible to ignore. Her name was Barachiel. She was, among other things, the Angel of Good Fortune, the Chief of Guardian Angels, and a regular thorn in Gadriel's backside.

"Good morning," Barachiel said cheerfully.

Gadriel narrowed her eyes. "No," she said. "No, absolutely not. I *told* you I was going to be a woman today. That means you're obliged to change and not me."[1]

If Barachiel was at all flustered by the obvious faux pas, then the emotion didn't show upon her face. She glanced innocently at Gadriel, clasping her wrists behind her back. "And here I thought you weren't very fond of rules," she said.

Gadriel scowled. "It's not about *rules*," she said. "It's about style."

Barachiel swept her eyes silently from Gadriel's head down to her feet. She didn't *say* anything, of course—proper angels liked to pretend that they were more polite than the opposition. But her expression clearly implied her scepticism that Gadriel could ever be considered *stylish*.

"Ah, well," Barachiel mused. "If you say so." She stayed right next to Gadriel, however, and it soon became obvious that she had no intention whatsoever of slinking out the door to change

---

1   Angels do not actually have genders. Or rather, they *do* have genders—but these genders are inexpressible to human beings, who tend to lose track somewhere after the fifth wing and the tenth burning wheel. As such, when said beings divine descend with the intent of having a coffee, they choose a more human-looking gender for the day in rather the same way that you and I might choose a shirt and trousers. This minor sleight-of-hand makes it possible for baristas to ask the question *And what can I get for you today,* instead of babbling incoherently.

But—as with any fashion choice—there is always the danger that one might end up at a luncheon wearing exactly the same gender as the friend with whom one is meeting. This is considered both gauche and embarrassing.

her gender.

"You are… infuriating," Gadriel muttered tightly.

Barachiel ignored Gadriel, peering over the fallen angel's head to consider the queue in front of the counter. "Well, look at that!" she said. "That whipped cream's put Mr Indecisive in a cheerful mood, hasn't it? I think he just left a few quid to pay for the woman behind him. How generous."

Gadriel whipped her head around to look, just in time to see the man with the chai latte strolling for the door with a smile on his face and a spring in his step. As he passed, the man whistled softly to himself.

Gadriel calculated numbers quickly in her head. As she finished her arithmetic, she stifled a groan. "I've put him into the positives, haven't I?" she muttered.[2]

Barachiel nodded. "Quite likely," she said. "And my goodness—you've moved the line along as well! Splendid news. Poor Becca up there was having a terrible morning, but things are really starting to look up for her. She's having troubles at home, you know, and every little bit helps." Barachiel jerked her chin towards the barista, who was looking very relieved indeed at the slowly shortening queue.

Gadriel glanced sideways at Barachiel. "Becca?" she repeated sourly. "On a first name basis, are you? I thought you were middle management now. You're not supposed to be anyone's *personal* guardian angel, are you?"

---

2   Buying the most expensive option out of gluttony is worth at least a quarter point of sin. Heartfelt acts of generosity, no matter how small, always add a full point of virtue to the tally.

Barachiel shrugged elegantly. "I'm allowed to make small talk with my regular barista," she said.

Gadriel raised one sceptical eyebrow.

Barachiel smiled. "I can't help it if I'm naturally curious. And Becca says I give good advice."

Gadriel shook her head. "One of these days, you're going to discover a rule so silly that you finally decide to break it outright," she said. "I look forward to it."

Barachiel frowned at that. It was an old argument of theirs—the Oldest Argument, in many respects. But Barachiel despised arguments, and so she diverted the subject instead of rising to the bait. "You've inspired something, Gadriel," she said. "The next customer just paid for the woman behind *her*, as well."[3]

Gadriel closed her eyes and sucked in a breath. "For the record," she said. "I hate you."

Barachiel laughed. It was a rich, pleasant laugh from deep in her chest—the sort which made you feel instantly warm and at ease. "I didn't do anything," she said. "Honestly, I often wonder if you botch the job on purpose."

Gadriel opened her eyes to fix Barachiel with a withering stare. "Perhaps neither of us knows the other quite so well as we'd like to believe," she said flatly.

Barachiel deflected that stare with another warm smile. "We could always find out," she proposed.

It was at this point that Gadriel realised Barachiel had started

---

3   Inspiring good deeds in others gains one half the value of the action so inspired. In this respect, particularly contagious good deeds can be compared to pyramid schemes.

shuffling an ornate deck of cards from hand to hand. The cards were long and thin—made of a sturdy, flexible material which most mortals would have mistaken for cardboard. Gadriel, who could see in several extra dimensions, knew that Barachiel preferred playing with fate.

Barachiel offered out the deck to Gadriel—who leaped backwards with a soft hiss of alarm.

Barachiel smiled innocently. "Why don't you pick a card?" she asked.

Gadriel eyed the gold-trimmed cards as though they were a cobra within striking distance. "The last time I touched that deck," she declared, "I played three hands and lost my metaphorical shirt."[4]

Barachiel assessed Gadriel's knitted vest critically. "You *could* do with a fashion update," she observed helpfully.

Gadriel wasn't fond of Barachiel's cards on the best of days—they were bossy, they knew too much, and they had a tendency to be smug about it. And while Gadriel was absolutely certain that angels weren't allowed to stack the deck, she had of late begun to wonder whether the deck was allowed to stack *itself.*[5]

Gadriel narrowed her eyes. "Stash the cards," she said. "Let's just get our business over with, shall we?"

Barachiel tilted her head thoughtfully. There was a spark of mischief in her dark eyes. "You could always try for double or

---

4   Gadriel's metaphorical shirt was a tatty old Beatles band shirt. One might therefore argue that her metaphorical fashion sense was even more out-of-date than her literal fashion sense.

5   It was allowed, and it often did.

nothing," she offered.

As temptations went, it was a fairly good attempt. But Gadriel was *very* familiar with temptations, thank you very much.

"No," Gadriel said emphatically. "No more bets. No more wagers. No more… *cards.*" The recollection sent a shudder through her. "I'm deep enough in debt with you already. So just tell me which favour you want this time, and I'll be off to do your bidding." Under her breath, she added: "I never learn. Ought to know better than to play cards with the Angel of *Gamblers.*"

"I am *not* the Angel of Gamblers," Barachiel protested. "I can't help it if they keep praying to me."

"Miss?" the barista at the counter called out timidly. "Er, miss? Could I take your order, please?"

Gadriel and Barachiel were the last ones in the queue.

Barachiel waved a hand at Gadriel, dismissing the argumentative tone between them once again. "Let's discuss over coffee," she said with a winning smile. "I'll pay."

Gadriel slouched after her, sulking. As Barachiel put in her order, Gadriel said spitefully: "GET THE ONE WITH CHOCOLATE."

Chocolate was always worth at least half a point of sin, and there was rarely any resistance to the temptation. It was the low-hanging fruit of sins—but Gadriel surmised she'd earned a bit of pettiness.

"I'll have the mocha please, Becca," Barachiel said pleasantly. "Oh—with extra chocolate, if you don't mind."

Gadriel shot a satisfied smile at the barista. "I'll have the same, thanks," she said.

It was only after they'd retrieved their drinks and settled into a corner table that an unpalatable thought occurred to Gadriel, souring her mood further.

"You let me have that one," she accused Barachiel.

Barachiel took a long sip of her very syrupy coffee. "You seemed like you could do with a pick-me-up," she said.

"Hm," Gadriel muttered. She slouched down into her seat. "Heartfelt act of generosity, that. Probably earned yourself extra points with the boss. Wanker."

"Is that a bad thing?" Barachiel asked. "I know you don't approve of the system—"

Gadriel scoffed. That was an understatement. Given the chance, she could rage for millennia about *the system*.

"—yes, I *know*," Barachiel sighed, holding up a hand. "We both know I can recite your rant from memory. *Chocolate shouldn't be a sin at all. Everyone deserves a bit of chocolate.* And then you'll say—"

"It's utterly ridiculous!" Gadriel burst out. The words slipped free before she could contain them. She threw up her hands, only narrowly avoiding the coffee cup she'd left on the edge of the table. "Did you know that taking the *last* piece of chocolate is worth an entire extra point of sin? What's the reasoning, I ask you? If no one *ever* takes the last bit of chocolate, then we'll have chocolate going in the bin for no reason! And binning food is a full point as *well*, so what's the solution there?"

Barachiel sighed and leaned back in her chair, waiting patiently.

Gadriel slammed her palm onto the table in front of her, unable to stop the torrent of irrational fury. "Have I told you about the—"

"—yes, the Cynics," Barachiel said. "The ones in Ancient

Greece."[6]

"Your boss probably loved them," Gadriel said sulkily. "They're exactly the sort who'd never eat chocolate at all, even if you offered it to them. Perfectly miserable people."

Barachiel nodded politely, but Gadriel knew that she'd probably exhausted the angel's attention span on the subject sometime last century, if not well before then.

Gadriel sucked in a deep breath all the same, preparing herself for Part 1.1.2 of her rant ("Regarding the Proper Disposal of Sweets"). But this time, Barachiel shot the fallen angel an exceedingly pleasant smile and opened her mouth to interrupt.

"I agree with you, you know," said Barachiel.

Gadriel closed her mouth with an audible *snap*. She stared at the angel, caught halfway between suspicion and satisfaction.

"I agree with you… *somewhat*," Barachiel amended herself. "At least as far as the chocolate is concerned. I've been thinking on the matter for the last century. I've come to believe that a little bit of sin is good for the soul—in moderation, of course." She sipped thoughtfully at her mocha. "Which is precisely why I think you're the best candidate for this job."

Suspicion abruptly overwhelmed satisfaction. Gadriel narrowed her eyes. "And… which job would *that* be, Barachiel?" she asked slowly.

---

6   The Cynics of Ancient Greece were an ascetic subset of the Stoics, particularly well-known for preaching self-sufficiency and the abandonment of earthly possessions. Many thousands of years later, the mere mention of Diogenes could still send Gadriel into fits of apoplexy.

Barachiel smiled, folding her hands together in front of herself. "I only want you to do what you do best," she assured Gadriel. "There's a mortal woman—Holly Harker. She has one of the lowest Cumulative Sin Metrics I've ever seen. Truly, she must be even more miserable than a Greek Cynic." Barachiel raised an eyebrow at Gadriel. "I want you to tempt her. Not *too* much, obviously. Just… enough to make sure she's enjoying her life."[7]

Gadriel eyed Barachiel carefully. "You're serious?" she asked. "You want me to—"

"—to do what you do best," Barachiel agreed. "I'd hazard, oh… twenty net points or so should do the trick." She lifted one well-manicured finger towards Gadriel in a display of imperious warning. "But Miss Harker only needs to sin a *little* bit, Gadriel. If you overshoot and get her damned, I will consider you even deeper in my debt than before. Understood?"

Barachiel picked up her cards again, shuffling them idly from hand to hand.

"Hm," said Gadriel. Doubt dripped from the sound. "That's

---

7   The angels in the accounting department define the Sin Metric thusly:

For every soul, let the Sin Metric be defined as a function of time, intentions, and actions of said soul. Let positive numbers be associated with sinful actions and negative numbers be associated with virtuous actions.

The Cumulative Sin Metric is therefore defined as the integral of the Sin Metric over time.*

*For a detailed infinite-sized matrix of recorded actions, please submit the appropriate prayers to Saint Peter.

it, then? I get this mortal to eat a bit of chocolate, nick a few flowers from her neighbour's garden… and then my debts are repaid?"

"That's it," Barachiel said cheerfully.

Though they were no longer on the same side, Gadriel and Barachiel had always considered themselves siblings. Oh, there had been an initial adjustment period following Gadriel's Fall— but there had never been any *real* animosity between them. Unlike many of her contemporaries in Hell, Gadriel wasn't out to wreck the world or doom humanity. In fact, for all of its foibles, she rather *liked* humanity. She just thought it deserved, well… better.

Perhaps the road to Hell *had* been paved with good intentions, as far as Gadriel was concerned. But she liked to think that Barachiel appreciated those intentions, even if the angel disagreed with her conclusions.

"It… *sounds* simple enough," Gadriel said slowly.

"Oh yes," said Barachiel. "Simple enough for *you*, surely."

"Surely," Gadriel mumbled. Still… she had the peculiar notion that this must be what a moth felt like when confronted with a lovely bright light. She *wanted* to believe that it was all just a convenient arrangement—but she also knew from experience that Barachiel always came out ahead, no matter the stakes. There was a reason that gamblers prayed to the angel, after all.

The gilded cards flickered back and forth between the angel's hands.

"So?" Barachiel asked. "We have a deal?"

The question was really just a formality, and they both knew it. Gadriel owed a debt, and Barachiel had called it in. The angel was being more charitable about it than she really needed to be; she could have handed Gadriel a far more challenging assignment. A bit of petty temptation was perfectly within her wheelhouse. Ideally, it wouldn't take very long at all.

"Yes, all right," Gadriel answered with a sigh.

Barachiel grinned. The cards stilled in one hand, and she offered them out to Gadriel again.

"Oh no," Gadriel said quickly. "I'm not falling for that again." She leaned back in her seat, trying to put as much distance as possible between herself and that accursed deck.

"I'm not offering a wager this time," Barachiel assured her. "I just thought you might want to take a peek at what's ahead."

Gadriel frowned. "Well, *obviously* I'm going to pull the Devil," she said. "I'm about to go and tempt someone."[8]

Barachiel arched an eyebrow. "I'd ask if you want to bet on it… but I suspect I know the answer." She flicked the top card off of the deck, offering it out encouragingly. "Go on. Aren't you curious?"

Against her better judgement, Gadriel reached for the top card. The deck didn't bite or burn her; she wasn't magically ensnared or teleported far away. But when Gadriel looked at the card she'd drawn, she sighed heavily all the same.

"Well?" Barachiel prompted. "Which one is it?"

Gadriel shot Barachiel a sour expression. She flipped the card around to show it to the angel.

The system may have needed work… but the boss still had

---

8   Gadriel has always had a great deal of sympathy for the Devil card. Naturally, she believes that the card has a poorly deserved reputation.

a sense of humour.

"The Wheel of Fortune?" Barachiel murmured. "Oh dear. And you swore you'd never gamble again, Gadriel."[9]

Gadriel flicked the card at the angel's head with a deep, dark scowl. She rose wordlessly from the table and strolled for the door, leaving Barachiel alone in the café.

---

9   The Wheel of Fortune represents an inevitable change in fortunes. In Barachiel's deck, it's also a literal roulette wheel.

Chapter Two

CUMULATIVE SIN METRIC (HOLLY HARKER): -932

Somewhere near the south end of Church Street, Gadriel realised she had forgotten an important detail.

"Bother," Gadriel muttered to herself. "Where *is* Holly Harker?"

She looked back in the direction from which she'd come. The idea of slinking back inside to confront Barachiel's amusement didn't terribly appeal. Technically, Gadriel had the angel's phone number—it was in her contacts under the name 'Bookie'—but Barachiel answered her texts about as reliably as she answered gamblers' prayers.[10]

"Surely, Harker's not *too* far," Gadriel mumbled. "Barachiel wasn't just craving coffee on Church Street, was she?"

Gadriel shoved her hands into her pockets with a broad scowl. She glanced around the street—perhaps hoping that she would see a woman nearby with a great big sign that read 'Too Good for My Own Good'.

---

10 Far too late—and often sarcastically, to boot.

Instead, she caught sight of a group of teenagers loitering around a bus stop. Given the time of day, they were almost certainly skipping school and therefore didn't require Gadriel's help to sin any further. But, lacking any other viable targets, she focused her attention on one of the younger ones—a girl with far too much eyeliner, a cleverly tattered skirt, and enough jewellery to open up a shop. Even as Gadriel watched, one of the boys tried to pass the girl a cheap bottle of vodka.

The girl hesitated, hunching her shoulders and hiding behind her curtain of long brown hair.

Gadriel strolled slowly past the group, making a show of fussing with the hem of her knitted vest.

"Go on, take a sip," she said. "You look stressed. Besides, you don't want them slagging you off."

To Gadriel's surprise, the words had no effect whatsoever. They were about as effective as a preacher's finger waggle. Indeed, Gadriel's inside voice was no more helpful than Abel's historically questionable attempts at diplomacy.

The brown-haired girl lifted a hand to stave off the bottle. As she did, Gadriel caught sight of a little silver pentacle around her neck, and the fallen angel's frown darkened.

"Wiccans!" Gadriel said beneath her breath. "Who ever expects Wiccans?"[11]

---

11   Neither angels nor their fallen brethren have any authority over those who follow non-Abrahamic religions. Wiccans have their own nasty chuds to deal with, just as Hindus have asuras and Taoists have guei-shen. Mostly, all of these different spirits stay in their lane, so to speak—though every once in a while, someone incites a global plague, at which point the administrators in the Celestial Bureaucracy

The unexpected failure only added to Gadriel's poor mood as the teenagers slowly dispersed. Again and again, her mind wandered back to that awful card. The Wheel of Fortune was a gambler's card, of course… but it *also* represented the promise of a sharp, sudden change in fortunes, for better or for worse.

I'm perfectly happy with my fortunes as they are, Gadriel thought warily.

Gadriel had never liked excitement very much, even before her Fall. Once upon a time, she'd worked for Barachiel as a guardian angel, moonlighting on the side as an Angel of Small Miracles. She'd always delighted in the tiny banalities of existence—the lucky coin on the street; the butterfly that lands on your shoulder; the bread that bakes perfectly on the first try. Somewhere along the way, Gadriel had decided that yes, small pleasures like plucked daffodils and bits of chocolate *were* more important than pleasing the boss.

This decision, it seemed, had been enough to turn her into the Fallen Angel of Petty Temptations. But while God's angels had since become very fond of smiting the fallen, they rather had their hands full with the louder, angrier rebels like Lucifer and Beelzebub; none of them could really be bothered to visit divine judgement upon someone who spent their time tempting mortals to eat just one more crisp.

Gadriel refused to participate in exciting things. Exciting things tended to be… loud. Abrupt. *Unpleasant.*

"Miss!" a woman's voice called breathlessly. "Excuse me,

---

start filing very passive-aggressive paperwork with everyone else's management.

miss!"

Gadriel continued walking. A moment later, however, it occurred to her that she had made herself visible for the purposes of ordering her coffee and had never bothered to disappear again.

Ah, she thought with annoyance. *I'm 'miss', aren't I?*

Gadriel turned with a frown. She was used to being overlooked, even when visible; her commonplace appearance did a lot for her in that respect. But the woman that had called after her—a tall, willowy brunette of Filipino ancestry with impeccable makeup and an off-the-rack suit—was waving urgently in Gadriel's direction.

Gadriel sighed and gradually backtracked.

For some reason, the brunette woman's smile wavered imperceptibly as Gadriel approached. But she straightened her posture and steeled herself. Then, in a desperately cheerful voice, she said: "Good morning, miss! Would you like to play our game?"

Gadriel stared at her in puzzlement. A moment later, she realised that the woman in question was standing in front of a cheap cardboard prize wheel, stuck upon a wobbly tripod. Brightly coloured wedges on the wheel said things like 'free belt with trouser purchase' and 'ten per cent off'.

LIMITED TIME, said the sign beneath the wheel. *DON'T MISS YOUR CHANCE.*

"Oh, well done," Gadriel muttered beneath her breath. "Very subtle, aren't you?"

The brunette blinked. "I'm sorry?" she said. "I couldn't quite hear you."

Gadriel considered the woman seriously. "What's your

name?" she asked brusquely. "I don't suppose it's—"

The brunette forced a fresh new smile. "I'm Sara," she answered quickly. "Pleasure to meet you. It's a lovely day, isn't it?"

Gadriel sighed. "Ah," she mumbled. "Yes, that would have been too simple." Holly Harker was clearly *somewhere* nearby... but someone upstairs was intent on having a laugh at Gadriel before she found her.

Gadriel straightened again and pasted on a pleasant smile in return. "It is a *lovely* afternoon, Sara," she emphasised. "Now, what is this here? Your... game, you said. For your shop? For advertisement purposes, I take it." Gadriel glanced at the shop window just past the prize wheel, where faceless mannequins posed in stances far too dramatic for their grey, business casual clothing. She looked back at the woman in front of her, who was still smiling with a hint of self-conscious misery.

"That's right!" Sara said brightly—as though Gadriel had committed an act of deduction worthy of praise. "Castle Clothing is running a promotion right now—"

Gadriel held up her hand. "No, stop," she sighed. "Don't say it like that. Are you trying to tempt me or not?" She strolled for the other side of the wheel, settling herself next to it. Gadriel cleared her throat once—and then she turned to address the brunette, who had paused to blink at her in bewilderment.

"Oh, hello!" Gadriel said, pretending surprise. "Thank goodness you're here. I haven't got much time left in this game, and I've still got so many prizes left." She pulled out her phone and mimed a small gasp at the time displayed there. "Only five minutes to go! Oh no, I really should give out some of these prizes. It'd be a shame if *no one* won them, wouldn't it?"

"Er," said Sara. "I'm sorry, are you talking to *me?*"

Gadriel smiled at her. "We don't do this very often at all," she said confidentially. "And the *best* prize is still on the board. I mean… there's only five minutes left. You might as well spin and see if you win it. What's the harm?"

Sara looked around herself, suddenly uncertain.

"Give the wheel a spin," Gadriel advised her.

The suggestion caught hold, digging in neatly. A genuine fascination flickered across the brunette's face, and she stepped forward to spin the wheel.

The two of them stood there watching, briefly transfixed by the way the colours whizzed past, and by the steady *click-click-click* of pegs passing under the flapper. Finally, the wheel slowed to a complete stop, landing upon a crimson wedge with the word 'makeover' written in bulky letters.

"Oh!" said Sara. "That *is* our best prize, actually!" She glanced back at Gadriel, suddenly confused. "I suppose that goes to you, doesn't it?"

Gadriel narrowed her eyes at the wheel. "I don't *need* a make-over," she said. She addressed the empty air around them, rather than the woman directly next to her. Predictably, no one replied.

Sara hadn't heard Gadriel. She rummaged in one of her jacket pockets for a little red piece of paper that matched the wedge on the wheel. "You've won a thirty per cent discount and a consultation with one of our employees," she said, offering out the voucher. "Would you like to schedule a time?"

"I would not," Gadriel said flatly. But she glanced one more time at the sign beneath the wheel—*DON'T MISS YOUR CHANCE*—and a heavy sigh escaped her. "I'd rather have my consultation now, if you don't mind. Is someone available?"

Sara, who had finally keyed to Gadriel's knitted vest, offered her an oddly sympathetic smile. "We can… certainly *make* time," she said soothingly. "Go in and ask for Holly. She'll sort you out in a jiff."

Gadriel smiled, despite the implied fashion emergency. *There you are, Holly Harker,* she thought. But all she said out loud was: "Excellent."

The fallen angel headed into the shop with a spring in her step, and a respectful nod towards one of the mannequins in the window.

The inside of the shop was an awful mixture of sterile light and dirty carpets, perfectly calibrated to quench any accidental cheerfulness in those who happened to behold it. Racks of synthetic clothing spread out across the shop, carefully arranged to look more flattering than they probably were.

Gadriel scanned the shop curiously, searching for signs of life. But only a few seconds later, she was forced to conclude that Miss Holly Harker was missing-in-action—unless, of course, she was hiding behind a mannequin. She wandered the room for a minute or two, checking behind flower-printed jumpers for stray employees. Eventually, she made her way to the counter at the back, which had a little bell upon it.

"Ugh," Gadriel muttered. "If I must, I suppose."

Ringing one of those annoying bells for service was technically worth a quarter point of sin. Gadriel wasn't normally one to worry about the points—but something about forcing an intelligent being to come running like a dog *did* ruffle her wing-feathers. It reminded her an awful lot of the way her old boss liked to test people for obedience.

Gadriel reached out, nevertheless, to tap the little silver bell.

Ring ring.

The sound echoed in the silence of the shop. But no employee appeared.

Gadriel frowned and hit the bell again. *Ring ring.*

Though she tapped the bell a few more times, it soon became clear that no employee was going to come running to fix her knitted vest situation.

Gadriel sighed and nudged the bell aside. Instead, she shoved her hands into her pockets and started directly for the door at the back, labelled 'employees only'.

The cramped, box-like office at the back of the shop was even less appealing than its front, without even a window to let in some light. A single dirty lamp shed its yellow light over a pink paisley sofa that had seen better days.

Draped unceremoniously over the sofa's arm was a pale, sleeping woman in a wrinkled white blouse and a black pencil skirt. Her honey-coloured hair, half-caught in a sloppy chignon, had lost several locks against her neck. Her hand still clenched a plastic fork with odd determination, though the takeaway container on the table next to her was mostly untouched. She would have been cute as a button if she hadn't looked so miserable, even in her sleep.

For just a moment, Gadriel dared to hope that Holly Harker had *already* sinned today by napping at work. But even a cursory inspection suggested that the woman had fallen asleep in the middle of eating, rather than sneaking off for a purposeful illicit break.

Gadriel cleared her throat.

The woman shot up in her seat, blinking quickly. As her senses caught up with her, she brandished the plastic fork at Gadriel with wide brown eyes, as though to hold her off.

"This—you—" she stammered dazedly. "Employees only!"

Gadriel nodded reasonably. "Oh yes," she said. "I must have missed the sign." She paused. "Are you Holly?"

The woman on the sofa flushed. "I… yes, I suppose I am," she mumbled. The colour stained the apples in her cheeks, making them stand out more prominently.

Gadriel squinted at her. "You *suppose?*" she asked.

Holly pushed up to her feet, brushing at her clothing with obvious embarrassment. "I mean—I am. Yes." Her eyes caught on the red voucher in Gadriel's hand, and she cringed. "You've… won a consult! Congratulations."

Gadriel rubbed at her chin. "Yes, very lucky," she murmured. She was only half-listening; most of her attention was on the woman in front of her.

Holly Harker was probably a woman in her late twenties— but the dark circles beneath her eyes and the permanent con- cerned wrinkle between her brows made her look somewhat older than that. Her nose stuck out prominently among her other features, like a very proud mountain. There was a faint speckling of freckles visible upon it, but they were difficult to see clearly in the yellow light of the room's single lamp.

I can work with this, Gadriel thought. The twenties were an excellent time for sinning. All she really needed was a few more details about the woman in front of her, and she'd be ready to get to work.

"—we'll get you and your knitted vest into this decade, no problem," Holly was saying. Gadriel blinked and brought herself back to the conversation.

"Pardon?" Gadriel said.

Holly flushed self-consciously. "Oh, I didn't mean—I'm sorry, I was trying to be funny. That wasn't very funny, was it?"

Gadriel considered this hopefully for a moment. Jokes in poor taste only counted for sin if they were purposeful, though. "The knitted vest is an obvious target," she advised. "But you've got an inch or two on me, if you want to make jokes about my height."

Holly stared at Gadriel blankly. Her eyes were wide now, like a deer in the headlights.

Gadriel sighed heavily. "I'd just like to be sure," she said. "You *are* Holly Harker?"

Holly blinked several times. "I... am," she confirmed. "Do we know each other?"

Gadriel shook her head. "Not *exactly*. More by reputation." She opened the door again, gesturing for the shop, and Holly crept past her with a confused expression on her face.

"Wait," Holly mumbled. "Did we... go to school together? You look awfully familiar."

Gadriel smiled. Barachiel might have had star quality, but there was something to be said for the boring everyman approach. "We never met directly," Gadriel assured her.

Holly nodded, now certain of her assessment. "And your name was..."

"Gadriel." The fallen angel in question waited patiently for the inevitable reply.

"I'm sorry?" Holly asked. "Gabriel?"

Gadriel shook her head. "Gadriel," she repeated. "With a 'd'. Very different, I assure you. Wouldn't want to mix us up." She paused. "It *is* a funny name. Plenty of jokes there, as well."[12]

Holly smiled nervously, and Gadriel cleared her throat.

"Go ahead," she said. "Crack a joke."

Every human being has a smug little part of their brain that enjoys feeling superior to other people. Gadriel aimed her suggestion at this specific part of Holly Harker's mind, pitching her voice to match its mutterings. The words caught there neatly, digging their way in...

...and then, for some unknown reason, they *snagged*.

"I really didn't mean to insult you," Holly assured Gadriel anxiously. "I promise, I'll leave off. It's just... I don't remember a Gadriel at school. I feel like I would."

Gadriel stared at her.

That should have worked, she thought. *I felt it start to work. What went wrong?*

Gadriel caught up to Holly's observation an instant later though, and she shook herself. "I let people call me Gabe sometimes," she said slowly. "I'm sure you never heard anyone say my full name, is all."[13]

---

12   Gadriel often received stray prayers from trumpet players and mail carriers which were clearly meant for the Archangel Gabriel. No one ever prayed intentionally to Gadriel, of course, and so she often saved time by responding immediately to all prayers with the words "sorry, wrong number".

13   It was true that Gadriel often capitulated to the nickname *Gabe*. She was inherently quite lazy, and the Gabriel thing just wasn't

"That... *does* sound more familiar," Holly observed dubiously. She turned to head for a rack of clothing, and Gadriel relaxed very slightly. "Er... what sort of outfit are you looking for, by the way?"

Gadriel followed after her, blinking. "Something from this decade?" she offered. "I thought you were supposed to tell *me*."

Holly winced. "Oh, you're right," she admitted. "You know, I've never done one of these makeovers before? There's nothing about them in the employee manual."

Gadriel nodded. "You're supposed to find me something expensive, I'd wager," she said. "Make me try it on, then tell me it's perfect."

Holly pursed her lips. "That's a bit cynical," she mumbled.

Gadriel snapped her head around. "It is *not*," she declared vehemently. "I don't care at all for Cynics, just so we're clear."

Awkward silence fell between them.

Holly cleared her throat first. "We can find you something to wear for work, then?" she suggested tentatively. "What is it you do for a living, Gabe?"

Gadriel reached up to pinch the bridge of her nose between her fingers. "Something very much like this," she said. *Though I'm normally much better at it,* she thought to herself.

"Ah, retail," Holly sighed. "You have my sympathies, obviously." She assessed Gadriel one more time before stepping off to pull clothing from the surrounding racks, draping items over her arms in quick succession. "We can try something with a blazer, maybe—"

worth the fight.

26

"I'll take it all," Gadriel interjected hurriedly. "Thirty per cent off, I think." She forced a smile at Holly. "You know, we should have a night out. Catch up over drinks. Fruity ones, with little paper umbrellas."

Holly blinked slowly, setting the pile of clothes onto the counter. "I… do like those little umbrellas," she admitted. "I'd really like to, actually. I'm just not sure if I have the time."

Gadriel caught the obvious flicker of interest in Holly's face. *Aha*, she thought. *I have you now.*

"No rush," she said casually. "We can work around your schedule." Gadriel levelled her gaze at Holly, and then added: "You deserve a night out."

Holly hesitated visibly. The flicker of interest in her face blossomed into outright longing, pried loose by the suggestion. Gadriel's inside voice caught upon that emotion, wriggling it free and dragging it up to the forefront of the woman's mind. Any moment now, she was going to say yes—

But an instant later, this suggestion snagged as well. The hook that had dug into Holly's desires cut loose, and all at once, her expression turned gloomy.

"I'm afraid I really can't," Holly sighed. "You'll have to drink an extra for me."

She started ringing up the clothes, while Gadriel stared at her in mute astonishment.

"Is something wrong?" Holly asked curiously.

"No, nothing," Gadriel said slowly. "I'm… *fine*. I just need a different approach, is all. I'm sure that's it."

Gadriel snatched the bag of clothing from the counter and headed for the door, already reorganising her thoughts.

Chapter Three

CUMULATIVE SIN METRIC (HOLLY HARKER): -932

Had Holly Harker been less tired, she might have noticed that she was having an exceedingly strange day.

For one thing, there was a small crowd outside of Castle Clothing. There was *never* a crowd in front of the shop—not even on the weekends. But at the very moment Gadriel had left, tapping furiously into her phone, another woman had come in looking very pleased with herself, waving around her green 'ten per cent discount' voucher as though it was a hard-won triumph.

"I won the last one!" the woman declared. "With only five minutes to spare, as well!"

"Five minutes until… what?" Holly asked her blankly.

"Until the prizes go away, of course," the woman said.

Outside, an older gentleman—more bewhiskered than his leashed terrier—spun the tacky wheel in front of the door. Holly's coworker Sara shot him an encouraging smile and handed him another green voucher, eliciting a triumphant cackle from him. Poor Sara had drawn the short straw today, which meant that she was stuck outside with the cardboard game the salespeople had quietly nicknamed the Wheel of Misery. Normally, the Wheel of Misery only brought in one or two spare customers—the sort who couldn't bring themselves to say no to an obviously humiliated employee. Today, however, it seemed to be unusually popular.

"Ah," said Holly. "I see." She didn't understand the situation at all, actually—but everyone involved seemed awfully satisfied with themselves, and so she decided to focus on doing her job.

Sometime right after Holly's fourth customer, however—a teenage girl with far more body piercings than her usual clientele—things began to get *noticeably* strange.

YOU LOOK TIRED, said a voice in her head. YOU OUGHT TO TAKE A BREAK.

It was the same voice in Holly's mind that normally said things like *I'm tired* and *This is demeaning* and *I'd rather die than stand in front of that silly wheel ever again.* But she had grown intimately familiar with such thoughts over the last few months; in fact, they were such *regular* thoughts now that she'd mostly learned to ignore them.

IT'S NOT LIKE THE BOSS IS GOING TO PAY YOU BY THE CUSTOMER, the voice added matter-of-factly.

For some reason, the voice in her head sounded a bit testier than usual.

"Oh, shove off," Holly muttered back. She reached out to refold another shirt on the display table near the front of the shop.

SHOVE OFF? the voice repeated disbelievingly.

Holly narrowed her eyes at the table. "One day at a time," she mumbled beneath her breath. "*Un jour de plus.*" The simple act of translating the words settled her mind, refocusing her on her goals. First, she would finish her shift. After that, she'd finish her *other* shift. Then, she would gather her things and hop on the Tube. She'd stop for groceries—she'd written *that* list in French as well—and then finally, it was just a matter of picking up Ella.

These things were all doable, she thought. They were all... little things, really. As long as she thought of them each separately, she could work her way through them.

The jarring tone of the door interrupted Holly's thoughts. She looked up and saw that Sara had entered with the Wheel of Misery folded beneath her arm.

"What a morning!" Sara sighed, planting a fist on her cocked hip. "I think I've tired myself out."

"That was some crowd!" Holly said. "What on earth happened out there?"

Sara tossed the wheel onto the table with a rueful smile. "I suppose I've discovered how shameless I can be when I'm starved for human company," she admitted. "I even had a proper conversation once or twice, in between the vouchers. Best social interaction I've managed all week. Isn't *that* pathetic?"

Holly frowned at her. "But weren't you dating someone?" she asked. "His name was, er... John? Jeremy? Jacob?" She was almost certain it had been a J name.

"John was a bigot, Jeremy yelled at waiters, and Jacob had two secret children," Sara said, listing off the men on her fingers. "If I find a man named Jingleheimer Schmidt, I'll have been through the entire children's song." She shot Holly a flat, helpless look. "I really can't pick men, can I? Or rather, I'm very good at picking all of the *wrong* men."

Holly winced. Casual conversations had never been her forte;

yet again, it seemed she'd managed to stick her foot in her mouth. "That *is* a bad run of luck," she admitted, hiding her embarrassment. "I suppose you're taking a break?"

"The Wheel of Misery and I are officially an item," Sara responded blithely. "May no man ever come between us." She reached out to caress the cardboard wheel with a feigned look of adoration, batting her eyelashes.

Holly shook her head. "That one is definitely going to let you down," she advised. "But it won't yell at any waiters, I suppose."

"My standards are exactly that low," Sara assured her. She frowned at Holly. "D'you mind taking your break and picking us up a snack? Honestly, I'm famished."

"I suppose I could," Holly mumbled. She grabbed her handbag from behind the counter. "Hold down the fort, will you?"

EXCELLENT, said the voice in Holly's head—though she wasn't sure exactly what *that* was supposed to mean.

"I'm finally going bonkers," Holly muttered to herself, as she headed out the door.

Chapter Four

CUMULATIVE SIN METRIC (HOLLY HARKER): -932

Once upon a time, a fallen angel pretending to be a serpent had tempted Eve into eating a forbidden apple. Somehow, this plan actually worked—a fact which never ceased to mystify Gadriel. Just what sort of human being, she wondered, found snakes to be uniquely persuasive? The few times she'd tried pulling the same stunt herself, she'd been stomped on, yelled at, and poked with a stick.

Serpents, Gadriel had decided, were off the list. Now with several thousand years of temptation under her wing, she'd long since concluded that *cats* were the perfect animal for the job.[14]

"Fifteen minutes," Holly mumbled to herself, as she clipped

---

14   Cats are responsible for 33.8% of time wasted on the Internet yearly. Indeed, cats are more efficient at temptation than most fallen angels are; a single well-placed cat can derail an entire online meeting in five seconds flat. This is especially infuriating to certain fallen angels, given that cats seem largely indifferent to their own powers of persuasion.

her way down the street. "That's barely long enough to get through the queue."

Gadriel the calico kitten threaded her way idly through the afternoon crowd, intent upon her target. Despite her tiny form, gasps went up immediately where she passed. Women clutched at their chest as though the sheer adorableness of Gadriel's existence had caused them physical pain.

I should have just started with cats, Gadriel mused silently, as she came within pouncing distance of Holly and her handbag. Surely, even saintly Miss Harker would be tempted to play with a friendly kitten for more than her fair share of break time.

"It's following her, mama!" cooed a child in the crowd. "How cute!"

Holly knit her brow and paused in place. Gadriel stopped just behind her, settling placidly onto her haunches. Slowly, the woman in front of her turned and looked down.

"*Mau,*" said Gadriel.

Holly blinked down at her. "Er," she said. "Are you... lost?"

Gadriel gave one very dignified lick at her paw. "Scratch behind my ears," she suggested. "We'll both enjoy it."

Holly frowned down at her uncertainly, obviously hesitating. At this, Gadriel heaved a tiny feline sigh.

Time to break out the big guns, she thought.

She set her paw back down onto the pavement. Then—very slowly and very deliberately—she rolled onto her back to show her excessively fluffy belly.

Several more squeals of joy went up among the people immediately surrounding them. A nearby woman swooned on her feet.

"Oh… bother," Holly mumbled. She reached down towards Gadriel's soft, downy belly… and promptly scooped the kitten up into her drawstring bag.

Cats may have had many fine qualities to their name—but Gadriel was, in that moment, absolutely *certain* that they were not meant to be picked up. Her instincts flared with alarm, and she twisted wildly, hissing and clawing at the bag.

"Ow, ow, ow!" Holly cried out. "I'm trying to *help* you!" She tugged the bag's drawstring closed, blocking out the sun—and suddenly, Gadriel was plunged into darkness.

"Ooh, that *stings!*" Holly moaned. "He got my hand!"

Gadriel, who was currently upside down and folded in between what felt like a wallet and a pair of sunglasses, felt no pity for her whatsoever.

"Excuse me?" Gadriel heard Holly asking, in a muffled voice. "Excuse me, do you know where the nearest animal shelter is?"

No, Gadriel thought. *No, surely not.*

"Well, he might get run over if I just *leave* him here!" Holly protested at someone. "There's all manner of traffic!"

Gadriel rolled inside of the bag, now clawing more frantically at the lotions and lip balms that surrounded her. She needed, *needed* to escape—if only to head off the inevitable good deed which had even now started speeding towards her like a dauntless locomotive.[15]

With great effort, she wriggled her little paws into the bag's opening, heaving with all of her might…

Gadriel burst from the drawstring bag with a yowl, landing

---

15   +10 Points of Virtue (Holly Harker): Rescuing a Lost Kitten.

heavily on the pavement with all four paws.

"He's got loose!" Holly gasped. "Oh, someone catch him, I don't want him getting run over!"

Gadriel hissed and sprinted, darting past several giant pairs of legs. Normally, being so tiny was an advantage rather than a problem—but in the moment, she was reminded abruptly just how *big* everyone else was in comparison to her current form. A few people snatched at her, gaining long scratches for their trouble, as Gadriel bolted angrily for an alleyway.

She finally stopped, halfway into the dingy, refuse-choked alley… and let out a frustrated growl.

What am I doing? Gadriel thought. *I don't have to put up with this.*

The fallen angel settled onto her haunches once again, and promptly went invisible.

Invisibility was really an angel's natural state of being, at least so far as mortals were concerned. As such, it commonly took more effort for a fallen angel like Gadriel to look like *anything* than it did for her to look like nothing.

Even as the last of Gadriel's whiskers and her tiny pink nose faded from view, Holly stumbled into the alley, gasping for breath. She looked around wildly for a few moments—even nudged away some rubbish bags with her foot—as Gadriel glared at her with unmitigated hatred.

"Go away," Gadriel hissed at her. "You've done enough."[16]

Holly sighed heavily, reaching up to shove back her hair with one bloody hand. "We'll just have to keep an eye out," she

---

16   -5 Points of Virtue (Holly Harker): Accounting Adjustment for a Failed Virtue. Partial Points for Effort.

mumbled. "Poor thing."

Holly searched for a few minutes more, halfhearted. By the time she finally left, Gadriel was still grooming herself violently—now in an even worse mood than she had been that morning.

The fuzzy belly had never failed her before. Not once, not *ever.*

I'm sure of it now, Gadriel thought bitterly. *I've been hoodwinked.*

Gadriel didn't know yet precisely what was going on… but she was absolutely going to find out.

It was about another hour before Gadriel had regained her composure and pulled together a human form to go back to Castle Clothing. By the time she got there, however, Holly Harker was mysteriously gone.

Chapter Five

CUMULATIVE SIN METRIC (HOLLY HARKER): -937

Holly did *not*, in fact, manage to buy any snacks. Rather, she was forced to spend the rest of her break in the lavatory with Sara, rinsing out the scratches on her hands and searching for the old plasters they kept beneath the sink.

"I still feel awful about losing him," Holly sighed later, as she picked at one of the plasters on her hand behind the counter. Despite the strange rush that morning, they'd now spent a full hour without seeing even a single customer.

"Well, maybe he was just an outside cat," Sara offered helpfully. "Did he look well-fed?"

"He… did," Holly admitted. "But he certainly *acted* feral. And who would let their cat wander around with all of these cars about?"

"Oh, you'd be surprised," Sara replied. "Anyway, he's not your problem for the moment." She paused at that and tilted her head, staring past Holly's shoulder at the clock on the wall. "D'you have another shift today?" she asked. "I could've sworn you did."

Holly's eyes widened. "Oh!" she squeaked. "Yes, I have got one." She snatched up her handbag and leapt to her feet—but her eyes flickered towards the register with consternation, and she hesitated. "I've still got to count up the till—"

"I've got it," Sara replied. "Go. Shoo."

Holly agonised for half a second more. "Yes, all right," she said finally. "But I owe you a coffee."

"I'll be sure to come and collect," Sara agreed mildly.

Holly didn't have the time to linger. She kicked off her heels, pulled on her trainers, and scurried for the door of the shop.

***

"Next in line, please!" Holly called out over her shoulder. "I'll be with you in a moment!" The espresso machine at Déjà Brew was dreadfully loud, and she was only half certain anyone would hear her over its ugly screeching. Still, she grabbed the café latte in front of her and turned back for the counter—only to come up short, blinking quickly.

"You have got to be joking," Gadriel declared. Her eyes were narrowed, as though Holly had somehow got herself hired at the coffee shop in the last hour purely in order to spite her. Despite Gadriel's earlier fashion consult, she was *still* wearing that worn-out argyle knitted vest. Worse—her short brown hair was tangled and ragged, as though she'd been through a miniature hurricane.

"I… ah…" Holly blinked again. "Fancy meeting you here," she said.

"Yes," Gadriel gritted out between her teeth. "Fancy that." She paused. "I don't suppose you have a regular customer. Tall

Black woman, movie star looks?"

Holly considered this. "I think... perhaps?" she said. "I'm afraid I'm not very good with faces. Or names. Or, ah... any of that, really." She forced a smile. "I take it you'd like a coffee, then?"

You would really like a coffee, she tried to convey with her tone. *Because otherwise, you would be holding up the line.*

Gadriel pressed her fingers to the bridge of her nose. There was a dull, long-suffering expression on her features. "Just a hot chocolate, please," she said. "And, ah... I'll buy you one of the same, if you like. As a tip." The glum tinge in her face deepened, and for some reason, a voice in Holly's head added: YOU COULD PROBABLY USE A BIT OF CHOCOLATE.

Holly frowned. The idea hit her strangely, like a pleasant little shiver down her spine. And briefly—for the very first time in her life, in fact—she thought that she *might* could use a bit of chocolate.

But the thought was foreign and uncomfortable, and she waved it away with a faint twist of her lips. "That's very kind of you," Holly said. "But I don't actually like chocolate."

"You don't like—" Gadriel's expression crumpled so completely that Holly felt nonsensically guilty for the comment. In fact, the other woman looked as though she were about to cry.

"Maybe you should have a sit down," Holly told her soothingly. "You look as though you've been having a day."

Gadriel met her eyes with an odd sort of pleading. "It has been... the closest thing to Hell," she said. "I'm not sure I could explain it if I tried."

Holly smiled tiredly. "Go settle in," she said. "I'll bring over your drink in a little bit. On the house."

Gadriel stared at her tearfully. "Was that... a heartfelt act of generosity, just now?" she choked out.

Holly reached out to pat the woman's hand awkwardly. "I suppose it might be?" she said. "But really, it's just a drink."[17]

Gadriel pressed a hand over her mouth. The poor woman looked so utterly overwhelmed that Holly stepped out from behind the counter to guide her to an empty chair.

As Holly dropped off the mug of hot chocolate at Gadriel's table a few minutes later, she saw that the woman had started typing into her smartphone with the sort of bitter violence one normally reserved for online political discussions.

"Are you winning the argument?" Holly asked her mildly.

"What?" Gadriel asked. She looked up at Holly blankly. There was a fresh wariness in her expression that Holly couldn't quite place.

"I assumed... you look very intent on something," Holly said. "Whoever's troubling you, they're probably not worth it." Holly wasn't entirely certain that this was the right thing to say— she had never been very good with people—but she had heard people say things very much *like* it on television.

Gadriel took in a deep breath and snatched the mug of hot chocolate from Holly's hands. "I am not winning," she said stilt- edly. Wounded dignity seeped from every word. "You know—I knew there was a catch. There's always a catch with her. I can't believe I was stupid enough to believe her, yet *again*."

---

17   +1 Point of Virtue (Holly Harker): A Heartfelt Act of Generosity.

Holly sighed. "Ah," she said. "Lady trouble. That might have been my other guess."

"I should say so," Gadriel agreed darkly. "Trouble. Walking trouble. But who would believe me? She's an *angel*." She threw back the hot chocolate as though it were a shot of whiskey. Her brown eyes flickered red for a moment, like burning embers. The sight was oddly captivating, and Holly soon realised she was staring.

Holly caught herself, nodding emphatically. The conversation had tugged at something buried deep within her. "I know exactly the feeling," she said. "Left you all alone, didn't she? But as soon as she needed something, she found your number all over again. Now you're obliged, and everyone just expects you'll clean up her messes, because that's simply how it's done." A lump formed in her throat. "A simple 'thank you' would be nice, every so often. But she wouldn't say it, even if she *was* here."[18]

Gadriel slammed her hand on the table. "That's right!" she declared, and her eyes surged again with banked crimson. "You're absolutely right, I—" Her brow furrowed. "Actually, that's not right at all. Who are you talking about?" She glanced up at Holly—and for some reason, her eyes widened. "That's one point!" she breathed. "What just happened? What did I do? How do I do it *again?*"

I shouldn't have said that, Holly thought. Her chest squeezed with guilt. A hot flush of embarrassment crept across her cheeks, and she took a tiny step back.

"I really should get back to work," Holly stammered.

---

18   +1 Point of Sin (Holly Harker): Speaking Ill of the Dead.

"Er—you're better off without her." This, too, was something she had heard on television, but it seemed like a proper way to end the conversation.

She fled for the safety of the counter, while Gadriel's eyes burned into her back.

Chapter Six

CUMULATIVE SIN METRIC (HOLLY HARKER): -937

G adriel had now sent Barachiel fifty-six furious text messages and counting.

> *Gadriel: ONE POINT*

> *Gadriel: ONE POINT OF SIN in the last six hours*

> *Gadriel: She's already cancelled it out!!! She's five points UP!*

> *Gadriel: I know you have something to do with this you ROTTER*

Barachiel had yet to respond. But the angel was clearly behind the curve on modern technology, because Gadriel could see the little check marks on each message which suggested they'd been opened.

Gadriel seethed over her third hot chocolate. The image of

Barachiel staring down at her phone with that infuriatingly mysterious, self-satisfied smile floated into her mind, and she gritted her teeth.

Gadriel: I KNOW YOU'RE READING THESE MESSAGES

Gadriel: I WILL NOT FORGET THIS

Gadriel tossed her phone back onto the table with a hiss of frustration. As she did, she caught sight of Holly Harker's vaguely bedraggled form rushing frantically for the door. Her honey-blonde hair had escaped its bun almost entirely now, despite several attempts to tame it over the course of the day. Her drawstring bag dangled uncomfortably from her elbow, only halfway closed.

Gadriel sighed and shoved up from her seat. Eventually, she *was* going to find (and strangle) Barachiel. But for now, she had agreed to this ridiculous temptation. And more than that— Gadriel really *hated* losing.

"There's a lesson in here, I'm sure of it," Gadriel muttered to herself, as she followed Holly out the door of the coffee shop. "Something about how I ought to learn to cut my losses, perhaps."

Nevertheless, Gadriel allowed herself to fall back into invisibility as she followed the other woman down the busy street.

"—so sorry, I'm on the other side of town," Holly was saying into her phone, as she wrangled with her handbag. "I'm not sure how long it will take me to get there." She fumbled inside of her bag one-handed, searching for her pocketbook.

Gadriel was only halfway paying attention to the conversation.

For the last hour, her mind had started picking at the problem of Holly Harker, considering new angles. Petty temptations were normally a simple affair—but it was quickly becoming clear that Gadriel's oldest, most reliable tricks were unsuited to this specific situation.

"You," Gadriel addressed Holly's back. "Yes, you, bane of my existence. I'm going to have to figure out what makes you tick."

Holly didn't hear the words. But then, she wasn't really meant to hear them.

"I completely understand," Holly assured the other person on the phone. Her voice had that quality now that suggested she was in the process of prostrating herself before a greater authority. A low-grade panic had started simmering just beneath the surface of her eyes. "No, I—I'm afraid there's no one else to call. I promise, I will be there as soon as I can be."

Gadriel scowled and started tapping at her phone again. Rather than sending more fruitless texts to Barachiel, however, she opened up a blank note on the device and started writing.

She titled this note with the words:

THE TEMPTATION OF HOLLY HARKER

"What do I know about you?" Gadriel mused, as she followed Holly down into an underground station. "Let's start there."

And she began her list thusly:

WHAT I KNOW
1. Holly Harker is very busy.

This was self-evident, given the manner in which Holly

pushed her way through the rush-hour crowd. She'd stashed her phone back inside her handbag, but her expression was clearly still that of a harried woman.

"But why are we so busy, Holly?" Gadriel muttered, as she followed Holly into one of the carriages. "I suppose I'll find out *something* shortly." The fallen angel glanced around for an empty seat, but there were obviously none to be had at this hour.

Gadriel scanned the people currently seated, searching for a likely option. Her eyes fell upon an older woman near the edge of the row who'd settled a heavy leather handbag into her lap. Peeking out from that bag was a tiny, ragged-eared chihuahua with obvious violence behind its beady-eyed glare.[19]

"You there," Gadriel said.

The chihuahua raised its eyes to her, despite her current state of invisibility. Gadriel *felt* its fury against her skin—far stronger and more concentrated than should have been possible for such a tiny form—and she cleared her throat uncomfortably, shifting on her feet.

"I doubt *you're* very religious," Gadriel continued, "so I'm unlikely to tempt you into anything. But I just couldn't bring myself to pass you by without observing how ugly you are."[20]

---

19   Animals can see many things which humans normally overlook, due to their extra senses. Cats are particularly well known for staring directly at angels who would prefer to go unnoticed, and even more well known for vomiting on their shoes.

20   You needn't feel bad for the chihuahua. Just as God created the platypus out of spare parts, Lucifer created the original chihuahua out of spare spite. There may be many greater evils in this world, but one would be hard-pressed to find a more *concentrated* form of evil than

SMALL MIRACLES

The chihuahua sat up abruptly, narrowing its gaze. A low, hideous growl rumbled from its tiny throat. The woman holding it glanced down, hushing the dog hurriedly.

"And then, I saw a hideous beast," Gadriel proclaimed, raising her hand dramatically into the air, "with a tiny body and an enormous head—rising from the depths of the handbag!"

The chihuahua barked in high-pitched fury, scrambling from the handbag to lunge at Gadriel. Its owner surged to her feet in a panic, snatching at the dog's silver-studded collar. The dog gave her an admirable run for her money, as it snapped at Gadriel's feet with murder in its little eyes.

Gadriel waved the dog goodbye as its owner clucked at it, hurrying off at the next stop.

Then, the fallen angel carefully smoothed her knitted vest and sat down in the empty seat, turning her attention back to her list. After another moment, she typed:

2. Holly Harker does not like chocolate.

This deserved its own line item, for perfectly obvious reasons. It was not, however, a terribly actionable item.

Gadriel glanced up at Holly, who had crammed herself uncomfortably between a tall man in a football shirt and a woman with a buggie containing a shrieking child. The subject of Gadriel's musings now looked as though she wanted to cry.

3. Holly Harker is absolutely miserable.

---

the average chihuahua.

49

Gadriel considered this last point very seriously.

Normally, she thought, miserable people were *more* prone to sin and not less. Getting through the day when you were miserable required an awful lot of willpower. Correspondingly, many of the tiniest sins involved a lapse in willpower—which was more common, of course, when you had already used up all of that willpower on other things.

Something else was going on here, Gadriel thought. There was a last piece of the puzzle missing; she just had to find it.

Gadriel continued turning the mystery over in her mind as she followed Holly out of the carriage. Two bus switches later, she found herself heading towards a large white stone building with far too many windows. It was a ghastly edifice—a blocky construction conjured from the dim imagination of an accountant who might have learned some architecture by accident. Gadriel stayed just behind Holly as the woman ducked her way through the glass doors at the front of the building.

The hallway inside was dour and cramped, but the white antiseptic walls were also covered in curiously colourful posters. One said: *JOIN THE SCHOOL DISCO PLANNING COMMITTEE!* Another said: *CHESS CLUB, 4 PM THURSDAYS*—only, someone had crossed out 'chess club' in permanent pen and written the words 'swot club' on the poster instead.

"Ah," Gadriel murmured to herself as they passed. "Secondary school humour. The height of sophistication."

Holly's once swift steps now slowed and started to drag as they continued down the hallway. Resigned foreboding tugged at her features—until finally, she came to a stop just outside of a thick wooden office door.

The two of them stood in front of that door for several seconds, as silence trickled in. The door might as well have had the phrase 'abandon all hope' inscribed above its frame.

"YOU COULD ALWAYS GO HAVE A BITE TO EAT AND SAY THE TUBE BROKE DOWN," Gadriel offered hopefully.

Holly sighed and reached up to rub at her face. "I can't just *leave* her here," she mumbled.

Gadriel mirrored Holly's gesture, running her own palms over her eyes. "IT WAS JUST A THOUGHT," she muttered sulkily.

Holly raised her head and squared her shoulders. She took a deep breath, covering her dread with a polite smile. Finally, she knocked once at the office door—and headed inside.

The room they stepped into was uncomfortably cramped, between the narrow wooden bench that had been set against the sidewall and the particle wood desk which took up most of the closet-like space. That cheap desk was situated in front of a second door with a pane of frosted glass such that its occupant—a pale, middle-aged woman with grey-streaked, frizzy red hair and thick-framed glasses—could guard said door with her polka-dotted dress and her stern-eyed gaze.

"Mrs Applebee," Holly greeted the woman weakly. "I hope your afternoon is going well?"

Mrs Applebee turned her stern glower upon Holly. "Miss Harker," she replied. "The state of my afternoon is predictably bleak. Unless, of course… you've brought biscuits?"

Holly smiled nervously. "No biscuits this time, I'm afraid," she admitted.

Mrs Applebee's expression had softened minutely in expectation—but at this, her facial muscles tightened and her eyes narrowed. "Well then," she declared primly. "Cutting it late, aren't we?"

Holly shifted from foot to foot, looking for all the world like a student caught in bad behaviour. Her eyes flickered to the floor. "I'm so sorry," she mumbled. "I had to beg off work, and I was across town—"

"You're here now, at least," Mrs Applebee interrupted— though it was clear from her clipped tone that Holly had *not* been forgiven. "Ella is in with Mr Parker. I have some paperwork for you to sign, and then she'll be going home with you. She's to remain off campus for the rest of the day."

Holly's mouth dropped. "Ella is *suspended?*" she asked. "What did she do?"

"Tripped a girl in the hall, as I understand it," Mrs Applebee informed Holly briskly. "The other girl sprained her ankle. Her family is furious. If you ask me, your niece is getting a slap on the wrist."

Holly goggled. She struggled to articulate an answer, even as Mrs Applebee slid a paper and pen over the desk in her direction. "This is her suspension letter," the older woman said. "If you could sign to acknowledge you've read it, please."

Holly took the paper and pen in a daze. Gadriel looked over her shoulder curiously.

"Ella Harker," the fallen angel read to herself. "Tripped Millie Wilson and called her a—*oh.*" Her tone became mildly impressed. "Someone has fallen *very* far from the chocolate-free tree, haven't they?"

Holly cringed, as if on cue. She signed her name at the bottom of the letter in messy, looping handwriting.

"It's not…" Holly sighed, and offered a pleading look towards Mrs Applebee. "I know none of this is ideal. She's just still having trouble, is all."

Mrs Applebee's expression remained supremely unimpressed. "Six months of trouble now," she said. "I'm afraid her trouble can no longer be everyone else's trouble, Miss Harker. Someone is going to have to take her in hand."

The older woman seemed sceptical that this someone might be standing in front of her.

Holly rubbed at her face. "I'll take her off your hands then," she murmured. "Thank you, Mrs Applebee."

Holly squeezed her way towards the door behind the desk, hiking her bag up onto her shoulder to keep it out of the way. She knocked once at the frosted glass and nudged the door open.

The room beyond was strikingly *less* like a sardine tin. It had a broad window at the back and a bigger, more expensive desk, which still left plenty of space for the leather chairs in front of it. A handful of old school trophies had been stacked on the shelves. The walls had a smattering of self-aggrandising diplomas and certifications, all framed in wood and glass.

A nameplate on the desk identified the man in the chair behind it as 'Headmaster Roy Parker' of Battenberg Grammar School. Said gentleman had gone fully grey; his plaid jacket and dated reading glasses would have made him seem dignified in a previous decade. This might have led Gadriel to consider him a kind of kindred spirit, except that he instantly turned a haughty look in her direction. Er, in Holly's direction, anyway. It was difficult to tell just who people were looking at sometimes when one was invisible and looming over a mortal's shoulder, but it somehow always *felt* personal in nature.

"Miss Harker," said the headmaster. His voice held the sort of haughty, patriarchal tone which one reserved for *disappointing* students. "I can't say it's a pleasure to see you again, given the circumstances."

"Headmaster," Holly greeted him tremulously. "I'm so sorry about all of this—"

"Why should *you* be sorry?" The voice that spoke this time emanated from one of the high-backed leather chairs in front of the desk. It was a young girl's voice, slightly nasal and heavily laden with sarcasm. Gadriel squinted and turned her head slightly; from her new perspective, she saw two small feet dangling from the chair, crossed impatiently at the ankles.

"That is quite enough, Miss Harker," Mr Parker upbraided the chair sternly. "You are already in very serious trouble."

The small feet uncrossed. A girl hopped down from the leather chair, hiking her satchel up over her shoulder and brushing out her school uniform. Like Holly, she had honey-blonde hair, pulled back into a ponytail, and a proudly prominent nose. Her face was softer and more rounded, though the rest of her had entered the awkward, lanky stage that announced one's early teenage years. Her mouth was stuck in a deeply sullen scowl.

"Why don't you apologise for the weather next?" Ella asked her aunt. "Oh, Mr Parker had a disappointing lunch. You could apologise for that as well."[21]

"Ella Harker!" the headmaster snapped. "Keep talking, and I'll suspend you tomorrow as well."

---

21   +1/10 Points of Sin (Ella Harker): Sarcasm.

Holly stared down at her niece in horror, as though she had been confronted with a wild, dangerous animal. The mild awkwardness she had shown when chatting with Gadriel that day now seemed to have multiplied tenfold.

"Oh dear," said Gadriel. "A teenager. No wonder you're in trouble."

Ella crossed her arms. Deep resentment coloured her features as she glanced between her aunt and the headmaster behind her. She pressed her lips together. "I'll wait outside then, while you talk about everything I've done wrong," she said shortly.

Ella stalked from the room, brushing directly past Holly. Gadriel danced instinctively aside, blinking at her as she passed.

Silence settled in behind the teenager, as the two visible adults in the room took a deep breath.

"I am... *so* sorry," Holly repeated in a small voice.

"You said that already," Gadriel told her. "Twice, I think."

Mr Parker shook his head disapprovingly. "I expect you'll have words with the young lady," he told Holly. "This behaviour cannot continue."

Holly's face fell into abject despair. "I have tried talking to her, sir," she admitted. "She doesn't want to hear it from me. Perhaps the school counsellor—"

"Mrs Lisbon is on maternity leave," the headmaster said. "Replacements are light on the ground. Besides which, a counsellor cannot replace a parent. I cannot imagine why it is you volunteered to raise a child if you are this unequal to the task."

Holly blinked. Gadriel blinked as well.

"Well, *that* was just uncalled for," said the fallen angel. She narrowed her eyes at the headmaster. "Speaking of volunteers..."

I'm going to have to think up something special for you."

"I would prefer never to see you *or* the younger Miss Harker in this office again," Mr Parker added, perfectly oblivious to the animus that he had just inspired in the invisible person at the door. "You are dismissed."

"*No,*" Gadriel gasped. She turned towards Holly. "You're a grown woman, Holly Harker. Please tell me you're not going to let that pass."

Holly's expression tightened. The freckles on her nose wrinkled, and her fingers closed into her fists.

"CALL HIM SOMETHING FOUL, I AM BEGGING YOU," Gadriel pleaded.

Holly smiled tightly. "*Espèce de branleur arriéré, enflure,*" she said.[22]

Gadriel sniggered.

Mr Parker frowned. "Pardon?" he asked.

Holly shook her head, reaching up to push her hair back from her face. "It's just a French phrase, sir. It means something like… 'absolutely, yes'."[23]

"Good enough," said Gadriel. "I'll accept that."

Mr Parker squinted at Holly dubiously. But Holly turned on her heel with one last nod of reply, and swept out of the office.

Ella had leaned herself against the wall in the hallway, with

---

22   +1/2 Point of Sin (Holly Harker): A Mean-Spirited Comment. Adjustment note: mean-spirited comments are normally worth a full point of sin—but this particular comment, being true, was worth only half a point of sin.

23   +1 Point of Sin (Holly Harker): Lying.

her arms still crossed. She shoved back to standing as Holly exited, falling into step next to her. "I need to get my guitar from the music room," she said.

"We have to leave, Ella," Holly replied. Her tone was low and forcibly level, though the freckles on her nose were still wrinkled with stress. "You're banned from the grounds. Besides which, you can't look after a guitar at the café."

Ella furrowed her brow. "At the café?" she asked.

Holly stopped in her tracks. Her patience had become visibly strained. "I had to leave work to come and get you," she said. "I still have half my shift left. If you can't go practice with your band, then you have to come to work with me."

Ella's eyes widened. "I don't need a babysitter!" she said. "I can go home on my own."

"You're staying with me, and that is final," Holly stated. She started walking again, a bit more quickly than before. "You're lucky you don't have to come to work with me tomorrow, as well."

Ella hurried after her with a sound of primal frustration.

Holly tried to force a sympathetic look onto her features as she glanced backwards—but the expression was clearly lacking, and all three of them knew it. "I know things are difficult right now, Ella," she began.

"Please don't," Ella warned her. "You're awful at this."[24]

"I wish I could help more," Holly continued helplessly. "I

---

24   +1/2 Point of Sin (Ella Harker): A Mean-Spirited Comment. Adjustment note: see above comment regarding truthful but mean-spirited comments.

just don't even know where to begin."

"I didn't trip Millie Wilson because my mum is dead!" Ella burst out. "I tripped her because she's a horrid—"

"—that's enough, definitely!" Holly interrupted quickly. She scowled at Ella. "Fine. You don't want to talk. That's fine. You can sulk alone at a coffee shop instead. Does *that* suit you?"

"It does," Ella said tartly.

"Good."

"*Good.*"

Ella pulled out a set of earbuds, shoving them furiously into her ears.

"What a mess," Gadriel marvelled.

She followed the other two back onto a city bus, typing intently into her phone all the while.

> 4. Holly Harker is locked in an epic struggle with her teenage niece.

"Maybe you should apologise to the bus driver too," Ella muttered beneath her breath, as she settled into one of the bus seats.[25]

"Excuse me?" Holly asked sharply. "What was that?"

Ella gestured at her earbuds with an innocently baffled expression. "Can't hear you," she said.[26]

Gadriel considered her phone very seriously for a moment, before adding:

> 5. The niece is winning.

---

25 +1/10 Point of Sin (Ella Harker): Sarcasm.
26 +1 Point of Sin (Ella Harker): Lying.

Chapter Seven

CUMULATIVE SIN METRIC (HOLLY HARKER): -935.5

The sign next to the pond said 'Do Not Feed the Ducks'. Despite this, several ducks had already become interested in Gadriel's presence on the park bench the next morning, which strongly suggested that someone—or likely, many someones—had ignored the sign completely. This, Gadriel thought, was an apt commentary on the human condition.[27]

Cautious at first, the birds sent out a scout. One brave duck waddled casually towards Gadriel, checking the ground for tasty morsels and glancing sideways at the fallen angel as it went.

"No," said Gadriel. "Shoo. I'm thinking." Gadriel had opted to be a man today, in an attempt to shake up his thinking. He often found that a change in perspective dug up new ideas. This did not, of course, require a *large* change in his appearance; his masculine form looked rather like a pleasantly forgettable sibling

---

27   Ironically, at least one fallen angel other than Gadriel happened to feed the ducks here. Had Gadriel known this, it might have injected some uncertainty into his ideas about human nature.

to the woman he had been just yesterday.

Holly and Ella had remained mostly silent with one another the previous evening, leading to little further illumination. But Gadriel's instincts insisted that the answer to all of his problems had finally presented itself, if only he could figure out an angle.

The bravest mallard was now standing directly in front of Gadriel's bench. The duck quacked at the fallen angel, clearly offended by his lack of interest.

"You're not *owed* bread, you know," Gadriel told the duck. "And I don't have any with me, regardless."

The duck turned its tail, shuffling away with an irritated waddle. A moment later, Gadriel heard a murmur of quacks travel through the flock, and he realised that the duck had responded to its fellows, rather than to his statement.

A young, plump faced boy had come hurtling down one of the nearby footpaths, running at top speed. His beleaguered mother fought to keep up while pushing an oversized buggie. "You come back here this instant, Ronald!" she yelled.

Ronald charged ahead without pause. "Ducks!" he cried triumphantly. He rushed into the flock, waving his arms and quacking. The birds scattered, flapping their wings with indignation as they retreated towards the water. Ronald followed them, gleefully splashing into the mud. Black, splotchy stains appeared on his little chubby legs, soon climbing their way up to his shorts and t-shirt. The ducks had outpaced dear Ronald, however, and the toddler soon squelched his way sulkily back to solid ground.

"Oh, god!" the boy's mother panted, still lagging far behind. "Why? Why me?"

Ronald paused in front of Gadriel, who cocked his head in

reply.

"Ducks?" said Ronald.

"No, not at all," Gadriel replied. "*Thinking.* I said that already."

Ronald nodded distractedly—as he did, his eyes locked upon the grass just next to his feet. The toddler leaned down curiously. When he straightened, he was clutching a dirty bit of old biscuit in his pudgy fingers. An impish glint came into the child's eyes as he glanced towards the ducks on the pond.

Ignoring signage was worth exactly one tenth of a point of sin. It was such a negligible sin that most fallen angels wouldn't have bothered. But Gadriel was feeling tetchy and even more rebellious than usual.

"GO ON," he said. "DO IT BEFORE YOUR MUM GETS DOWN HERE."

The boy looked at his grungy biscuit. He looked to his mother, and then to the ducks, and then back at the biscuit.

Finally, a surge of wild determination overcame his features—and he stuffed the entire grimy old biscuit into his mouth.

Gadriel stared at the toddler. "You know," he said. "That's on me. I should have seen that coming."

The boy's mother hurried past the bench. "Spit it out!" she howled. "What have you eaten this time? Good lord, you're enough trouble for two!"

Gadriel slammed his fist into his palm. "That's it!" he declared suddenly. He stood up from the bench, searching for his phone. As the screen came up, he typed in a brand new line item.

6. Ella Harker sins enough for both women combined.

"It's time to try an easier target for a bit," Gadriel announced, as he tucked his phone back into his pocket.

Ronald's mother was still wiping uselessly at the child's face as Gadriel passed them both. "Ducks," the boy muttered furiously.

"You'll get them next time," Gadriel assured the boy distractedly.

***

The halls of Battenberg Grammar were far more densely packed as Gadriel made his way through their glass double doors. The children in the crowd were only slightly taller than his waist, however, which made it easy to see where he was going. All of the students wore very similar uniforms—white shirts, navy knitted vests, and matching trousers or skirts—and while Gadriel obviously had a fondness for knitted vests, he found himself subconsciously stifled by the sea of conformity.

"Small mercy I never had to go to school," he mumbled to himself.

Students shot him wary looks as he passed, searching for suggestions of authority. He shooed at them with one hand, and they backed out of his path like herd animals without a leader.

As Gadriel slipped into the tiny reception area in front of the headmaster's office, the noisy din of the hallway was slightly muted—only to be abruptly replaced by the loud, aggrieved voice of an older woman.

"I have a *note!*" protested the woman, who'd installed herself directly in front of Mrs Applebee's desk. Her American accent stood out sharply against the backdrop of the setting. "You are required by law to offer appropriate accommodations for my child!" At first, Gadriel thought she was a tall woman, given the way that she loomed over Mrs Applebee—but on second glance, she was wearing high black heels which made her appear far taller than she really was. Her cream silk blouse and red trousers were custom-tailored, and her short black hair had been cut at a sharp, dramatic angle in order to frame her pale face. Though she was clearly upset, she was splitting her attention as she spoke, tapping quickly into her smartphone as she spoke down to the receptionist.

Mrs Applebee, for her part, seemed remarkably unfazed. She had yet to rise from her chair; in fact, she had settled her chin into one hand as she gazed up at the woman in front of her desk over the top of her thick-framed glasses. "We already have a note on file informing us that Beatrix has trouble understanding written instructions," Mrs Applebee said. Any celestial bureaucrat would have envied the inscrutable patience she displayed upon her face. "Will that be all, Mrs Relish?"

Gadriel squeezed himself past the woman in front of the desk to stand beside Mrs Applebee's chair. "Apologies," he interjected mildly, "but I'm here to fill in for the school counsellor."

Mrs Relish let out an exasperated sound, now speaking loudly over Gadriel. "You should have *two* notes, Mrs Applebee," she said. "Dr Rodriguez sent a follow-up saying that Beatrix has trouble understanding *spoken* instructions. She'll require extra time on all oral assignments—"

"Well, which note would you like us to keep on file, then?" Mrs Applebee asked drolly. "I'm unclear as to your preferences, Mrs Relish." She glanced over at Gadriel. "No one told me we'd found a replacement counsellor," she said.

Mrs Relish narrowed her eyes. "I'll require both notes on

file," she replied. "And I expect you to explain to your teachers that Beatrix will—*by law*, I remind you—require that extra time on all written and oral assignments."

"So… *all* assignments?" Mrs Applebee asked tartly.

Gadriel smiled at the receptionist. "You seem to have your hands full," he said. "If you can just get me a badge and give me some directions, I'll be right out of your hair. It's Mr Gadriel Sweet, by the way."

Mrs Relish slapped her phone down on the desk with an infuriated noise from the back of her throat. "This is a very important conversation, Mr Sweet!" she declared. "I'll thank you for waiting your turn."

Gadriel pressed a hand to his chest. "I'm so sorry to interrupt," he said. "I didn't realise the office was going to be so busy." He glanced sideways at Mrs Applebee and murmured: "SAY WHAT YOU'RE REALLY THINKING. YOU'LL FEEL BETTER."

Mrs Applebee *had* been reaching for the landline phone at her desk—but at this, she pushed her glasses back onto her nose and fixed a withering look upon Mrs Relish. "Madam," she said, "you *insisted* that your daughter was so gifted that she ought to be educated with the older children—against the school's recommendation, I might add. Perhaps she would be doing better in her classes if she were still with the younger cohort. Or perhaps Dr Rodriguez could write a note explaining that she has been saddled with an overbearing mother?"

Mrs Relish's eyes widened. "Well, I *never*—"

"YOU REALLY CAN'T BE BOTHERED WITH ANYTHING ELSE RIGHT NOW," Gadriel told the receptionist. "YOU'D RATHER JUST WRITE ME A NAME TAG AND SEND ME OFF."

Mrs Applebee pried open a drawer, snapping up a permanent pen, a paper name tag, and a plastic badge. She scribbled furiously for a moment as Mrs Relish caught her breath. "Here you are!" she told Gadriel shortly. "You're room 113."

Gadriel took the name tag with a last pleasant nod, stuffing it into its plastic badge. He flicked his eyes towards the woman in the suit, who was still sputtering incoherently. "You'd like to speak with the headmaster, right this instant," he informed her.

"I want to speak with the headmaster, right this instant!" Mrs Relish declared finally. "Mark my words, I *will* post this on social media! I have over twenty-thousand followers, and if even half of them decide to call your office, it will ruin your afternoon! I have doctors and reporters and politicians who all follow me, you know."

Gadriel sidestepped back for the door. He shot Mrs Applebee one last sympathetic glance, before adding: "Let her talk with the headmaster. They deserve one another."

He slipped back out into the hallway just as the first period bell rang, strolling for room 113. On his way, he looked down at the name tag, which read: *Mr Gabriel Sweet.*

He sighed once, and pinned it to his knitted vest.

Room 113 was even smaller than reception had been—though it had a tiny window behind the desk, at least, which let in a bit of natural light. There were three hard, uncomfortable looking chairs in the room, as well as an empty bookshelf which looked as though it hadn't been dusted in weeks. The rest of the walls were white and bare. The only spot of colour in the room came from a miserable plastic plant on the windowsill, which looked about ready to jump from a height in order to end its dreary existence.

"Hm," muttered Gadriel. "This won't do at all." He turned back for the hallway, peering idly through windows as he walked its length. Eventually, he discovered a dingy-looking room with a kitchenette and several padded chairs. The door was guarded by a keypad—but the physical lock it controlled was no match for a plastic name tag and several thousand years of determined delinquency. Gadriel flicked it neatly open and headed into the room, humming idly to himself as he went.

The half-empty pot of cheap coffee on the counter confirmed Gadriel's suspicion that he'd found the staff room. He briefly lifted the pot to sniff at it, but replaced it just as quickly with a disgusted expression. He rummaged next in the small fridge, piling plastic containers and lunchboxes on the floor beside him.

"No," Gadriel muttered, as he went through the lunchboxes. "No, not you. Ugh—cold peas, really?" He paused while searching through a particular lunchbox, though, and reached in to pull out a chocolate bar. "Perfect! Thank *you*, Ms Schmidt."

Gadriel tucked the chocolate bar into his pocket and refilled the fridge. Then, without further ado, he hauled two of the padded chairs over his shoulder and headed for the door.

Chapter Eight

CUMULATIVE SIN METRIC (HOLLY HARKER): -935.5
CUMULATIVE SIN METRIC (ELLA HARKER): +212.7

Lately, Ella Harker's least favourite day of the week had been Monday. Today was Thursday, however, and it was very quickly shaping up to take the lead.

First period Thursday was maths with Ms Schmidt. Ella loathed maths only *slightly* less than she loathed history. She'd avoided her maths textbook all week long, reassuring herself that she could cram for this morning's test at the last moment and still get by. But yesterday, Millie Wilson had called Beatrix Relish an American cow, and after that, Ella had had little choice but to trip Millie—and after *that*, things had rather… devolved. Somehow, Ella had ended her evening in a loud, busy café without any of her textbooks.

And now, here she was—staring down the barrel of one of Ms Schmidt's cutesy maths tests without a clue in the world.

Ella focused blankly on the paper in front of her, with a seething ball of anxiety in her stomach.

Ms Schmidt has owned 12 animals over the course of

her life. She has owned 4 more cats than all of her other animals combined. How many cats has she owned?

Ella leaned forward, thudding her head into the desk. *Thanks for nothing, Aunt Holly,* she thought bitterly.

Deep down, Ella knew it wasn't really her aunt's fault that she'd ended up in this position. But yesterday had been infuriating enough, even *before* her aunt had come rushing in to apologise for her behaviour. Perhaps, Ella thought, if she hadn't been so frustrated, she might have remembered about the textbooks.

Too late, Ella thought glumly. *Time to face the music.*

Ella pried her forehead from the paper, sitting back up in her chair. She scanned the classroom as though it might contain some inscrutable clue to the problem before her… but all she saw was her fellow classmates dutifully hunched over their own papers. Her eyes fell upon the back wall, where Ms Schmidt's favourite cat poster loomed ominously over the desks. 'Think PAWsitive!' it said at the top. The tabby cat in the picture had all but knocked the exclamation point off the end of the sentence.

At least, Ella thought, she wasn't stewing alone in her anxiety—poor Beatrix was already chewing nervously on the end of her pencil. No amount of extra time was likely to help Beatrix with a maths test, no matter how brilliant her mother thought she was. Once, Beatrix had *loved* maths—a strange and concerning condition which Ella was willing to overlook in favour of her sunny personality. But from the first moment Beatrix's mother had jumped her into the next academic year, she'd started struggling to maintain that interest. These days, Beatrix Relish was far more fraught and far less sunny than she had been.

Ella leaned her chin into her hand, letting her gaze wander to the boy on her immediate left. Stupidly fit, stupidly smart Jasper O'Neill was working diligently through the equations on the test with a confidence that Ella couldn't help but envy. Everyone knew that *Jasper* studied for his tests—though just how he managed it in between all of the football practice was anyone's guess. Occasionally, a teacher would ask him to read the correct answers off his own paper when they were discussing their marks in the next class.

YOU COULD TAKE A PEEK AT HIS WORK, whispered a voice in Ella's head. JUST ENOUGH TO FIGURE OUT A CLUE.

Ella darted her eyes towards Jasper's tidy handwriting. *I'll just see how he's working the problem,* Ella reasoned to herself. *It's not like I'm stealing all of his answers.* She gave the rest of the room one last, furtive glance before hurriedly copying the string of numbers Jasper had written out for the first problem.[28]

"Ms Schmidt!" Millie Wilson whined abruptly across the classroom. "Ms Schmidt, Ella is *cheating!*"

Ella shot Millie a furious glare. "I am *not!*" she snapped, curling her arm defensively over her paper to shield the copied numbers. "Why don't you mind your own test, Millie?"[29]

Millie narrowed her eyes at Ella, screwing up her face into an expression which was probably meant to be insulting. Her platinum blonde fringe was overly long and messy, always escaping her pony tail; it shadowed her eyes intensely in a way that Ella believed made her look like a cartoon villain.

Millie knocked her temporary crutch meaningfully against

---

28   +2 Points of Sin (Ella Harker): Cheating.

29   +1 Point of Sin (Ella Harker): Lying.

OLIVIA ATWATER

the side of her desk.

Ella rolled her eyes in response—but she couldn't help glancing at Ms Schmidt's desk to see what their teacher thought of the situation. Her heart sank slowly as she saw the woman striding across the classroom towards them.

As far as Ella could tell, Ms Schmidt spent most of her life being *very excited* about maths in a way that very few people could relate to. The woman's loud, flowery blouses contrasted starkly with her black skin and frizzy hair; the blouses, Ella knew, were a sort of camouflage to set unwary people at their ease so that Ms Schmidt could ambush them with cheerful trivia about *how often we use maths without ever noticing!* The maths teacher did, however, have a rare second mode of existence; sometimes, when her brows drew together and her broad nose wrinkled, she could find her way to being *very concerned* instead of *very excited*.

Ms Schmidt now wrinkled her nose and straightened her pink orchid blouse as she strode between Ella and Millie's desks, glancing between the two girls.

"Girls," Ms Schmidt said, shooting them a warning look over her horn-rimmed glasses. "I know you haven't been getting on, but I don't want you using my classroom for your arguments."

"I wasn't doing anything!" Ella protested, shooting another dirty look at Millie. "*She* started it!"[30]

Millie crossed her arms over her chest. "Oh, and I made you look at Jasper's paper?" she asked. "Just like I *made* you trip me in the hallway?"

Ella's mouth dropped open. "And I suppose you were just

---

30   +1 Point of Sin (Ella Harker): Lying.

minding your own business both times, were you?" she shot back.

"Girls!" Ms Schmidt said again sharply, demanding their attention. "That is enough! Everyone else is trying to finish their tests."

Millie shifted sulkily in her seat, glancing away. "Ella is trying to finish *Jasper's* test," she sneered softly.

Whispers skittered through the classroom. Contrary to Ms Schmidt's statement, no one seemed at all focused on finishing their test any more. Instead, Ella felt the entire room's attention pressing down on *her*. Jasper had turned a dumbfounded stare upon her, as though the idea that anyone might cheat was entirely foreign to him.

Ella stood up abruptly, clenching her fists at her sides. "I swear, if you don't shut your trap, Millie—" she started.

A knock at the door drew everyone's attention at once. Even Ella startled, temporarily distracted from the sentence that probably would have resulted in another suspension.

The door opened before anyone could really respond to the knock. A pale, mousy-looking man in a knitted vest peered inside, blinking owlishly at the room.

"Oh dear," he said. "I seem to have mixed up the timetable. I was sure this was an empty period. My apologies."

Ms Schmidt blinked. "Can I help you, sir?" she asked carefully. A temporary armistice had fallen over the classroom, as though everyone at once had decided that it was far too embarrassing to keep arguing in front of a stranger.

"I suppose it's a bit late to duck out," the man admitted sheepishly. "I'd hoped to introduce myself. I'm the new counsellor, Mr Sweet."

Ms Schmidt exhaled with relief. "Thank *god*," she breathed.

("Oh, I wouldn't do that," the man mumbled—but Ms Schmidt didn't seem to hear him.)

"Your timing couldn't be more perfect, Mr... Gabriel Sweet?" Ms Schmidt squinted at his name tag, then nodded once to herself, gesturing between the two girls. "Ella, Millie. I don't know what's caused this problem between you, but I want it to end today. You're both to go with Mr Sweet until you've worked things out."

The counsellor paled. "Er... both girls at once?" he asked weakly. "Perhaps it would go better one at a time—"

"What?" Ella demanded. "I don't want to go anywhere with Millie!"

Millie let out an indignant noise. "Why should *I* go?" she asked. "I didn't do anything wrong!"

Ms Schmidt winced. "It isn't about who's right or wrong!" she said. "If I wanted to punish you, I'd send you to the head-master. But I'm sending you with Mr Sweet in order to have the matter *solved*. That's what a counsellor does—isn't it, Mr Sweet?"

Mr Sweet sighed. "I suppose it is," he said dolefully. "It's... fine. I can work with this." He glanced at Ella. "I take it you're in the middle of a test? The girls will simply have to make it up at a later date."

Ella opened her mouth to protest again... but as she did, Mr Sweet levelled an exasperated look at her.

YOU WOULDN'T WANT TO TAKE A TEST IN YOUR CURRENT STATE, WOULD YOU? said the voice in her head.

Ella closed her mouth again abruptly. *Why should I argue?* she realised. *I'm getting out of maths! I'll have another chance to study.*

"I thought not," said Mr Sweet. "And you... Millie, was it? Would *you* like to stay and finish your test? Or would you rather sit down and have a friendly conversation while we sort this all out?"

Millie bit at her lip. Not a single student in the class would have insisted on staying put, when the question was framed *that* way.

Well. Perhaps Jasper would.

"Fine," Millie said shortly. She forced herself up from her desk onto her crutch, exaggerating her wince as she hobbled for the door.

Ella rolled her eyes and grabbed her bag. "Stop screwing up your face like that," she muttered at Millie on her way past. "You just look constipated."[31]

Millie's face dropped back to a carefully neutral expression.

Mr Sweet coughed into his hand. Ella shot him a suspicious glance—but he continued his coughing fit quite convincingly, and she decided that she must have been imagining the laugh after all.

"This way then," he said, as he opened the door for them both. "Let's go have a chat, shall we?"

***

Mr Sweet had put his feet up on the old desk in the counsellor's office. Millie and Ella settled warily into the chairs in front of the desk—padded with two threadbare, daisy-patterned pillows—as he pulled a chocolate bar from his pocket and slowly began to

---

31   +1 Point of Sin (Ella Harker): A Mean-Spirited Comment.

unwrap it.

"Would either of you like some chocolate?" he offered.

Ella frowned at him. "Are we… in trouble, or not?" she asked.

Mr Sweet idly snapped off two pieces of chocolate, sliding them across the desk. "Oh, you might be in trouble with *some-one*," he said, "but you can't be in trouble with me, since I don't know the first thing about what's going on. I only got here this morning."

"*I'm* not in trouble," Millie insisted, with her head held high. "I'm not the one who cheated on the test!" But her hand flashed out swiftly, snatching her piece of chocolate from the desk. Ella seized her piece just as quickly, suddenly aware that Millie might take it next if she didn't.[32]

Mr Sweet chewed thoughtfully on his own piece of choco-late. He ignored Millie's statement entirely, keeping up the friend-ly chatter. "Was that maths test difficult?" he asked. "Looked like an awful lot of numbers. And letters, too. You just can't trust maths once the letters get involved, can you?"

Ella nibbled carefully at her chocolate. She *had* been very upset when she'd walked in… but chocolate always seemed to soothe things. "And an awful lot of cats," she agreed. "Ms Schmidt always likes giving us questions about cats." She matched his friendly tone, as yet uncertain of his intentions.

Millie licked the chocolate off her fingers and promptly crossed her arms. "I don't know why you've brought us here, but I'm not buying this cool counsellor bit," she said suspiciously.

---

32   +1/2 **Point of Sin** (Ella Harker): Chocolate.

"You're like one of those lame youth pastors, trying to be hip."

Mr Sweet coughed again—and this time, Ella was *sure* that he was laughing. "You're right, that's brilliant!" he said. "I should try that one of these days. I bet they'd even let me into church."

"You should have just let him think he was doing well," Ella muttered at Millie. "We could've got more chocolate."

"What's this?" Mr Sweet asked, arching an eyebrow. "I thought you two hated each other. Now you're closing ranks on me?"

Ella glanced sideways at Millie, who met her eyes back. The only thing worse than being stuck in a room with her mortal enemy was having an adult there to *meddle*. She was fairly certain that Millie felt the same way, judging by the faintly disgusted look on her face.

"It doesn't matter," said Mr Sweet. "I'm not trying to be *hip*, actually. I was just establishing the stakes before we get started." He held up the remainder of the chocolate bar, clearing his throat. "In the next five minutes, I am going to ask several questions. Whichever one of you answers them to my satisfaction stays here with the rest of this chocolate for the remainder of the period; whichever one of you is *less* forthcoming gets to go play with mathematical cats again. Ms Schmidt will later hear how very disappointed I was with your lack of cooperation."

Millie goggled at him. "Are you blackmailing us with maths?" she demanded.

Mr Sweet pointed at her approvingly. "I am!" he said, in an upbeat tone. "But please, Miss Wilson—I'm the one asking the questions now. And remember, both of you, that there can only be one winner. In precisely five minutes, one of you will have chocolate and one of you will have a test in front of you again."

"That's not fair!" Ella blurted out. "We'll have less time on the test!"

Mr Sweet ignored her too, now. He steepled his fingers, surveying them both. "Let's start with an easy one," he offered. "How long have you both been attending this school?"

Ella looked at Millie again. Millie looked back warily. "Don't," Ella warned her. "You see what he's doing—"

"Two and a half years now," Millie interrupted quickly. "We're Year 9."

Ella stomped her foot on the floor. "You're giving him what he wants!" she hissed.

"Very good, Miss Wilson," said Mr Sweet. "I foresee several imaginary kittens in Miss Harker's future."

"You said you didn't know what was going on!" Ella challenged him. "How do you know our last names?"

Mr Sweet smiled pleasantly at her. "Next question," he continued. "What started your altercation in the hallway yesterday?"

At *this* question, Millie pressed her lips together. Ella crossed her arms in front of her, narrowing her eyes at the counsellor.

"Ah," Mr Sweet sighed heavily. "I misspoke earlier, actually. There can be *one or fewer* winners in this particular situation. If no one answers this question, then I suppose I'll be forced to eat the rest of this chocolate myself, while the both of you return to your tests." He popped off another piece of chocolate, chewing it over with a satisfied sound, and his eyes flickered over to Ella.

You don't want to let her win, surely, said a voice in Ella's head.

Ella ground her teeth together. Why *was* she bothering to

protect Millie? The other girl had already proven she was willing to snitch, after all.

"Millie was talking about Beatrix behind her back," Ella blurted out. "Her and the other girls were all laughing and calling her stupid because her mum's American."

Millie kicked at Ella's shin—but Ella had been prepared for just such a response, and the other girl's foot slammed into a chair leg instead. Millie choked back a yelp of agony.

"No one called her stupid," Millie protested, in a voice faintly strained with pain. "I said she was insufferable. She thinks she's so smart she belongs the next year up, but she needs extra time on everything! And her mum does online videos every day about how *special* Beatrix is, how she's too good for this school—"

"Beatrix can't control her mum!" Ella shot back heatedly. "How long d'you think you'd be grounded for if you tried to tell off *your* mum?"

"Good, excellent," Mr Sweet said brightly. "Now we're getting somewhere. Let's talk about parents. How do your parents feel about this little fight you've been having, girls?"

Ella shut her mouth abruptly, as her stomach twisted with nausea. Silence settled in around them; even Millie shifted down into her chair uncomfortably.

"I've hit upon a sore subject then," Mr Sweet observed.

"My mum knows it's not my fault," Millie mumbled. "Obviously." Suddenly, she couldn't look at Ella. They both knew Ella didn't *have* parents any more.

Mr Sweet had no such trouble. He considered Ella directly, waiting patiently for her answer.

"My Aunt Holly's upset with me," Ella said shortly.

"Your aunt?" Mr Sweet asked. "She's your guardian, is she? How long has that been the case?"

"About half a year," Ella mumbled.

Mr Sweet focused upon her intently. "And do you normally have a good relationship with your aunt?" he asked.

Ella pressed her lips together. "No," she said. "I barely know her. I only met her for the first time at—" She stopped, and gritted her teeth. "I'd rather go take the test now, I think."

"Do I get the chocolate, then?" Millie asked immediately.

Mr Sweet scribbled something on a notepad and tore off the top piece of paper. He snapped off a piece of chocolate, and offered both the paper and the chocolate out to Millie. "This is your bribe, Miss Wilson," he informed her. "According to this note, you are far too upset to sit for a test today. If you take it, I expect you to avoid talking about Beatrix or her mother for the entire next week. We'll discuss further bribery after that, assuming you hold up your end of the deal."

Millie blinked slowly, staring at the note and the chocolate. Ella stared along with her. The old counsellor, Mrs Lisbon, had never offered *bribes*.

"Yes or no, Miss Wilson?" Mr Sweet prompted her, waving the note in front of her. "I have the power to make your school year *much* easier. I can absolve you of later play dates with cats... or even get you entire days off of school. But I want to see that you're willing to make it worth my while. Prove that you're willing to play ball, and I'll see you back in this office to discuss the possibilities."

Millie raised her eyebrows. Gradually, she reached out to take both the note and the chocolate from the counsellor.

"Excellent," said Mr Sweet. "I love it when a deal comes together." He inclined his head at Millie. "You may leave, Miss Wilson."

Millie stuffed the chocolate in her mouth and grabbed her crutch, pushing up to her feet. She hobbled her way out of the room with one last curious look at the counsellor.

As the door closed behind her, Ella leaned back in her chair. "Was that… legal?" she asked.

"Oh, probably not," said Mr Sweet. "But it's more effective than asking you to hug it out, isn't it?" He tapped his pen against the desk in front of him, considering. "You're a loyal friend, Miss Harker. I'm happy to work with that. If you help me get what I need, I can significantly improve Beatrix's life. Does that sound workable?"

Ella knit her brow. "I don't understand," she said slowly. "What is it that you need from me?"

Mr Sweet smiled. "For starters," he said, "I want you to finish telling me how you met your Aunt Holly. After that… I want you to complain at me. At least once a week—though preferably more often."

Ella slouched down further in her seat. "You're bribing me into therapy?" she asked sceptically.

"Why not?" Mr Sweet asked. "You barely know me, and I'm asking you to talk about difficult things. You deserve to get something in return for that, don't you?" He tapped his pen against the desk again. "I'm a practical person, Miss Harker. I'm not going to punish you into compliance—we both know that wouldn't work, regardless. If you'd rather walk out that door, you can. But here's what's going to happen if you stay: next week, once Miss Wilson has proven that she can follow instructions, I am going to convince her to say *nice* things about Beatrix to the other girls. And wouldn't that be helpful?"

Ella chewed at her lip. "There's no way you'll get Millie to do that," she said. "She wouldn't *ever*."

Mr Sweet popped another piece of chocolate into his mouth. "Oh," he mumbled past it, "but don't you want to see if I can pull it off?" He slid the rest of the chocolate bar across the desk, holding her eyes.

MIGHT AS WELL, something whispered in her mind.

Ella reached out to take the chocolate.[33]

"...I met Aunt Holly at the hospital," she said quietly. "My mum died before she made it there."

"And why was your mother in the hospital?" Mr Sweet asked.

"She was in a car accident," Ella mumbled. "Um." She swallowed back a knot in her throat. "She might've been drinking."

Mr Sweet nodded slowly. "And your father?" he asked. His voice was low and soothing now.

Ella chewed numbly at the end of the chocolate bar. "Never met him either," she muttered. "I don't even know his name."

"Ah," said Mr Sweet softly. "That *is* a mess, isn't it? One awful accident, and suddenly both you and your aunt have had your lives turned upside down."

Ella let out a sharp breath. "Yes, it's really awful for Aunt Holly," she said sarcastically. "I'm sure she cries every night over being stuck with me."[34]

---

33   +1/2 Point of Sin (Ella Harker): Chocolate.

34   +1/10 Point of Sin (Ella Harker): Sarcasm.

Mr Sweet nodded thoughtfully. "I'm starting to see the shape of the problem," he said. "I don't fully understand it yet... but it's certainly getting clearer."

The bell rang for the next period. Ella pushed up from the chair, avoiding his gaze.

"What's your least favourite class?" Mr Sweet asked her, before she could leave.

Ella gave him a wary look. "History with Ms Wood," she said. "It's Monday and Wednesday next week."

Mr Sweet scribbled on his notepad and tore off a sheet, offering it out to her. "Well then, Miss Harker," he said. "I'll see you on Monday."

Chapter Nine

CUMULATIVE SIN METRIC (HOLLY HARKER): -935.5
CUMULATIVE SIN METRIC (ELLA HARKER): +217.1

Friday morning found Gadriel standing in line at Déjà Brew, despite the miserable downpour outside.

It was very *early* in the morning. But he'd acquired himself a job for some silly reason, and—as it turned out—people expected you to show up for those things nearly every day.

"What was I thinking?" Gadriel muttered. "I don't enjoy *working*."

"Working?" asked a deep male voice next to him. "You?"

Gadriel turned sharply. The voice's owner was a tall, handsome Black man in a sharp charcoal suit, with an impeccable jawline and a closely shaved head. He flashed a bright smile at Gadriel. "Fancy seeing you here again," Barachiel said.

"No!" Gadriel sputtered. "Not again! Don't you have *any* sense of shame? We look like tacky gender twins!"

Barachiel shrugged. "You're the one who demanded I change genders last time," he said. "How was I supposed to know you were going to do the same?"

Gadriel narrowed his eyes. "I *know* you're doing this on purpose," he accused the angel.

Barachiel offered him a friendly, unaffected smile. "I didn't mean to upset you," he said soothingly. "But here, I'll make it up to you—let me buy you a hot chocolate."

Gadriel crossed his arms sullenly. "A mocha," he muttered. "I need caffeine. Lots of it." He eyed Barachiel sideways. "I know you got my texts."

Barachiel slapped at his forehead. "Ah, I did!" he said. "I was busy at the time. I absolutely meant to respond, but I'm afraid I got caught up in something. Well—I'm here now, I suppose. What did you need, Gadriel?"

"What do I *need?*" Gadriel seethed. He fought back the urge to grab Barachiel by the lapels of his very expensive-looking suit. "You sent me on a wild goose chase! The woman can't be tempted! I *still* haven't managed to increase her Cumulative Sin Metric, not even by one point."

Barachiel raised an eyebrow. "I warned you she would be a difficult case," he said. "That's precisely why I sought you out. You're the expert on petty temptations, after all." He considered Gadriel curiously. "You have a plan, though, don't you? You just said you were working."

Gadriel groaned. "I'm making nice with the niece," he said. "I've become a school counsellor. That lie isn't going to hold up for long, by the way—eventually, some agnostic administrator is going to ask me for my credentials, and I won't be able to distract them."

Barachiel stroked at his well-chiselled chin. "I could request a real identity for you," he said. "Only if you really think this counselling job will help you succeed, of course."

Gadriel knit his brow. "You can *do* that?" he asked.

Barachiel raised an eyebrow at him. "Working for the Man has its advantages," he replied. "I hear your side does something similar, on occasion."

"I'm not surprised it's *possible*," Gadriel clarified. "I'm just surprised that your side is willing to do it. Isn't lying a sin?"

"It certainly is," Barachiel agreed. "That's why we only do it when the gain in virtue is overwhelmingly worth the cost."

Gadriel scoffed. "And you don't find that just a bit hypocritical?" he asked.

Barachiel shot him a wry smile. "It's not at all hypocritical if you prefer the Jewish interpretation of the system," he said. "And I do."[35]

Gadriel narrowed his eyes at the angel. "I know my Torah just as well as you do, Barachiel," he said. "No one's in danger of dying right now. How do you square that?"

Barachiel ignored the question. "If I do this for you, I expect you to be a *good* school counsellor," the angel warned. "Heaven's resources are supposed to be used for virtue, after all."

Gadriel snorted. "Hah," he said. "You *can't* square it, can you?" He shook his head. "I'm not capable of being a good school counsellor. I am what I am. The best I can promise is that I won't go out of my way to damn anyone."

---

35 Jewish law allows, and even requires, that an adherent break lesser mitzvot in order to save a life. Normally, this requires an urgent situation—but angels, being immortal, have a very different definition of the word "urgent" than humans do.

Barachiel sized up Gadriel, pondering this offer. Finally, he offered out his hand. As Gadriel took it, the angel gave him a long, slow handshake.

"Do you know," Barachiel said, "I trust you more than I trust some angels, Gadriel. You always did get the job done. It's a terrible shame you won't come back."

Gadriel scowled, tugging his hand free. "You know I won't," he said. "Not even if someone up top goes mad and decides to offer. I'd tell you why all over again, except that we haven't got years to stand here arguing."

"I know all about the chocolate and the Cynics," Barachiel assured Gadriel hastily. "I'm not going to try and change your mind right now. But just… think on it. Perhaps I could subcontract you. I'm sure there's *something* I could offer you in return."

Gadriel rolled his eyes, wiping his hand on his knitted vest. "I can't imagine anything of the sort," he said. "In either case—"

"Next, please!" Holly's voice called across the line, and Gadriel realised that they were at the front. He strolled for the counter, dragging Barachiel behind him.

"Miss Harker!" Gadriel said pleasantly. "I didn't realise you were on shift."

Holly was a bit less harried today—her honey-blonde hair was almost completely confined to its bun, and her deep brown eyes were clear and alert. She glanced between the two men, blinking in puzzlement. "Barry!" she said, with a note of pleasant surprise. "I didn't realise you knew Gabe."

Gadriel raised his eyebrows at Barachiel. "*Barry?*" he repeated.

Barachiel smiled warmly. "I know Gadriel quite well," he said. "He's my sibling, in fact."

Holly blinked again slowly. "I see," she said. "And... he's..." She coloured abruptly. "Oh, that's none of my business."

Gadriel knit his brow. "What's none of your business?" he asked.

Holly's flush deepened, spreading once more to the apples of her cheeks. "I don't mean to be insulting," she assured Gadriel quickly. "It's just that... I could swear that you were... weren't you a woman before?"

Gadriel blinked. "Oh!" he said. "I forgot entirely. I suppose most people don't just change that when they feel like it?"

"It's *truly* none of my business," Holly told him again. "Only, er—I wouldn't want to offend. How should I call you?"

Gadriel offered her a look of mild confusion. "I'm not particular," he said. "I promise you won't be able to get it right, even if you try—no one ever has."

Barachiel nudged him lightly. "There *was* Ezekiel," he reminded Gadriel. "He got very close, didn't he?"

"Oh, that's true," Gadriel admitted. "Well, we can't all be Ezekiel."[36]

Holly stared at them both blankly.[37]

---

36 The biblical prophet Ezekiel remains one of the few human beings ever to see an angel's true form. He still got the details a bit garbled, but everyone is very proud of him for having tried.

37 The reader might be wondering why Gadriel and Barachiel see no problem discussing metaphysical matters in such a cavalier manner. The answer, of course, is that very few mortals would believe the truth even if it were told to them directly. Most of the time, in fact, human beings will rationalise away such things all on their own, without any sort of extra divine encouragement.

Barachiel cleared his throat. "One mocha and one coffee with milk, please," he said. "And one of your lovely brownies, if you have them today?"

Holly straightened at that, and her dark eyes lit up with pride. "I do have brownies today!" she said. "I baked a whole batch just yesterday. I'm almost out of them, but you'll have the second to last one."

"You baked brownies?" Gadriel asked her in confusion. "But I thought you didn't like chocolate!"

"Oh, I don't!" Holly said cheerfully, as she ducked beneath the counter. "I enjoy baking for other people, though. Don't you remember? It's the only way I ever made any friends at school."

Holly reappeared with a plate—upon which sat the biggest, most tempting brownie Gadriel had ever seen. Nearly the size of his entire hand, the brownie was *just* moist enough, while still being perfectly firm in the middle. Partially melted chocolate chips stood out within its crust, beckoning to the depths of Gadriel's chocolate-covered soul. This, the fallen angel thought, was a brownie to trump all other brownies—a silent temptation which required no extra encouragement at all.

"Is that... a triple-chocolate brownie?" Gadriel asked reverently.

Holly smiled slyly at him. "It *might* be," she said. "I do have one more, if you were interested. It's the very last one, in fact."

Gadriel rummaged swiftly for his wallet. "Both," he said

Occasionally, of course, someone *does* decide to start ranting about angels and demons in their midst. This does not tend to go very well for said person, but it does still neatly solve the problem.

fervently. "I'll take both. Barachiel isn't supposed to eat chocolate anyway—isn't that right, *Barry?*"

Barachiel spread his hands helplessly. "Technically true," he said. "I suppose you'll have to eat them both for me, Gadriel." He set a note down on the counter. "Ignore him and his money—I'm sure this will cover it. By the way, how is Ella doing?"

Holly sighed. "I honestly don't know," she said. "I'm so awkward with her, Barry. Even when I give it an honest try, I feel like she's *trying* to wind me up. I just wasn't meant to interact with children."

Gadriel had already snatched the brownie from its plate. He took in a deep breath, inhaling its heady scent, before he took his first careful bite. Rich chocolate exploded on his tongue, and he moaned softly.

"Well, perhaps Gadriel here can offer some advice," Barachiel said genially. "He's always been good with children, I like to think—he's just taken a job as a school counsellor, in fact."

"He has?" Holly looked hopefully towards Gadriel, who'd already taken another bite of brownie. He froze, suddenly put on the spot.

"I haff—" Gadriel swallowed the bite of brownie quickly. "I *have*," he corrected himself. "I wouldn't actually say that I'm good with children, mind you. I just know how to bribe them. They're similar to adults that way."

Holly laughed at this as though he'd made a joke. "Well, you've certainly got a leg up on me there," she said. "I've tried biscuits and brownies and all sorts of things on Ella. It's the closest I ever get to peace with her, but it's still not enough to make her *like* me."

Gadriel chewed another bite of brownie—he couldn't help himself. He held up one finger at Holly to stall her as it went down, and then took a deep breath. "Every human being has a heart's desire," he said didactically. "Children are no different. Let me ask you this: if your girl suddenly had to pack up and flee the country, what one item would she bring with her?"

Holly blinked. "Er," she said. "That's a novel question, isn't it? Well... I suppose she'd bring her guitar."

Gadriel nodded. He opened his mouth to speak again—then paused. "Where's the second brownie?" he asked.

Holly reached slowly down behind the counter. She brought out a second brownie—even bigger than the first!—and settled it neatly onto Gadriel's plate.

"As I was saying," Gadriel continued blithely, "heart's desire, yes. Now, *why* is that guitar her heart's desire?"

Holly pressed her lips together. "Ella's mother bought it for her," she said. Her tone had gone quiet and uncertain.

"Even better," Gadriel declared. "Today is... yes, it's Friday, isn't it? Well, as soon as Ella comes home from school, you'll offer to take her to the music shop this weekend to buy something small for her guitar. Let her talk at you the entire time. Ask her questions about her music. People *love* talking about their heart's desire." He picked up the plate of brownies with a wary, sideways glance at Barachiel. "These are both mine. You said so."

Barachiel held up his hands. "Go right ahead," he said.

Holly, meanwhile, was staring at Gadriel as though he had grown a second head. "It's that simple?" she asked.

"Well, why not?" Gadriel asked impatiently. "When you know what someone loves, it's easy to get them to do what you want."

For some reason, Holly glanced briefly at Barachiel… and then back at Gadriel. "Er… Gabe," she started. "Gadriel, was it?"

Gadriel nodded silently, as he popped another piece of brownie into his mouth.

"Why don't you give me your phone number?" Holly suggested. "I could let you know the next time I bake something. I was thinking of bringing in chocolate biscuits next week. I'm sure you'd love the recipe."

Gadriel sharpened his gaze on her. "Really?" he said.

"It was always my most popular recipe at school," Holly continued. "I hear the biscuits are a bit addictive."

Gadriel licked his lips. "I see," he said. "Well. It's not *that* far to the school. I could see my way to dropping by before work, if you let me know. Do you have something to write with?"

Holly smiled brightly. She'd already procured a pen from somewhere in between sentences; she held it out to him now expectantly. "I will *certainly* let you know," she assured him. Gadriel scribbled his phone number down on a napkin, and she snatched it neatly away from him, tucking it into the pocket of her apron.

Barachiel cleared his throat. "Oh," he interjected, "before we go sit down…" He reached into his coat pocket to retrieve a familiar deck of cards. "Would you like to know your future this morning, Miss Harker?"

Holly chuckled as though this were a running joke. "I suppose it couldn't hurt," she said.

"Oh, but it *could*," Gadriel muttered darkly. He inched away from the deck surreptitiously, putting further space between himself and the angel.

Holly shot him an amused glance, as Barachiel offered out the deck. She peeled off the top card and glanced at it. Upon it, Gadriel caught sight of a blazing figure wreathed in red and orange flame.

"Ah," Barachiel murmured. "The Princess of Wands. I fear someone untrustworthy has entered your life. A dark figure plots against you, Miss Harker."

Gadriel peered at the card over Barachiel's shoulder with an unamused frown. "Very funny," he mumbled. "And whose fault is *that*?"

Barachiel pivoted smoothly towards Gadriel, holding out the deck. "What about you, Gadriel?" he asked. "Go on. It could be useful."

Gadriel recoiled instinctively, searching Barachiel's face for any sign of treachery. Finding none, however, he eventually sighed and reached gingerly for the top of the deck.

The card that he pulled showed a single human figure with its face split between man and woman, mixing fire and water together within a cauldron.

"The Art," said Barachiel. "*Solve et coagula.* You'll require a bit of the old and a bit of the new in order to solve your current problem."[38]

Gadriel shoved the card back at the angel. "I'm sure *you'd* like

---

38   Medieval alchemists (also known as practitioners of the Art) were fond of the phrase "dissolve and coagulate", which they believed to be the key to creating the fabled Philosopher's Stone. In fact, the phrase is part of an ancient recipe for alcohol—but that is neither here nor there.

that," he mumbled.

Barachiel shrugged. "I'm just trying to be helpful," he replied. "You know I'd like you to succeed."

"I'm not *always* sure of that," Gadriel said bluntly. "You're very twisty for an angel, you know."

"An angel?" Holly asked. She slid her card back across the counter towards Barachiel, who snapped it up deftly, shuffling it back into his deck.

"Well, just look at him," Gadriel told her, gesturing emphatically at Barachiel. "Most innocent man alive, isn't he? That's what he'd *like* you to think. I'm the only one who ever suspects him. But who would believe me—I don't have those movie star looks, do I?"

"Sibling rivalry," Barachiel told Holly with amusement.

"Hah," Gadriel muttered. "You think I'm jealous of you? I don't want your job. I quit for a reason."

"We're still very fond of one another," Barachiel assured Holly. "You know how it goes."

Holly's expression fell minutely at that. She forced a fresh smile, though, and turned for the espresso machine. "I'll get those drinks right out to you," she promised. It was a polite but obvious dismissal.

"I didn't need your help just now," Gadriel grumbled, as he settled into a chair across from Barachiel. "I was handling things perfectly well on my own." He picked up a brownie from the plate in front of him, biting off an entire mouthful of chocolate.

"Yes, of course," Barachiel agreed. "I just thought I'd help speed things along. I know you're eager to be done with all of this. I don't think you've followed around a single mortal for this long since... well, since you left." He paused, then added: "You're going to make yourself sick on chocolate."

Gadriel narrowed his eyes. "Will not," he replied shortly. "And I *would* like to be done with all of this. But I've recognised that this job is going to require some extended work. Assuming you sort out my identity problems, I'll have near-unlimited access to the niece—and she's already singing like a canary."

Barachiel raised his eyebrows. "And using Ella, you'll uncover Holly's heart's desire?" he guessed.

"Hah," Gadriel said with a snap of his fingers. "I already have." He shot Barachiel a crooked smile. "Holly Harker would like nothing more than to have her niece adore her. And now that I know *that*, I can tempt her into all manner of things."

"Hm," said Barachiel.

Gadriel squinted suspiciously at him. "You're not convinced," he said.

"I didn't say that," Barachiel replied.

"No, of course not," Gadriel muttered. "You said *hm*, though, which is nearly the same thing."

"You *are* the expert," Barachiel assured him. "I'm sure you have all of your ducks in a row."

Holly hurried breathlessly over to their table. "One coffee with milk and one café mocha," she managed, as she set down their drinks in front of them. "Here you are." The line had grown since they'd first entered, as the morning rush arrived.

"My apologies," Barachiel said as he pushed up to his feet. "Could I take mine to go?"

Holly plucked his coffee from the table again without missing a beat. "Of course," she replied obligingly—though she shot a wary look back towards the growing line at the counter. "Just give me a moment, please."

"Take all the time you need," Barachiel told her mildly.

Gadriel frowned at him as Holly rushed away. "Leaving so soon?" he asked.

Barachiel straightened his tie. "I have a busy morning ahead of me," he said. "Apparently, I have arrangements to make."

Gadriel grinned lazily at him. "It's Mr Gadriel Sweet," he said. "If you put the 'b' in there, I'll hold it against you for the rest of eternity."

"So noted," said Barachiel.

Chapter Ten

CUMULATIVE SIN METRIC (HOLLY HARKER): -935.5
CUMULATIVE SIN METRIC (ELLA HARKER): +217.1

Gadriel wandered into school at well past nine in the morning. The black-and-white chequered halls were empty this time when he showed up, though those dreadful school posters were still there to keep him company.

Even as Gadriel passed the headmaster's office, however, Mrs Applebee cracked open the door to call out to him. "Mr Sweet!" she said, with a hint of crankiness. "I've been searching for you all morning! Surely, you're not *late* to your second day of work?"

Gadriel forced a warm smile as he turned upon her. "No, no, of course not," he lied. "I was just walking about the school, getting a sense for where everything is."

Mrs Applebee frowned at him suspiciously. But few people can really grudge a man in a knitted vest, and her expression eventually smoothed over. "Well, I did find your paperwork this morning," she said. "I thought you ought to know."

"How... unusually efficient," Gadriel observed carefully.

"Er—not you, Mrs Applebee, just bureaucracy in general. The wheels turn slowly, don't they?"

Mrs Applebee inclined her head stiffly. "Well, it's good I found you," she said. "I believe you have a student waiting in your office."

Gadriel suppressed a scowl. "A student," he muttered. "Yes, naturally. That is… my job, after all."

"I'll leave you to it, then," Mrs Applebee said briskly.

The office door closed again with a soft *click*. Gadriel shook his head. "And here I am, entirely unprepared," he mumbled. He ducked for the staff room, heading for the fridge to dig through lunches once more until he found the one that he was searching for. "Ms Schmidt, Ms Schmidt… aha! Aren't you reliable, Ms Schmidt." Gadriel plucked a chocolate bar from the lunchbox.

The chocolate in Ms Schmidt's lunch had a sticky note on it today—'This chocolate belongs to Ms Schmidt. DO NOT TAKE IT'. Gadriel casually plucked off this sticky note and tossed it in the bin, stuffing the chocolate bar into his pocket.

He slipped back down the hallway to his new office, whistling idly to himself. Obviously, he should have expected other students showing up in his office on occasion—but he couldn't imagine the school would toss him a situation any more dire than sinless Holly Harker. And hadn't he already made a bit of progress on *that*?

Gadriel pushed open the door to his office—and stopped in his tracks.

"Bother," he said.

Beatrix Relish looked up at him from the chair in front of the desk. Though she was only one year younger than most of the other girls, this still made her noticeably smaller than the average Year 9 student. The way that she hunched her shoulders and shrank down into the chair made her look a bit like a black-haired mouse in a navy skirt. The expression which she currently wore behind her thick, rectangular glasses instantly suggested both guilt and embarrassment.

"Ah, er," said Beatrix in a tiny voice. "Hello, Mr Sweet. Sorry to bother you."

Gadriel closed the door behind him, circling warily for the other side of the desk. "No bother," he said pleasantly. "I *am* a counsellor. Counselling is what I do. I do it all the time, in fact."

Beatrix smiled hesitantly at this, though her smile was visibly forced. "Yes, of course," she mumbled. "Well, I still… oh, this is awkward."

Gadriel settled into his chair, twirling the pen that he'd stolen from the café. "And what is it your mother would like from me today, Miss Relish?" he asked.

Beatrix's smile crumpled abruptly. "You know about her already," she sighed miserably.

"I ran into her on my way in yesterday," Gadriel replied matter-of-factly. "Oh, don't worry, Miss Relish. I'm not in a mood to cause myself any trouble today. Let's both have some chocolate, and then we'll hear it and have done." He plucked the chocolate bar from his pocket, already unwrapping the top.

Beatrix eyed the chocolate bar glumly—but she took the piece that Gadriel offered her, nibbling quietly at the edge of it. "I'm supposed to tell you that my grandmother has died again," she said. "I told Mum about what happened with Ella and Millie yesterday, about them leaving the maths test. I really should have known better."

Gadriel nodded sagely. "And your mother would like you to have counselling during the next maths test?" he guessed.

Beatrix shook her head. "History," she admitted. "Ms Wood's tests are the worst. No one does well in her class—not even Jasper. All of her questions are tricks, so you put down the wrong answer even if you did study. And sometimes, she asks questions that are technically in the book, but they're details that no one would ever think to notice!" She threw up her hands. "Do *you* know what instrument Nero played when Rome burned?"

"Oh, I love telling that story," Gadriel laughed. "People *say* he played a fiddle, but those weren't invented until a few hundred years later. Actually, it was a lyre, and he wasn't even very good at it—" He shut his mouth at Beatrix's stricken expression. "I have… personal reasons to know that," Gadriel admitted. "Certainly, I wouldn't expect the average secondary student to know it."[39]

Gadriel chewed on a piece of chocolate, narrowing his eyes at Beatrix. "Well… so your mother wants to get you more time to study for the next history test. What do *you* want?"

Beatrix bit at her lip. "Honestly, Mr Sweet, it's not like avoiding the test will make it any better," she said. "I'll still have to take it later, and it will be just as bad when I eventually do. Everyone

---

39   Gadriel does not, as a rule, truck with things like Roman arson. But he may be counted fully responsible for some of the more ridiculous stories out of the Roman Empire, including but not limited to: Nero's predilection for composing awful music, Vespasian's fondness for bad jokes, and Caligula's brilliant idea to appoint his favourite horse as a Roman consul.

else will know it was my mum's idea to put it off too, and they won't let me hear the end of it."

Gadriel nodded along, licking the chocolate from the fingers of one hand as he tapped his pen on the desk with the other. "I take it you've already tried telling your mother *no*," he mused. "You have that defeated look in your eyes."

Beatrix slumped even further in her chair. "Mum doesn't listen to *anyone*," she said. "She's proud of being that way. She has all of these followers online, and she's always telling them that the only way to be exceptional is to never accept no for an answer." She paused and drew in a shaky breath, as though preparing herself to say something truly egregious. "She calls herself 'An American Mama Bear In London'."

Gadriel cringed. He briefly lost his grip on the pen between his fingers; it went flying for the wall, where it clattered to the wooden floor. He worked to collect himself again, as Beatrix smiled in pained agreement. As he settled once again, he hurriedly passed her another piece of chocolate.

Gadriel cleared his throat loudly. "You can't make an ally of your father?" he asked conversationally.

"Not at all," Beatrix sighed. "He's always busy with work. He doesn't want to hear about my schooling."

Gadriel reclined in his chair, considering the girl in front of him. "Well, I've already got a student in here for Monday, in either case," he said. "So we're just going to have to come up with a different solution." He paused thoughtfully. "Have you tried cheating?"

Beatrix stared at him, with a piece of chocolate halfway to her lips.

"What?" Gadriel asked. "If no one does well in Ms Wood's class, then clearly the tests aren't fair in the first place. The system isn't always equitable, Miss Relish. There's no virtue in letting it stomp all over you, simply out of principle."

"I… I don't know if I'd be brave enough to cheat, even if I knew how to do it," Beatrix said. Her voice was now sheepish, and her face was pink with confusion.

Gadriel waved a hand. "It's a very good thing you're speaking with an expert then, isn't it?" he said. "Ask, and ye shall receive." He leaned forward, folding his hands upon the desk while he held the girl's eyes. "How would you like to ace your next history test, Miss Relish?"

Beatrix took in a deep, uncertain breath.

"Wouldn't it be nice to beat that old bat, just once?" Gadriel asked her.

Beatrix let out the breath and straightened in her chair. "Okay," she said. "But… how?"

Gadriel stood up from his chair and offered out his hand. "I'll require your assistance," he said. "I hope you brought your phone to school with you. Now—where does Ms Wood keep her tests?"

***

Shortly after the bell rang for the end of the period, Gadriel waltzed his way casually into room 201, slipping past the last students who hurried for the door. He kept his phone to his ear, chatting amiably into the receiver.

"You have her in your sights?" he asked.

"I do," Beatrix's voice whispered back. *"She's headed for the staff*

room."

"Excellent," said Gadriel. "That should give me a sizeable window of opportunity. Next time, you won't have an inside man, so you'll need to come up with an excuse for someone to be in here in case they're caught. Simple lies are always best, I find. 'I left my notebook behind', that sort of thing. It works even better if you can actually leave something on purpose to corroborate the excuse."

One or two of the students in the classroom shot Gadriel curious looks, though they quickly lost interest as they saw his posture; he had long since perfected the art of looking as though he belonged. He headed for the desk at the front of the room, noting details idly as he went.

Room 201 could have been plucked from the greyest, most anodyne level of Purgatory. There were no flags or pictures or posters on the walls—not even of boring historical paintings. The entire room was depressingly simple and, above all else, painstakingly *neat.*

Ms Wood, Gadriel quickly decided, was a bit of a monster. Her desk was smooth and clean, entirely unhampered by papers or folders. The only prominent item upon it was a single white mug, which was generously filled with red pens.

There were *just* red pens there. Gadriel took a moment to check, sure that he must have missed something. But Ms Wood kept no blue or black ink anywhere in sight.

"The tests are in one of the desk drawers, I take it?" Gadriel asked, as he frowned at the mug.

"I think it's the bottom drawer on the right," Beatrix replied. *"I'm not entirely sure, though."*

Technically, Gadriel could have simply gone invisible and copied the test answers for Monday without so much as a hitch. But he was aching for a more substantive bit of larceny, and besides—this was so clearly a perfect teaching opportunity.

He reached for the bottom right drawer, halfway hoping that it would be locked. But the drawer opened smoothly to display several neatly kept files, each one marked by a period and a day of the week. At the very front of the drawer, in front of the folders, was a single open bag of salted black liquorice.

This woman is most definitely a monster, Gadriel thought.

"Aha," he said. "Monday, first period." He pulled the file from the drawer, flipping it open on the desk. Several blank tests were stacked within, and he found his eyes unerringly drawn to the first question.

> On what date did Russia's October Revolution begin?[40]

Gadriel stared. "Bloody hell," he said. "You weren't joking, were you? That is elegantly devious."

"Of course I wasn't joking!" Beatrix huffed. *"I don't know how anyone is supposed to pass a test like that—"* A door opened in the background, and she cut herself off abruptly. *"Ms Wood is leaving!"* she hissed.

"Don't panic," Gadriel said. "Just do what we talked about.

---

40   At the time of the October Revolution, Russia was using the Julian calendar, which marked the date as October 25th. The modern day calendar would mark the date as November 7th. This question therefore has two different answers.

You'll be fine." He flipped through the tests until he found an answer key at the back—all written in red pen. For some reason, the sharp, spidery lines of ink reminded him of blood. Gadriel blinked once, shaking himself from the thought, and then snapped a few pictures with his phone.

"Ms Wood!" Beatrix called out. *"Ms Wood, I have to talk with you."*

The voice that responded on the other end of the phone was distant and garbled—but Gadriel heard a note of cold annoyance within it, nevertheless.

"Oh, it's my father on the phone," Beatrix lied. *"He wants to make sure I'm being given extra time on my tests, like the headmaster said."*

Gadriel pinned the receiver against his ear with his shoulder as he carefully rearranged the tests within the folder, stuffing it back into the drawer.

"Let me see that," said a woman near Beatrix's phone. The line made the woman's voice sound unnaturally thin and hollow, but Gadriel couldn't help but wonder if it might sound exactly the same in person. *"Hello?"* said the voice. *"Is this Mr Relish?"*

The woman *sounded* like a mug full of red pens.

"Yes, yes it is," Gadriel said. He did his best to lower his pitch, adding a stern note to it for good measure. "My wife told me just yesterday that you're denying our daughter accommodations for her medical condition. Is that true?"

"And which medical condition would that be, Mr Relish? Can you name it?" Ms Wood's voice was now silky and dangerous. Gadriel found himself shifting uncomfortably on his feet, despite himself.

"Oh, she has one," Gadriel blustered. "Or two. I don't know. My wife says—"

"Perhaps your wife should be the one discussing the matter with me then, Mr Relish," Ms Wood said shortly. *"Now, if you'll excuse me—I have a class to teach."* She paused. *"By the way... I'll be keeping Miss Relish's phone until the end of the day."*

"What?" Gadriel said. "Well, that's entirely—"

The line went dead.

Gadriel blinked and spun for the door. "—unnecessary," he finished, tucking his phone into his pocket. "What an awful woman."

He slipped out of the classroom and around the corner, just as a sharp *click-clack* of heels sounded up the stairs nearby.

"—give me my phone back, please!" Beatrix said. "If my mother calls and I don't answer, I might get in trouble!"

"That is hardly my problem, Miss Relish," said that high, hollow voice. "You can come and request your phone back at the end of the day. Now, I'd recommend that you run for your next class—you're about to be late."

The door to room 201 snapped shut with a final sort of sound, just as the bell rang in the next period.

Silence fell upon the hallway for a moment, before Beatrix's steps headed slowly around the corner. Finally, her tiny figure came into view. At first, her expression was tired and forlorn—but as she saw Gadriel, it lit up with sudden delight.

"I did it!" Beatrix said excitedly. "I actually distracted her, like a real-life thief! She didn't even suspect anything!"

Gadriel offered out his palm, and Beatrix high-fived him enthusiastically.

"And that's why you always commit crime with a partner, Miss Relish," he instructed her sternly. "Lone wolves get caught.

You should only work with people you trust, of course—there's nothing more debilitating than a snitch."

Beatrix nodded emphatically, taking in the advice. "Do you—did you get it?" she whispered.

Gadriel turned his phone towards her in reply, showing off the photo on his screen. Beatrix stared at it in disbelief.

"That is *so* cool," she whispered.

Gadriel patted her fondly on the shoulder. "Let's go print this out, shall we?" he said. "I'll make sure you've got a late pass afterwards." He started walking for the stairs… but then he slowed as an afterthought occurred to him. "Miss Relish?" he said.

"Hm?" Beatrix asked.

Gadriel smiled to himself. "I believe Miss Wilson would be *awfully* grateful to see these answers, too. Sharing is a virtue, after all."

Chapter Eleven

CUMULATIVE SIN METRIC (HOLLY HARKER): -935.5
CUMULATIVE SIN METRIC (ELLA HARKER): +217.1

Holly's working day had been just as long and difficult as it usually was—but somehow, it *felt* shorter. After months of nothing going right, she'd stumbled abruptly into the answer to all of her prayers. Now, she had expert advice only a phone call away—for the relatively low price of a batch of chocolate biscuits, anyway.

Better yet, she had a *plan*. Holly had always lived by plans; she had a list for every occasion, a schedule for every week, and goalposts by which to check her progress. Until now, her niece had been befuddling, mysterious—a factor for which she simply couldn't plan.

But somehow, Gabe had broken things down in a way that finally made sense. And now, there were steps that she could take in order to reach her goal.

"Step one," Holly muttered to herself, "pick up Ella." She jogged up the steps to the school and swept through the glass double doors with a determined stride. The hallways were nearly empty at this hour; her shift at Castle Clothing had run late again, but that was par for the course. Thankfully, Ella had other concerns to keep her busy after the school day was out.

Room 128 was tucked away at the very back of the school, as far away from the other classrooms as possible. The room had never been properly soundproofed, though the administration made noises every year about finally adding some. The low strains of an electric guitar trickled through the hallway as Holly approached, bouncing strangely off the walls. The tune sounded vaguely familiar—but Holly wasn't terribly good at remembering bands, and so she couldn't place it.

Holly knocked once politely at the door and slipped her way inside.

The music room was bigger than most of the other classrooms, though not by much. Metal cages of varying sizes lined the back wall, each one padlocked to protect the instrument inside. Curved plastic chairs and metal music stands cluttered the room, though several of them had been stacked or tucked away in order to create more room for the two girls at the front.

Ella had settled herself on the edge of a chair with a bright red electric guitar that was easily too large for her. She plucked out chords with a grim, determined concentration that looked somewhat out of place on a thirteen-year-old girl.

Beatrix sat behind a drum set nearby, watching Ella from her stool. The younger girl always seemed small next to Ella, but the addition of those drums made her look comically tiny. Her modest size, of course, did nothing to prevent her from torturing a shocking amount of volume from the drums before her. There was more than one reason Beatrix's mother insisted she keep the drums at school and not at home, Holly thought.

"Next measure, hit it!" Ella called out to Beatrix.

Beatrix counted down one more measure—and then, in a manic flurry of motion, she snapped out her drumsticks. Holly wasn't sure whether to be fascinated or put off by the violent glee on her little face as she beat the cymbals.

As the drums picked up, Holly paused just inside the door, considering the girls. They were tolerably good, actually. She was far from an authority, but the song seemed to be steady and well-tuned. *Am I allowed to be proud?* she wondered. *Ella's been practicing for years. I wasn't even here for most of it.*

One of the guitar chords slipped, and Ella cursed. Beatrix stopped a moment later, waiting patiently for the signal to restart. Holly took the opportunity to clear her throat.

"Ella?" she called. "It's time to go."

Ella glanced over at her with a heavy sigh. "Whatever," she said. "I need to tune this thing, anyway." She nodded seriously towards Beatrix. "We're still doing good. I think we've almost got this one."

Beatrix smiled brightly. "I think so too!" she chirped, hopping down from her stool. "That's almost a whole set. That makes us a proper band, Ella!"

Ella lifted her chin. "We were *already* a proper band," she said. "But you're right. We need to book a gig one of these days." She shrugged the guitar strap from around her neck. Holly snagged the sticker-covered guitar case from a chair near the door, carrying it over helpfully.

"I wish I could help," Holly said. "I don't think the café has room for drums, though, even if they wanted to host you." She stepped back respectfully as Ella packed up the guitar—she'd learned very early on that no one else was allowed to touch the instrument directly.

"Everyone wants a singer, anyway," Ella muttered darkly. "God forbid we just play music."

"You're a fine singer," Holly told her encouragingly. "Why don't you do it?"

Ella shot her a long-suffering look. "I have a nasally voice," she said. "Even I don't want to hear me sing." She secured the guitar case again, hauling it up from the floor with effort—but as Holly offered out a hand for it, Ella passed over the case reluctantly. Playing the oversized guitar was one thing; carrying it around was another thing entirely.

"I see," Holly said slowly, ginning up her resolve. "Well. I know we normally go straight home, but... maybe we could stop off somewhere today?"

Ella groaned. "Please tell me we're not going to the café," she said.

Holly suppressed a bolt of irritation. "I was going to suggest we stop by the music shop," she replied. "But if you'd *rather* we go to the café—"

Ella straightened abruptly. "Why the music shop?" she asked. The cautious interest in her voice washed away Holly's irritation, replacing it with a surge of victorious glee.

Gabe was right! she thought. *It's working!*

Holly did her best to hold back the unreasonable exhilaration that had blossomed in her chest. "We've both had a hard week," she said. "I thought you might want to browse around a bit, maybe pick out something small to buy."

Beatrix clapped her hands together. "Can I come?" she pleaded. "I'll call my mum and ask. I don't want to go home and do homework just yet."

Holly bit at her lip. The Plan had called for some alone time with Ella, in order to bond with her. But Ella's smile had broadened at the suggestion of bringing Beatrix, and it was clear that denying her would only muddle things.

"As long as your mum says yes," Holly agreed reluctantly.

Ella and Beatrix shot each other determined, conspiratorial looks as they fell in behind Holly. "Tell your mum you need something for your drums," Ella hissed at Beatrix. "Oh—tell her we'll get dinner while we're out too, so she won't have to cook!"

"We're getting dinner now too, are we?" Holly muttered. But she kept it to herself. It was rare to see Ella so excited about *anything*. She mentally reshuffled her plans for the evening with a bit of effort. It was Friday, after all—she wouldn't have to wake up early the next morning in order to get Ella off to school.

There was a brief, wheedling phone call as Holly led them back to the bus stop. For the space of about five minutes, both girls put on their sweetest, most well-behaved manner as they spoke into Beatrix's phone. This sudden angelic behaviour disappeared almost completely as soon as they'd reached an accord with the woman on the other end of the line—though the excitement that followed was admittedly infectious.

I should have done something like this sooner, Holly thought distractedly, as Beatrix squished into a single bus seat with Ella. Between the sudden move, the funeral arrangements, and her work schedule, Holly realised, she'd been convinced that every moment of their lives needed accounting for in order to keep things afloat. But now that she'd made the room, a brief Friday night outing no longer seemed quite so intimidating.

"Our stop is next!" Ella called over, pointing at her phone screen. "Let's go, Aunt Holly!"

The three of them squeezed out of the bus just in front of Music City—a tiny corner shop which might have been more aptly called 'Music Village', if there was such a thing as truth in marketing. The shop was musty inside, with several instruments mounted on the wall and locked inside of glass displays. The entire back wall was filled with row upon row of vinyl records, old CDs, and sheet music. Rock music played over the shop's speakers at a tinny, frantic pace, as Joan Jett declared her apathy towards people's opinion of her reputation. A single tired-looking teenage boy in a ratty-looking Led Zeppelin t-shirt sat behind the counter, studiously avoiding Holly's eyes on their way in out of fear that she might ask him to *do* something.

"I can relate," Holly mumbled to herself, as the two girls unleashed themselves upon the aisles of sheet music and accessories. Her first instinct was to go hide in a corner while Ella and Beatrix looked around—but she was supposed to be connecting with her niece, and so she suppressed the instinct and headed over to join the girls instead.

"Any ideas of what you might want to buy?" Holly asked.

Ella had pulled an entire stack of sheet music booklets from the shelves, spreading them out across the floor. She and Beatrix were sorting them into piles based on some mysterious criteria known only to them. "We're almost done learning all the music we have," Ella said. "I figured we could pick up a new song while we're here."

Holly looked over the sheet music curiously. As she did, her eyes caught on one booklet in particular that had merited its very own pile. "Oh!" she said. "I didn't know you listened to The White Stripes. They're a bit before your time, aren't they?"

Ella raised an impatient eyebrow at her aunt. "There's only so many two-man bands out there," she said. "And their songs aren't super complicated."

Holly picked up the booklet, glancing it over. "Ivy loved The White Stripes," she said. "She played their music all the time when we were growing up."

Ella smiled at the comment. It was such a rare expression on her face that Holly was briefly taken aback. "I learned to play *Seven Nation Army* for Mum's birthday," she said. "We sneaked Beatrix's drum set into the flat and waited for her to get home. I made her sing the words."

"Oh my god," Holly laughed. "I'm sure she loved that."

"She danced on the sofa," Beatrix added. "It was kind of dorky."

"That's funny," Holly mused. "I was always the dorky one. I suppose becoming a mum does a number on your cool factor, though."

Ella reached out to pluck the sheet music from Holly's hands. Her smile had gone misty now—but it was still a soft, pleasant sort of expression. "Well, I guess I *have* to get this one now," she said. "Unless you know any of Mum's other favourite bands?"

Holly's own smile faded a bit, despite her best efforts. The sincere longing in Ella's voice was precious and unusual. But talking about Ivy was always a difficult tightrope act, and the stress of it sent nervous flutters through Holly's stomach.

"That was a long time ago," Holly said quietly. "I'll… try to remember, though."

Ella nodded mutely, hugging the booklet to her chest. The grateful vulnerability on her face sent a surge of guilt through Holly, and she glanced away.

"Why don't you pick up some spare guitar strings while we're here?" Holly added, after a moment. "It's not like they'll go to waste."

Ella and Beatrix restocked the sheet music onto the shelves before scurrying for one of the shop's other racks to pick through strings. Holly leaned against the shelf, sighing heavily.

Couldn't we bond over just about anything else? she wondered wearily.

It was progress, at least. She couldn't deny it.

Holly searched her handbag for her phone, pulling up a number under the name 'Mx Chocolate'. She typed in a text message.

> Holly: I owe you biscuits. I'll bring some with me to my shift at Castle Clothing on Sunday, if you think you can stop by.

Something *dinged* in a nearby aisle. Holly glanced around curiously—but the source of the sound was nowhere to be found. She shook her head and started putting her phone away, just as it trilled a response.

> Mx Chocolate: I'll be there.

Chapter Twelve

CUMULATIVE SIN METRIC (HOLLY HARKER): -935.5
CUMULATIVE SIN METRIC (ELLA HARKER): +217.1

It was Sunday afternoon, and the Wheel of Misery was earning its name, as Holly Harker stood before it with an expression of unrivalled despair.

"Would you like to play a game, miss?" Holly asked a passing woman, in a voice barely louder than a mumble. "Oh—that's fine, yes, you're busy." Her face burned visibly with embarrassment, as her hands dropped awkwardly to her sides.

This, Gadriel thought, was hard proof that divine rebellion had been the correct decision. What just god could look upon that cardboard wheel and resist the urge to destroy it? Why, if she'd had the ability to smite things, she would have turned it into a burning wreck right then and there. The crater left in its place would be a biblical warning to all future bosses regarding silly pavement games.

"You're not cut out for this," Gadriel observed to Holly, as she approached Castle Clothing. "You look like a trapped animal getting ready to chew off its own leg to escape." Gadriel had decided to be a woman today, just in case she ran into Barachiel—though, knowing Barachiel, the angel had probably changed genders *again*, just to tweak Gadriel's nose.

Holly's face fell further as she saw Gadriel. She clasped her hands behind her, fidgeting awkwardly. "I was hoping you might come by *after* we'd closed," she sighed. "I forgot it was my turn with the wheel today."

Gadriel arched an eyebrow. "You've got the goods inside?" she asked.

"I do," said Holly. "Er. You make it sound so illicit. They're just biscuits."

Gadriel shrugged. "Force of habit," she admitted. She surveyed the wheel critically, running one finger along the top of it. "It's about thirty minutes before you get off shift, I think? Why don't we make a little wager to pass the time?"

Holly knit her brow. "You want to gamble on the Wheel of Misery?" she asked sceptically. "Oh, um—please don't tell anyone I called it that."

"I'm no stool pigeon," Gadriel assured her. She flicked the wheel back and forth a few times, watching the pegs spin. "How about this? If I land anything referencing jumpers, belts, or clearance, you pack this thing up early and we both go inside." Holly opened her mouth to protest, and Gadriel held up a finger. "If I land anything *else*, you go inside alone, and I run the wheel for the last thirty minutes."

Holly blinked. "You don't know how to run the wheel," she said. "Er... do you?"

Gadriel turned to crook a finger at a pair of elderly women who were passing arm-in-arm. "What's your name, madam?" she asked one of them.

The woman that Gadriel had addressed now slowed, eyeing her curiously. She was a broad matronly sort who obviously fancied the same hats as the Queen. The woman hiked her oversized handbag further up her shoulder. "My name is Agnes," she said mistrustingly. It was clear that she suspected Gadriel was getting ready to pull one over on her.

"Agnes," Gadriel repeated, rolling the name thoughtfully on her tongue. "Well, Agnes—I've got a quid that says you won't win a prize on this wheel."

"What—you can't do *that!*" Holly sputtered, pulling Gadriel back by her shoulder. "We haven't got a gambling license!"

Agnes narrowed her eyes at Gadriel in a calculating manner. "There's more prizes than not on that wheel," she pointed out, watching the fallen angel's face.

"You're right, there are," said Gadriel. "I'm proving a point." She rummaged in her pocket, pulling out a coin. "One quid. Are you in or out?"

Agnes considered for a second longer. But one quid was hardly a grievous risk. Finally, she dug into her handbag for a coin. "I'm in!" she declared. "Spin the wheel, young lady!"

"You heard the woman," Gadriel told Holly, nudging her back towards the display. "Spin the wheel."

Holly reached hesitantly for the Wheel of Misery, flicking it into motion. Pegs and colours whirred by, *tick-tick-ticking* away, before the wheel finally settled on 'free belt with trouser purchase'.

"Haha, I won!" Agnes pumped her fist. "I'll take your quid now, thank you." She snatched the coin from Gadriel's hand before the fallen angel could offer it over.

Gadriel blinked, but she let the matter pass. "Give the woman a voucher, Miss Harker," she said. "And incidentally—I just landed something mentioning trousers. That means it's time to pack up the wheel."

Holly blinked at Gadriel as she handed a voucher to the woman. "But I didn't agree to—"

"You said your main objection was that I couldn't run the wheel," Gadriel pointed out. "I've just proven you wrong. Ergo, we have a wager."

"We could always go for double or nothing," Agnes suggested, waggling the coin in Gadriel's face.

"There's a betting shop right down the street," Gadriel told her blithely. "You've got a free quid to spend there now." She kept her focus on Holly, and added: "PACK UP EARLY. NO ONE WILL KNOW."

The words sank into Holly's mind, tugging at the deep longing that Gadriel knew to be there. For a moment, Gadriel was worried the suggestion had snagged again, as it wavered on the edge...

But all at once, Holly sighed and reached for the cardboard wheel. "It's only about twenty minutes until closing now, anyway," she mumbled.[41]

Gadriel barely resisted the urge to whoop with victory. It was the first time Holly Harker had accepted *any* of her temptations without some sort of complication.

"Allow me," Gadriel said. She snatched the wheel from Holly

---

41   +2 Points of Sin (Holly Harker): Skiving Off Work.

and gallantly opened the door to the shop for her. "*Après vous madame.*"

Holly took the invitation with a dazed blink. "*Parlez-vous francais, madame?*" she asked.

"*Avec la bonne motivation,*" Gadriel replied smoothly.

Holly laughed, and her skin flushed with pleasure. There was something oddly satisfying, Gadriel thought, about painting a bit of pink into those apples in her cheeks.

Sara stood up from behind the counter as they entered, peering over at them curiously. "Oh!" she said. "It's you again!"

"Yes, it is I!" Gadriel proclaimed. "I have come for victory biscuits." She strode for the counter, firmly plunking down the Wheel of Misery. "I'm in an unusually good mood today, so I *might* even be convinced to share."

"I made plenty of extra biscuits," Holly assured them both, as she ducked behind the counter for her handbag. "I wouldn't dream of shortchanging you, Gadriel."

Gadriel paused. "Do you know?" she said. "That's the second time you've used my name right. I think you must be the only person in the last week who's done that."

Holly reappeared with an old blue biscuit tin, about the size of a dinner plate. "Barry gets your name right, doesn't he?" she asked.

Gadriel shrugged. "Barry doesn't count," she said. "He's known me for literal ages." She found herself perfectly distracted from the thought, however, as Holly cracked open the tin to reveal a veritable mountain of chocolate-covered biscuits. "Are those—*dipped* in chocolate?" she marvelled.

"I wanted to try my hand at tempering chocolate again,"

Holly admitted. "I've always found it tricky before, but I think it turned out all right this time."

Gadriel had a biscuit in her mouth before the word 'chocolate' had fully left Holly's lips. It crunched delectably against her teeth, and she sighed with delight. "Perfuct," she mumbled.

Holly eyed her curiously. "I suspect you'd say that even if they *weren't* perfect," she observed. "You're very easy to please as long as there's chocolate involved, aren't you?" A fond expression flickered across her features as she watched Gadriel reach for another biscuit.

Gadriel blinked. "Issat a bad fing?" she asked, around a mouthful of chocolate.

"No, not at all!" Holly assured her. "It's wonderful, actually. Very good for the ego."

Sara glanced between the two of them. "I didn't realise you knew one another," she said.

"I wouldn't say we know each other *well*," Holly admitted. "But I'm very familiar with her brother. He's one of the loveliest men I've ever met, actually—"

"Boo," Gadriel said petulantly, as she swallowed the rest of her biscuit. "Let's not talk about him, please. Let's talk about tonight instead."

"Tonight?" Holly asked.

"Tonight!" Gadriel tapped her hand emphatically upon the counter. "I happen to be a woman right now. That means we can have a girls' night out, all three of us. Drinks and karaoke, what do you say?"

Holly hesitated. "Well…" she mumbled, drawing out the word with audible temptation. She sneaked a shy glance at

Gadriel. Her cheeks had gone red again for some reason.

"I would kill for a night out," Sara sighed. She glanced sideways at Holly. "You said Ella's staying the night with her friend, didn't you? That means you're technically free."

Gadriel gestured at Sara, as though to say 'exactly'. "You're technically free," she repeated helpfully. "And besides… I want to hear all about how things went with your niece."

Holly straightened perceptibly at that. "I… yes, that *does* sound fun," she declared suddenly, with her face still aflame. "And you know what else? We've got fifteen minutes left in the day. I say let's start cleaning up now. We can leave right at closing that way."

Gadriel nodded strongly. "Excellent!" she said. She swiped one more biscuit before packing up the tin and tucking it beneath her arm. She paused, however, as her eyes caught upon the Wheel of Misery.

"Hm," said Gadriel. "On second thought—why don't we take this with us?"

***

"Spin the wheel! Spin the wheel! Spin the wheel!" Sara and Gadriel slammed their fists into the karaoke room's table as they chanted. Holly obliged their demand with solemn fanfare, as though she were a television game show host. The Wheel of Misery whirred several times, before landing on the words 'makeover'.[42]

"Aha!" Holly declared, slightly tipsy. "I get to give a consult! I

---

42   +5 Points of Sin (Holly Harker): Borrowing Company Property Without Permission.

choose…" She pointed firmly at Gadriel. "…you! I hereby advise you to have another glass of sake!"

"You are as wise as you are benevolent," Gadriel told her seriously. She threw back the contents of the tiny wineglass in front of her and set it firmly down upon the table. "*Kanpai*."

"You're supposed to say that *before* you drink," Holly reminded Gadriel, with a dazed shake of her finger.

"Oh, quite right," said Gadriel. "My mistake. Would you please do the honours, Sara? I don't think I'm supposed to pour for myself." Sara poured more sake into the glass, and Gadriel held it up again. "*Kanpai*," she declared, before downing it entirely once again.

The night was already going well; Holly had indulged in at least twelve points of sin since they'd begun, if you counted leaving work early and borrowing company property (and Gadriel *did* count both of those). Technically, drinking alcohol wasn't a sin in and of itself, but Holly had long since passed the two-drink maximum such that each successive drink was considered to be naughty.[43]

"Now," Gadriel said, "since I drank, I get to choose the next song." She fumbled with the karaoke remote, punching in a number.

Sara squinted at the screen. "Not more Beatles?" she asked dubiously.

"There is nothing whatsoever wrong with the Beatles," Gadriel said defensively. "They age like fine wine. Besides,

---

43   +5 Points of Sin (Holly Harker): Excessive Indulgence in Alcohol.

everyone knows the words to their songs."

"No more Beatles," Holly said with a trickling laugh. "Vetoed. Choose something else."

Gadriel considered her for a long moment. Finally, she cancelled the song on the screen and flipped through the songbook to punch in a new number.

Despite the unqualified success of the evening, something troublesome had continued to nag at the back of Gadriel's mind. In fact, it had been nagging there for days, ever since Barachiel's dramatic *hm* and then after Holly's minor coup with her niece at the music shop.

I Just Don't Know What to Do with Myself faded onto the screen.

Holly stared at it blankly. "The White Stripes?" she asked in a dull voice.

"Is it?" Gadriel asked innocently. "I'm fairly sure someone else did the song originally."

Holly sat down heavily on the sofa, pulling her legs up beneath her. "Veto again," she mumbled in a dazed voice. "I don't want to sing The White Stripes."

Gadriel hit the pause button. "Of course," she said. "Is something wrong? Did, um… did the singer run over your dog?"

Holly lolled her head back against the sofa. Her hair had halfway escaped its confinement all over again, framing her face asymmetrically with its tangled strands. "I don't wanna talk about it," she murmured. "Put on some Queen?"

There was something there, Gadriel thought. Some emotion that didn't *belong*. It wasn't quite grief. Nor was it anger, or sadness. In fact, she wasn't quite certain what it was, though this was now the second time she'd seen it. But she nodded amicably and plugged in one more number. "Fine," she said. "But you have to help sing the operatic parts."

Several songs and a few more points of sin later, and the atmosphere had returned to its previous highs. An employee soon knocked at the door to inform them that the lounge was closing, however, and the three women stumbled out with a bit of grumbling.[44]

"I don't wanna go to bed," Sara groaned. "Next week is going to be so *dull*."

Gadriel narrowed her eyes. A different sort of temptation had been buzzing at her mind for hours, urged on by the alcohol. Presently, it took centre stage, demanding to be recognised.

The fallen angel reached into a pocket and pulled out a deck of cards. "All right," she said. "I have a different game in mind. Who lives closest?"

---

44   +2 Points of Sin (Holly Harker): Further Excessive Indulgence in Alcohol.

Chapter Thirteen

CUMULATIVE SIN METRIC (HOLLY HARKER): -921.5
CUMULATIVE SIN METRIC (ELLA HARKER): +217.1

S ara's one-room flat was small enough that it reminded
Gadriel of Mrs Applebee's tiny reception area. The old
sofa in the middle of the living room was so close to the
coffee table that there wasn't any room for their knees.

Being the host, Sara had volunteered to throw down a pillow
on the floor so she could sit opposite Gadriel and Holly as they
played cards. This meant, of course, that Gadriel could see almost
all of Sara's cards whenever she reached for a drink and tipped
her hand.

"All right," Gadriel declared, several hands into the evening,
"we need to play for better stakes than pennies. I think it's safe
to say we're too pissed for dares… so truths it is. The winner of
each round gets to ask the loser one question."

"I'm game," Holly said. She squinted at Gadriel. The dark
pupils of her eyes had already overtaken her irises almost entirely—but they flared even further now with suspicion. "One
condition: I want to deal. You've won the last three hands. I'm

not sure I trust you and your knitted vest any more."

Gadriel pressed a hand to her chest. "I don't need to cheat, Miss Harker," she said loftily. "You're just that bad at the game."[45]

Sara *ooh*'d audibly.

"Then you won't mind handing over the cards, will you?" Holly challenged her back.

Gadriel offered the deck to her graciously. Holly snatched it away from her, dealing out hands to each of them. Finally, she settled the remainder of the deck at the centre of the table.

"Oof," Sara mumbled, staring down at her cards with glassy dejection. "Rubbish for me." She tossed down her cards. "I fold."

Gadriel goggled at her. "You're not supposed to just *say* that," she protested. "You're supposed to bluff like you've got a flush. Now you've lost by default."

Sara shrugged apologetically. "It's getting late," she admitted. "I'm not sure all the lights are on upstairs, if you take my meaning."

Holly set her jaw at Gadriel. "I'll raise you," she said. "If I win, I get to ask you *and* Sara both one question. If you win, you'll get to ask me one as well."

Gadriel narrowed her eyes. "I'll take that bet," she said. She discarded two cards face-down onto the table. "Deal me two."

Holly dutifully replaced the cards. "I'll stand," she said smugly. "And call." She displayed her hand with a flourish—four queens, all in a row—and Gadriel cursed.

"You had that from the beginning?" Gadriel demanded.

---

45   Nonetheless, Gadriel did cheat. She considered cheating to be her prerogative as a fallen angel.

Holly smiled. "Go on," she said. "Let's see your cards, since I'm so bad at this game."

Gadriel revealed her two pairs with a grumble. "You were bound to win at least *one* hand," she said grudgingly. "That's just statistics."

Holly dragged the cards to the centre of the table, shuffling them back into the deck. "I think it's because *I'm* dealing now," she said primly. "Now then... Sara. Let's figure out your man troubles. What are you looking for in a boyfriend?"

Sara leaned back onto her hands, considering the question. "I mean... I like a fit man," she admitted. "One who's confident, and willing to buy me a drink."

Holly frowned. "But that's not what you're *looking* for," she said. "I assume all of the men with J names were confident and bought you drinks, and you wanted more than that from them."

Sara wrinkled her nose. "All right, yes," she admitted. "Let me think on it more." She stared up at the ceiling, turning the question over in her mind. "Hm... I'd like a man who's figured himself out," she declared finally. "And I suppose someone with a career would be nice. Oh! I'd like him to be good with kids—though no more *secret* children, I should hope."

Holly nodded encouragingly. "Does he *have* to be fit?" she asked. "I mean—be honest, either way."

Sara reached for her glass of wine, ruminating. "Fit *enough*," she decided. "But I could forgive a lot if he liked cats. There's just something about a man with kittens that makes you melt into a puddle."

"Well then!" Holly slurred, pointing across the table. "We've answered your problem! You need to stop looking in bars. There aren't any kittens in bars, Sara."

"Where am I supposed to go looking instead?" Sara asked, knitting her brow in confusion.

"Animal shelter," Gadriel advised neatly. "Mostly people with stable careers volunteer there. And they're all guaranteed animal lovers."

Sara's mouth dropped open. "*Genius*," she said. "Why didn't I think of that?"

"I *am* a genius," Gadriel said modestly. "But really, I was just thinking of all the most disgusting bastions of virtue I know. Believe me, animal shelters—that's the ticket."

Holly turned her attention on Gadriel then, crossing her arms. The freckles on her nose had wrinkled again. "What on earth do I want to ask *you?*" she pondered dimly. "I only have a few dozen questions."

Gadriel shrugged. "You could ask my favourite kind of sweet," she suggested, with a winsome smile. "Just in case you needed to know for future reference."

Holly shook her head. "No," she said firmly. "I know what I want to ask." She squared herself towards Gadriel, taking in a deep breath. "Why don't you like your brother? He seems so… *nice*."

Gadriel blinked. For some reason, the question had caught her entirely off guard. Very slowly, she reached for her own glass of wine. "Well, I… hm." She took a long swallow, eyeing Holly over the glass. "You know, that particular discussion could go on for years. I think I'd literally have to start with the Cynics."

Holly scowled at her. "Don't wriggle out now," she said. She poked her index finger accusingly into Gadriel's chest. "*Make* it simple."

Gadriel glanced down at her finger with amusement. She reached down gently to brush aside Holly's finger. "I suppose, if you want the *simple* version…" She set her glass down on the table and leaned back into the sofa. "Barachiel has many good qualities. He genuinely loves people; he's always the first to lend a hand when someone's in trouble. But…"

"But?" Holly prompted. To Gadriel's surprise, there was an urgent note in her voice that suggested she really *wanted* to know. An odd sympathy coloured her dark eyes as she stared at the fallen angel, waiting for the answer.

It was the compelling *need* in her eyes, more than anything, that made Gadriel answer truthfully.

"But Barachiel believes in the Rules," Gadriel sighed. "He thinks they're all there for a reason, even if he doesn't know what the reason is. I can't be like that. I have… *questions*. I want to know why a Rule is there in the first place—especially if it's making people miserable." She rubbed at her face. "We understand one another. We respect each other, even. We just… fundamentally disagree on so much."

Holly digested that quietly. Her posture softened with a mixture of vulnerability and confusion. "That's not quite what I was expecting," she admitted. "Given that…"

"…yes, the knitted vest," Gadriel muttered. "You know, that's a form of rebellion too. It's comfortable. I think we *all* ought to wear more comfortable clothing, no matter what anyone else thinks. It just makes your whole day more pleasant."

Holly cracked a shaky smile. "I was going to say 'given that you're a school counsellor'," she corrected Gadriel softly. "I've decided I rather like the knitted vest."

Gadriel blinked. For some reason, she caught herself flushing at the words. "Oh," she stammered. "Well. I think most children benefit from a bit of healthy mistrust in the system. It's not always out to help them, after all. Isn't it best they learn to spot the difference early on?"

"You're a school counsellor?" Sara interrupted. There was a dazed consideration in her eyes now, somewhere behind the alcohol. She leaned forward with interest. "You must be good with children, then!"

Gadriel shot her a bewildered glance. "I don't know that I'd say—"

"Oh, she *is* good with children!" Holly said emphatically. She patted Gadriel on the shoulder encouragingly. "I took her advice about Ella, and ever since then, things have been nearly pleasant!"[46]

Sara narrowed her eyes speculatively. "I don't suppose you like kittens?" she asked.

Gadriel choked on a sip of wine, glancing wildly between the two women—one of whom still had her hand on Gadriel's shoulder. "Are you entirely sure you want to continue down this line of questioning?" she asked Sara. "I wasn't even aware that you dated women."

"I don't!" Sara exclaimed, with drunken epiphany. She slammed her hand down on the table. "But what if that's my problem? What if what I *really* need to do is go to an animal shelter and find a stable woman who loves kittens?"

---

46   +1 Point of Virtue (Holly Harker): A Heartfelt Compliment.

Holly snorted and dropped her hand from Gadriel's shoulder. There was a warm spot where her hand had been, already swiftly fading. Gadriel *missed* her hand there, for reasons she couldn't quite pin down.

"I'm afraid Gadriel already has a girlfriend," Holly informed Sara, as she collected the cards and started shuffling them again.

Gadriel shot her a double-take. "I do not," she said—with perhaps a *bit* more emphasis than was strictly necessary. "Where on earth did you get that idea?"

Holly blinked. Her hand slipped, and she fumbled a card. "I thought you had lady troubles," she said, as she reached over the edge of the sofa to retrieve the card.

"I did," Gadriel stuttered. "I mean, I do. I mean—not like *that.*" She flushed, watching Holly as she floundered awkwardly, scraping the runaway card up from the floor with her nails. "My troubles sometimes take the form of a woman, is all."

Holly, who'd only been partially listening, now tumbled off the sofa entirely. Gadriel snapped a hand out to catch her, dragging her back with an arm around her waist.

Holly looked up at Gadriel, blinking. The last-minute leap had sprawled her halfway across Gadriel's lap. The apples of her cheeks were pink again, and Gadriel suddenly found herself thinking about other biblical apples and their famous attraction.

"Victory is mine," Holly laughed breathlessly. She held up the missing card with a silly grin.

Gadriel slowly helped the other woman straighten. She released her grip with a strange reluctance, smoothing down her knitted vest and recomposing herself. "Perhaps, ah. Perhaps you should deal the cards," she said.

Holly obediently counted out a hand for each of them again, though her reflexes were clearly starting to suffer. "I think that must be a sign," she said in a dizzy tone. "This ought to be the last game for me."

Gadriel frowned sharply at that. *Only one more chance,* she thought. The question that had been plaguing her all evening drifted back to mind. She tried shoving it away again—the night had been a success, blast it!—but she couldn't quiet the uneasy suspicion that something was still *off.*

Gadriel looked down at her hand cautiously. *Three jacks.*

"Ooh!" said Sara, clutching her cards close to her chest. "I have a *good* hand this time!"

"You're really not supposed to say that," Gadriel sighed at her distractedly. She chewed at her lip... and reached for her phone.

"I thought we'd agreed not to check the time," Sara protested.

"I'm not," Gadriel assured her, as she tapped awkwardly at the phone with one hand. "I'm just... texting someone."

Gadriel: jack of ♥ plz

A little check mark appeared beside the text message, and Gadriel knew that Barachiel had read it. She narrowed her eyes at the phone.

Gadriel: need it 4 harker case

Someone started typing on the other end of the text message chain.

"Gadriel?" Holly asked distantly. "Are you staying in the game?"

"Absolutely," Gadriel said, staring down at her phone. "I'll be drawing two. Just give me another second."

Bookie: That is by far the least respectful prayer I have ever seen.

Gadriel let out an exasperated sound.

Gadriel: O great angel of good fortune, JACK OF ♥ PLZ, amen

No one responded to the text message this time. Gadriel rolled her eyes and set the phone aside, putting two of her cards down on the table. "Two more, please," she said.

Holly dealt out two replacement cards, with a quizzical look at Gadriel's phone. Gadriel picked the cards up and smiled.

"I'll call," she said.

Gadriel laid out four jacks and an ace. Holly revealed her pair of threes with a grumble, while Sara displayed her pair of nines.

"I thought you said you had something good!" Gadriel accused Sara.

"You told me to bluff!" Sara said with a shrug. "Make up your mind."

"All right, well…" Gadriel cleared her throat. "That leaves me one question for Miss Harker." She eyed Holly intently, searching carefully for the right words. "Why were you so put off by that song, earlier this evening?" she asked finally.

Holly sighed heavily, lolling her head back against the sofa. "It's… complicated," she muttered.

"Make it simple," Gadriel told her.

Holly shot her a reproachful look at the familiar words. "Fine," she said. "If you really want to know. My sister… really loved that band."

Sara cringed. "Ooh," she mumbled, drawing her knees up to her chest. "I guess that's still painful."

"It is," Holly said. Her voice held a thread of drunken irritation. Her dark eyes blinked slowly. "But it's not because I miss her. It's… it's because I *don't* miss her."

Sara's lips parted in an *oh*. The words had briefly stunned her into silence.

"*Oh*," Gadriel whispered, for both of them at once.

"I'm not s'pposed to admit things like that," Holly slurred. "Especially not in front of Ella. But no one really wants to hear it, do they? Dead people are sacred. Family is sacred. The truth is… you know… irrelevant." She waved a hand glumly. "I'm not allowed to… *not* miss her. I have to pretend, or else I'm a monster."

Gadriel turned to stare at Holly. Her honey-blonde hair was nearly loose around her shoulders now. There was a flat, resigned look to her eyes, tinged with just a bit of self-loathing.

"We were estranged when she died," Holly said. "I didn't want her in my life. I didn't even know she'd had a daughter—that's how rarely we spoke."

Gadriel leaned her elbows onto her knees, absorbing the revelation. "Whatever happened must have been awful," she said slowly.

Holly couldn't look at either of them. "Ivy left me with Mum," she said. "The moment my sister got a boyfriend, she moved out and just… left." Tears pricked at her eyes, and she reached up to wipe at them. "I spent three years all alone with our mum, while Ivy pretended not to have a family. When I finally finished school and got out, Ivy showed up acting like nothing had ever happened. But I... I couldn't just forget. I told Ivy she'd spent three years acting as if I didn't exist, and she could just go on that way forever for all I cared."[47]

"You've never mentioned your mum before," Sara mumbled quietly. She had the cautiously neutral tone of a woman who knew she was walking on verbal landmines.

"I enjoy pretending that *Mum* doesn't exist," Holly said flatly. "We're a broken family, all of us. It makes perfect sense, Ivy drinking herself into a car wreck. Mum is exactly the same." She gestured halfheartedly at the open bottle of wine on the table. "Tonight is the first time I've had any alcohol in months. I've been too scared to touch it since the funeral. I'm always wondering if I might turn into them, if I drink too much."[48]

Gadriel very rarely had occasion to feel guilty. But this particular statement pricked at her conscience. A knot formed in her throat. "I'm sorry," she said in a thick voice. "I didn't realise I was pressuring you. I thought..." She rubbed at her face. "You seem so unhappy. I've been trying to figure out how to help you have a bit of fun."

Holly turned a watery smile on Gadriel. The sight of it made Gadriel's heart twist uncomfortably in her chest. "That's very sweet, actually," Holly managed. "I *am* having fun, you know. I've been so focused lately on trying to keep everything together that I guess... I've been afraid that if I do even one thing wrong, it'll all come apart at once."

Sara heaved an uncomfortable sigh. "Well... I don't think

---

47 +1 Point of Sin (Holly Harker): Speaking Ill of the Dead.
48 +1 Point of Sin (Holly Harker): Speaking Ill of the Dead.

you're a monster," she said finally. "I just think you've been under an awful lot of stress. And anyway, family is complicated. I can see why you wouldn't want to talk about it in front of Ella— but you can talk about it with *us*." She glanced questioningly at Gadriel. "She can, right?"

"Yes, of course," Gadriel said softly. Holly's eyeliner had run a bit, and the muscles of her face were trembling in a way that suggested she still wanted to cry. The sight tugged at something within Gadriel—a dusty, distant impulse that hadn't bothered her in centuries.

She shifted across the sofa to pull Holly into a hug.

Holly stiffened for just an instant—but slowly, she relaxed into Gadriel's embrace. She returned the hug tightly, shivering slightly. Gadriel stroked reassuringly at her hair, and Holly laughed into her knitted vest.

"You give very lovely hugs," Holly mumbled.

"Of course I do," Gadriel murmured back. "It's practically a job requirement." There was a strange sort of relief to holding someone in her arms. Once upon a time, she'd done such things regularly—but somewhere along the way, she'd fallen out of the habit. Holly smelled quite a lot like alcohol; but she also smelled of soap and coffee, and there was something very nice about that.[49]

Holly sighed and buried her face in Gadriel's shoulder. "I don't know what to tell Ella," she said in a muffled voice. "I feel like I'm lying to her. But I don't think telling the truth is an option

---

49 Guardian angels—former or otherwise—give the very best hugs in the universe.

either, is it? Won't that, um. Traumatise her, or something? I don't know how children work, Gabe."

"Ooh," Gadriel muttered in a faltering tone. "Moral dilemmas? I don't really think I'm the person to ask."

Holly pulled back, staring up at Gadriel. Her eyes were dark and wide again. "I could swear you said you were a counsellor," she mumbled.

"You did," Sara chimed in helpfully from the floor. "Or... *someone* said it."

Gadriel cleared her throat. "I think... the *right* thing to do is to get you home," she said finally. She released Holly in order to push up to her feet, and offered out her hand. "Shall we?"

"Oh, wait," Sara said dimly. "Just give me one second." She shuffled through the cards on the table, grabbing at one of the jokers and scribbling on it with a pen. She swayed to her feet and offered out the card to Gadriel. "In case you change your mind," she said, in a slurred but sunny tone.

Gadriel looked down at the card. The joker now had a slightly shaky phone number written across his face.

"I'm afraid I'm entirely *too* much your type," Gadriel told Sara sympathetically. "In more ways than one." But she took the card and tucked it into the pocket of her knitted vest, regardless. "I appreciate the thought."

"Well," Sara sighed, "there's always more karaoke."

Holly took Gadriel's hand, leveraging herself unsteadily to her feet. Gadriel caught her as she listed to one side like a spinning top. "There will *certainly* be more karaoke," Gadriel agreed.

Chapter Fourteen

CUMULATIVE SIN METRIC (HOLLY HARKER): -920.5
CUMULATIVE SIN METRIC (ELLA HARKER): +217.1

Beatrix Relish was beating her drumsticks against the inside of Holly's head. At least, that was the dream from which Holly awoke on this sunny Monday morning.

"Oh, god," Holly mumbled. "I'm going to die." She groped around for the edge of the knitted throw blanket that currently dangled off of her, pulling it up to her chin.

Something warm shifted beneath her, and she blinked her eyes blearily. The sunlight slatting in through the window of her flat highlighted an unmistakable argyle pattern just next to her cheek.

"Even *I've* got a hangover," Gadriel groaned. "That takes some doing."

Holly squinted up at the woman. Gadriel's short brown hair was stuck up at odd angles, and her eyes were faintly bloodshot. The bewildered look on her narrow face was oddly... adorable. "You're in my flat," Holly murmured in surprise. "On my sofa."

Gadriel rubbed painfully at her forehead. "So I am," she said hoarsely. Her other arm was still curled around Holly's waist, somewhere beneath the blanket. Dimly, Holly decided that this was actually a very pleasant way to wake up, apart from the pain in her head and the awkward knot in her neck.

Holly stared at the other woman. Her heart was doing funny things in her chest for some reason. Or, no—perhaps that was just the hangover.

"I think… I need to call in sick," Holly rasped.[50]

Gadriel let her head fall back against the sofa pillow. "Good idea," she mumbled. At first, it appeared she might drift right back to sleep… but then, her eyes opened abruptly to slits, and she said: "Did I remember to bring the biscuits back with us?"

Holly laughed despite herself. She shifted off of Gadriel, rolling off the sofa with an undignified *thud*. "You're worried about the *biscuits?*" she asked incredulously.

"Those were perfectly good biscuits!" Gadriel protested.

"I can always make more," Holly reassured her. She forced herself up to her knees, searching the small living room for her phone. There were *two* phones on the table, actually, and she picked up the wrong one at first. A short text message currently showed on the lock screen.

Bookie: I expect several Hail Marys in return.

Holly blinked down at the phone in confusion. "Your bookie wants you to perform some Hail Marys," she told Gadriel.

Gadriel snatched the phone from her with a groan. "That's Barachiel," she said. "And I'm sure he thinks he's very funny."

---

50   +2 Points of Sin (Holly Harker): Skiving Off Work.

Holly rubbed at her face. "You have your brother in your phone as 'bookie'?" she asked dimly.

"He may as well be," Gadriel grumbled. "I've never once beaten him at cards." She tapped blearily at her phone. "I suppose I ought to call the school as well."

Holly flushed, reaching for the correct phone this time. "I didn't mean to keep you out so late," she said in a guilty voice.

"Do I look like I'm complaining?" Gadriel asked. She blinked against the sunlight that still trickled in from the window. "Honestly, I *needed* last night. This job has been rough." She brought the phone up to her ear, curling around it wearily. "Hello?" she rasped. "Yes, this is Gadriel Sweet. I'm afraid I'm feeling poorly. You'll have to go on without me. Of course, thank you."

Gadriel hit the 'end call' button, tossing the phone aside. She lurched up to a seated position with a groan of effort and ran her fingers back through her tousled hair, before fixing Holly with a haggard gaze.

"Incidentally," said Gadriel, "how do you feel about breakfast?"

***

Two cups of tea and one ibuprofen later, Holly was feeling at least marginally human once again. She and Gadriel had staggered into a little café in search of breakfast. They were both still rumpled, in the same clothing they'd worn the evening before— but Holly knew from personal experience that no one there was interested enough or even awake enough to judge them for it.

They sheltered at a corner table, avoiding both windows

and sunlight, with a surprising air of camaraderie. This, Holly thought, must be what it felt like to run with the wrong crowd. Or perhaps it was the slightly-less-right crowd; neither of them looked like hooligans, precisely, no matter how much they could have both used a shower.

"You weren't the sort to cut class, were you?" Gadriel asked Holly conversationally, as she downed another full cup of tea. To call it 'tea' was probably being generous—it might have been more sugar than liquid at this point. The rest of their full English breakfast spread dotted the table, half picked over.

"I've never been very good at breaking rules," Holly admitted. "I hate to disappoint you, but I'm much like Barry that way."

Gadriel leaned back in her chair, assessing Holly critically. "I don't think it's the same," she said finally. "I don't think you believe in the rules—I think you're *scared* to break them. You don't like going off-script."

Holly blinked. "That's… probably an accurate assessment," she acknowledged sheepishly. "I lived the loud and unexpected life with Mum, back when I didn't have a choice. Now that I have some control over things, I just prefer everything in its place. I *like* my life quiet and unexciting."

Gadriel pointed at her with a fork. "*That* I can relate to," she said. "I enjoy causing a ruckus now and then, but I like it on my terms. It's far less entertaining when someone else comes along and upends your life without asking." She reached out to spear a breakfast sausage emphatically. "I don't think you'd be happy raising Hell. But you could do with breaking *little* rules every once in a while. I mean—this is nice, isn't it? Having a bit of lazy breakfast, instead of begging passers-by to spin a bloody wheel?"

Holly nodded reluctantly. "I have to admit, you're far better company than the Wheel of Misery," she said. She avoided Gadriel's eyes as she spoke, feeling unaccountably shy. Her own fork paused halfway to her eggs though, and she looked up at Gadriel, wide-eyed. "Did we... leave the wheel behind at karaoke?" she whispered.[51]

Gadriel stared back at her. Holly couldn't help it; an incredulous laugh trickled out, escaping her control. Soon, they were both laughing so hard that Holly had to wipe tears from her eyes.

"More tea?" The waitress paused next to them, hovering with a carafe. Her gaze flickered warily between the two of them.

"Yes please," Holly wheezed breathlessly.

"More sugar, too," Gadriel managed. "I think the table's fresh out."

They worked to recollect themselves as the woman swept off again. Occasionally, Holly lost control of another helpless giggle while Gadriel gave her a warning look, trying desperately to control her own response.

Just as Holly began to think that they'd conquered the mood, however, Gadriel looked at her straight-faced and said: "Do I still get a free belt?"

It was another five minutes before they could speak again. The other people in the café were starting to edge their chairs subtly away from their table.

"I already want to do this again," Holly admitted guiltily. "I'm not sure whether that's a good thing or not."

---

51   +5 Points of Sin (Holly Harker): Carelessly Losing Company Property.

"*Qui vivra verra*," Gadriel said into her tea. "You won't know until you get there." A thought seemed to strike her then, and she squinted at Holly. "Speaking of which—I'm dying to know. What's with all of the French?"

Holly blinked. "Oh, it's… it's habit," she said. "I've been studying French for years. I was nearly fluent when the accident happened, and I don't want to lose that. As soon as Ella's gone off to university, I should be able to get back to…" She trailed off, suddenly uncomfortable.

"Back to?" Gadriel prompted.

Holly looked down into her tea. "I'm supposed to be in France right now," she said. "I had a patisserie course lined up at *Ecole Lenôtre*. I had to put it off, obviously."

Gadriel frowned. "Obviously?" she asked.

Holly knit her brow. "Ella just lost her mum," she mumbled. "I'm not going to uproot her from her home and her language and all of her friends as well. Besides, it's an intense program. I doubt I'd be able to look after her properly while I finish it." She sighed. "It's only five years until Ella finishes school. I can survive until then."

Gadriel held up a hand. "Please, let's rewind a bit," she said. "You're telling me you threw away all of your hopes and dreams in order to work at Castle Clothing and Déjà Brew while you raise a niece you don't even know?"

Holly threw up her hands. "What else was I supposed to do?" she said. "If I don't raise her, Gabe, she'll go to my mum. How could I possibly put someone else in that position? I'd be—"

"—a hypocrite, yes!" Gadriel finished for her. "*Most* people are hypocrites, Holly. That you aren't one is… frankly bizarre."

She shook her head. "You called yourself a monster last night. I can't parse it. Monsters don't get up every day and do what you do." She levelled a flat look at Holly. "Let me ask you something: do you love Ella?"

Holly's face fell. "I… I don't know," she admitted quietly. "I think so, sometimes. But I haven't known her for very long. Can you love someone that quickly—even family?"

Gadriel nudged the bacon closer to Holly. You should take the last piece, said a voice in Holly's mind. She reached out automatically for the plate, popping the end of the bacon strip into her mouth.[52]

"From where I'm sitting," Gadriel continued matter-of-factly, "you love your niece very much. Believe me, plenty of people claim they love someone because they get the warm fuzzies around them—but love is something you *do*. Quite often, it's something you choose. Why, I used to decide I was going to love someone before I ever met them."[53]

Holly tilted her head. "Before you ever met them?" she asked in puzzlement.

Gadriel worked her mouth soundlessly, suddenly stymied. "Er… as a counsellor," she said finally. "You know, you have to… love the people you're helping, in a way."

Holly smiled at Gadriel. The idea warmed at her heart, wriggling its way into a special place there. "I like that," she said softly.

---

52   +1 Point of Sin (Holly Harker): Taking the Last Piece.

53   It is, in fact, part of a guardian angel's duty to love the person they protect. It is commonly understood to be one of the most heartbreaking requirements of the job.

"That's a nice way to put it." She leaned her chin into her palm, studying the other woman intently. The beautiful sentiment *felt* uncharacteristic—but the more that Holly thought about it, the more she realised that it only felt that way because Gadriel preferred so often to act like a rebel with a cause.

"Do you still fall in love with people all of the time?" Holly asked Gadriel gently.

The question tugged Gadriel's lips down into a frown. "I don't," she said. "I've changed a lot since then. I mostly have… short-term clients now. Far less hassle, on the whole."

Holly nodded seriously. "Everybody needs a change of pace sometimes," she said. She studied the table in front of her, choosing her next words carefully. "You… really don't think badly of me? Even after everything I said last night?"

"Of course I don't," said Gadriel. "Or, well… all right," she admitted. "I'm hardly the best person to ask for the average person's opinion." She rubbed at her jaw. "The thing is, the dead don't need anything from you—not love, not forgiveness. Those are things you offer because *you* need them. The main person who needs anything from you is Ella, and all *she* really needs is for you to show up every day—"

Gadriel stopped abruptly. A funny sort of expression crossed her features.

Holly raised her eyebrows. "Is everything all right?" she asked carefully.

Gadriel stood up quickly, clearing her throat. "Er," she said. "As it turns out—I have an appointment I forgot. So sorry."

Before Holly could manage a response, the other woman had already collected her things and bolted out the door.

Chapter Fifteen

CUMULATIVE SIN METRIC (HOLLY HARKER): -912.5
CUMULATIVE SIN METRIC (ELLA HARKER): +217.1

It is very difficult to fly in a straight line while one is still hungover. As such, while Gadriel had certain advantages over the underground system, she still arrived at the school in a less than timely manner. Though she hadn't dared to check the hour on her way, she was absolutely certain that she'd missed most of first period by the time she finally arrived.

"Drat!" Gadriel muttered angrily to herself, as she rummaged through the fridge for Ms Schmidt's lunch. "Rookie move. I had the kid all stitched up, too. This is definitely going to derail things."

The chocolate bar was missing from Ms Schmidt's lunch today. This stymied Gadriel for all of a few seconds, before she turned to rummage through the freezer.

"Aha!" she said, as she found the chocolate bar hidden behind an old tub of ice-cream. "An excellent attempt, Ms Schmidt. But you can't con a con woman." She snatched the chocolate bar from its hiding place and stowed it in her pocket. She then hurried for the stairs, leaping them two and three at a time.[54]

The bell rang just as she reached the second floor. Teenagers spilled out of their classrooms in a rush of chatter, hurrying for their next period. Gadriel cursed several times beneath her breath, rubbing at her face.

"Mr Sweet?" Beatrix's voice carried over the din. Gadriel scanned the students quickly and caught sight of both Beatrix and Ella standing just outside of room 201. To Gadriel's surprise, neither of them looked terribly upset—in fact, they were both wearing broad smiles.

"I am... *so* sorry," Gadriel managed, as she cut across the crowd towards them. "Called in sick. Nearly forgot I had an appointment on the books."

Ella frowned at Gadriel. "Wait," she said. "Were you always a woman?"

Gadriel shook her head. "Not at all," she wheezed, still gasping for breath. "Woke up that way today."

Ella crossed her arms and furrowed her brow. "You got sick and turned into a woman?" she said sceptically.

"No, goodness!" Gadriel said breathlessly, resting her hands on her thighs. "I decided to be a woman today on my own. I called in sick for other reasons."

Ella considered this for another second... and finally

---

54   In point of fact, you *can* con a con woman. Some of the most famous grifters in all of history have fallen prey to other grifters in the mood to prank them. But it is well within the nature of con women to lie and *claim* that they cannot be conned, and so the proverb stands.

Incidentally, and for no reason whatsoever: many fallen angels like to think of themselves as con artists.

shrugged. "Well. You're not contagious, I hope, whatever it is."

"Not at all," Gadriel said distractedly, as her breathing finally steadied. "I was up all night with your aunt at karaoke. Oh—we played poker as well! It was incredibly irresponsible, and I'm very proud of her for it."

Ella goggled at her. "With my *aunt?*" she repeated. "You didn't tell me you knew Aunt Holly!"

Gadriel waved a hand impatiently. "I met her last week," she said. "She sold me a blazer. That's not important at the moment, though. I didn't get you out of history, I'm afraid, but I *do* have some chocolate—"

"It's fine!" Beatrix said cheerfully. "We both aced the test today!"

Gadriel stopped talking to eye the two girls. "You *both* did?" she asked.

Beatrix shot Gadriel a smug, self-satisfied look. "Me and Ella and Millie *all* did very well on our history test today," she said. "We won't know for sure until the papers are back, but I have a really good feeling about it this time."[55]

"Not that *you* had anything to do with it, of course," Ella said archly, raising an eyebrow at Gadriel.

Gadriel let out an exasperated sound. "Beatrix!" she said, turning on the twelve-year-old girl. "What did we say about snitching?"

Beatrix coloured. "Oh," she said sheepishly, fiddling with the edge of her shirt. "Well, I only told Ella. I thought that didn't count."

---

55   +2 Points of Sin (Ella Harker): Cheating.

Gadriel ran her hands back through her wind-tousled hair. "And to think, I flew all the way here," she groused. "With a *hangover*, no less."

Beatrix patted her sympathetically on the shoulder. "You could always slip out the back door before the other teachers see you," she suggested.

"I think I *will* do that—" Gadriel started.

But as she spoke, she happened to glance into room 201... and suddenly, all of the breath left her lungs at once.

Inside the history room, behind the painfully neat desk full of red ink pens, there stood a pale, gaunt-looking woman in a very professional black business suit. She would have been tall for a woman, even without her red high heels—but the slim, straight line of her body and the elongated nature of her features added a particularly intimidating cast to her person. Her white-blonde hair was swept up into a painfully tight bun at the back of her head—but most striking by far was the poisonous red lipstick she wore.

All at once, she turned her head—and two cold, serpentine eyes fixed *directly* upon Gadriel.

"Ms Sweet?" Ella asked. "You're not going to throw up, are you?"

Gadriel ducked around the corner of the wall, sucking in a breath. The world had started tilting dangerously in a way that had nothing to do with alcohol and everything to do with the woman in room 201.

"Oh no, oh Hell," Gadriel muttered fearfully. "Maybe she didn't see me. No, she definitely saw me. Maybe she didn't recognise me? I hope she didn't recognise me. What is she *doing* here?"

Beatrix peered curiously into the room. "You mean Ms Wood?" she asked, with a hint of confusion. "Well… she works here, obviously."

Ella raised an eyebrow at Gadriel, clearly unimpressed. "Aren't you being a bit dramatic?" she asked.

"*A bit dramatic?*" Gadriel repeated incredulously. "Do you have any idea who that woman—" She paused. "No, of course you don't."

"Hello, Gadriel," said a voice from the doorway. It was high and hollow… and dreadfully amused.

Gadriel leapt to her feet with a startled shriek. Several students shot her shocked glances. She waved them off weakly, turning around to face the woman that had spoken.

"I thought that was you," said Ms Wood. She laughed in a manner which was probably meant to be friendly—but *nothing* about that hollow voice ever sounded friendly. Her flat green eyes glittered, and her red lips curved up into a cruel slash of a smile.

"Fancy meeting you here, Wo—Ms Wood," Gadriel whimpered. "I had no idea you were in the area."

"Oh, I know," Ms Wood mused, waving one well-manicured hand. "It's far from my usual haunts. But what a pleasant surprise it is to see you here. We ought to catch up."

Ella glanced between Gadriel and Ms Wood, taking in the atmosphere. "I'm supposed to have an appointment with you shortly, Ms Sweet," she interjected.[56]

Gadriel shot her a grateful look—but Ms Wood laughed

---

56   +2 Points of Virtue (Ella Harker): Saving Someone From an Uncomfortable Situation.

again and threaded their arms together. "I'll send *Ms Sweet* right back to you in a few minutes," she told Ella. She turned her attention back to Gadriel then, in a clear dismissal of the children. "Let's take a walk, Gadriel."

Gadriel pressed her lips together. "If I don't come back, you know who took me," she told Ella seriously.[57]

Ms Wood patted Gadriel's arm fondly, turning them both to stroll down the hallway. "Always the joker, aren't you, Gadriel?" she said, as they left the girls behind them. "Incidentally... it seems we're both women today. How *embarrassing*."

"I'll change immediately," Gadriel said quickly. "Why don't we do this later? I'll go find a closet and pick a different gender—"

"Oh, that's not necessary," Ms Wood said sweetly. "I'm sure you'll sort it out as soon as we've spoken."

Gadriel swallowed very hard.

"I didn't know you were in London," Ms Wood continued idly. "We could have done brunch. I've always appreciated your eye for the little details, you know."

"Yes, the little details," Gadriel said weakly. "Er, speaking of which... isn't this a bit small-time for you? Shouldn't you be, I don't know... planning the end of the world or something?"

Ms Wood sighed heavily. "We're still in negotiations with the other big stakeholders," she said. "It's been taking *forever*. Last I'd heard, the Buddha was still insisting we agree upon a strict definition for the 'world' before we end it, but he's never happy enough

---

57   -1 Points of Virtue (Ella Harker): Adjustment for a Failed Virtue. Partial Points for Effort.

with what we send him."[58]

"Hah," Gadriel mumbled. "Paperwork. Am I right?"

"I did spend a short stretch with Mammon in Silicon Valley," Ms Wood added conversationally. "But I swear, Gadriel, I was going to strangle him if he brought up NFTs even *one* more time."

"NFTs?" Gadriel asked blankly. "I'm sorry, I'm not up on all of these modern acronyms—"

"Let's pretend I didn't mention it," Ms Wood said briskly. "What's important is that I'm taking a break. Absolutely no high-stakes, high-pressure work—not for the next decade, at least. I'm indulging exclusively in tiny disasters for the next little bit." Her long, pointed nails dug lightly into Gadriel's arm. "That's why it's so good to see *you*. Why, you've never done anything important in the whole of your existence. I'm sure you have plenty of pointers to offer."

Gadriel forced a brittle smile. "How flattering," she said. "Well, er… I suppose it depends on the sort of tempting you had in mind. I always try to start with a bit of chocolate—"

"Chocolate?" Mild surprise flickered behind Ms Wood's cold green eyes. "Oh my. You really *do* go small. You shouldn't be afraid to aim a little higher, Gadriel. Just because you're only

---

58   Despite their long-lived nature, most fallen angels have little knowledge of other religions. Had anyone on the negotiation team bothered to take a comparative religion class, they might have realised that Buddhism insists that the world cannot be perfectly defined, and that it cannot truly end *or* begin because it is inherently an illusion. Moreover, someone might have pointed out that the number one hobby of Buddhist masters everywhere is playing pranks upon those who ask them very serious questions.

ruining one person's life doesn't mean you have to restrict yourself to little half-point sins. You can't kill someone with *chocolate*."

"Kill someone?" Gadriel repeated faintly. Her head had started to feel very light now.

"You're sceptical, I can see that," Ms Wood said soothingly. "But I've done plenty of large-scale work with despair. I can't imagine it's much different on a personal level. Here, just as a for-instance: several of those little gremlins just tried to cheat their way through my class. I'm giving them a few days to gloat and enjoy their victory, right before I get them all expelled." She paused thoughtfully. "I think I'll do it in front of the entire class."

Gadriel stared straight ahead, trying very hard not to react.

"Well!" said Ms Wood cheerfully. "Let's do lunch this week. How does Wednesday work for you?"

"Sounds lovely," Gadriel said hoarsely.

Ms Wood stopped, and Gadriel realised that she'd brought them full circle, all the way back to the stairs. "Excellent," she said. "Good luck with your appointment, Gadriel. Give out lots of… chocolate." She released Gadriel's arm, chuckling as though she'd make a joke—and then, she was gone.

"Always a pleasure, Wormwood," Gadriel mumbled weakly.

***

Ella Harker was waiting in Gadriel's office when she finally dragged herself back inside. The adult-sized chair which Gadriel had stolen from the staff room was tall enough that her feet dangled just a few centimetres off of the floor.

"You're not dead," Ella said. The wariness in her tone suggested it was only half of a joke.

Gadriel threw herself into the chair behind the desk, pressing a hand to her eyes. "Not at all," she said dully. "We're on for lunch on Wednesday."

Ella leaned across the desk, eyeing her intently. "You're really scared," she observed. "And not in the funny way."

Gadriel rubbed at her face. "Have you ever read Revelation?" she asked. "The part of the Bible about the end of the world, I mean."

Ella frowned, shifting back in her chair. "I have," she said. "Mum's therapy group made us both read the whole thing."

"Oh, good," Gadriel said. She glanced up at Ella through the sieve of her fingers. "You remember the part about Wormwood? Fallen angel, herald of the end times?"

Ella nodded, though she still looked understandably confused.

"That's her," said Gadriel.

Ella chewed uncertainly at her lip. "Is this some sort of fancy metaphor?" she asked suspiciously. "Are you saying Ms Wood is basically a demon?"

Gadriel sighed and let her head fall into her arms. Her forehead thudded gently against the desk. "Sure," she said. "Yes. I'm being metaphorical." She brooded miserably on the matter for several seconds, as thoughts chased themselves around her head.

"I don't know how it came to this, honestly," Gadriel said finally. "Ruining people's lives? That's not what I signed up for. I just had questions, and the higher-ups said that wasn't allowed. I jumped ship because I wanted to make people *happy* instead of telling them off all the time." She closed her arms more fully over her head, as though to hide from the situation. "When did it become a choice between making people miserable for their own good and making them miserable because someone down below thinks it's fun?"

Gadriel heard a shuffling noise from the other side of the desk—followed by a curious sort of *snap-crunch*.

She looked up slowly from her arms, as Ella slid half of a chocolate-covered biscuit across the desk towards her.[59]

"Aunt Holly gave me some biscuits with my lunch," Ella said quietly. "I already ate most of them early. But I guess you can have half of the last one."

Gadriel stared at the half a biscuit. As she did, she was forced to shove away her existential dread in favour of a brief, soul-deep consternation.

"Please tell me it's not that simple," she said. "Tell me you did not just solve several centuries of bureaucratic angst by pulling a chocolate King Solomon."[60]

Ella blinked. "If you don't want it, I'll eat it," she warned.

Gadriel picked up the half-biscuit warily, nibbling at the edge of it.

"Do you want to talk about it?" Ella asked. A hint of genuine concern now coloured her features. The expression made her look quite a lot like her aunt, in fact.

"I *do* want to talk about it, actually," Gadriel mumbled past the biscuit. Once she started speaking, the words spilled out in a torrent. "I'm way out of my depth here. The smart move would

---

59   +1 Point of Virtue (Ella Harker): Sharing.

60   It was exactly this simple, of course. One cannot technically eat the last piece of chocolate if one is sharing it with someone else.

be to just go along with it all and keep her happy. But—I don't want to *hurt* anyone. I don't. That's not at all my thing."

Ella picked at the chocolate coating on her half-a-biscuit, licking it off one finger. "I still don't know exactly what you're talking about," she said patiently. "But you could probably just run? Ms Wood has plenty of people here to bully. I doubt she'd go looking for you if you switched schools or something."

Gadriel groaned. "That's the rub, isn't it?" she asked. "I *could* run. I could leave everyone else to deal with her. And that's probably the best decision, honestly. I'm within spitting distance of finishing my real job. She's not *my* responsibility. And—even if she was my responsibility, what would I do about it? I can't face up to an angel of the apocalypse, even if she is on holiday!"

Ella nodded reasonably. "Makes sense to me," she said. "Don't pick fights you can't win. I mean—unless you're really cheesed off and you just don't care."

"Exactly!" Gadriel said, pointing emphatically at her. "No reasonable person would send a two-bit fallen angel to deal with the Third Calamity—"

Gadriel stopped abruptly, staring down at what remained of her biscuit.

"Er… Ms Sweet?" Ella asked. She waved a hand carefully in front of Gadriel's face. "Hello? Anyone home?"

"That dirty, two-faced, oversized pigeon!" Gadriel hissed loudly. "He *knew* she was here! Of course he knew!" She stood up from her chair, fisting her hands in her hair. "I'm going to kill him."

Ella looked up at her. "Does this mean our appointment's over?" she asked dryly.

Gadriel straightened and headed for the door, pulling out her phone. "You'll have to excuse me," she said. "I've got to deal with some family business."

***

Gadriel paced furiously in front of the pond, typing away at her phone. She'd long since lost track of the number of texts she'd sent Barachiel, but it didn't matter—she had plenty more to say.

> **Gadriel: WORMWOOD**

> **Gadriel: WORM. WOOD.**

> **Gadriel: I don't know what you were thinking**

> **Gadriel: I don't owe this to you**

> **Gadriel: NO CARD GAME IS WORTH THIS**

No check marks appeared next to the texts. Either Barachiel hadn't seen them yet, or else he'd finally figured out how to turn off the feature.

One of the ducks had started pacing behind Gadriel, following her back and forth as she went. As she stopped in place, the duck bumped into her foot and let out an irritated *quack*.

Gadriel whirled on the duck. "For the last time, I don't have any bread!" she burst out. "Go and bother someone else!"

The mallard backed away with a soft hiss.

Gadriel looked down at the phone in her hand, weighing it

seriously. This, she decided, was grim business. It was unprecedented, really. If there was ever a time for desperate measures, then truly, this was it.

Gadriel hit the 'call' button.[61]

The line rang several times. Just as she'd suspected, however, no one picked up.

"*The angel you are trying to reach is not available right now,*" said a cheerful automated voice on the other end of the line. "*Please leave a prayer, or try again later.*"

The phone beeped.

"Oh, I'll leave a prayer, all right!" Gadriel growled into the phone. "Now you listen here, O Chief of Underhanded Card Tricks! Whatever you think you're going to get out of me, it is *not* happening. We agreed that I'd tempt Holly Harker into having some fun, and that is exactly what I'm doing. I've got exactly half a point of sin to go, and then I'm out of here—so if you're looking for someone to meddle with Wormwood's plans, then you'd better start hunting for a new patsy."

The line closed with another beep. Gadriel shoved it back into her pocket with an infuriated hiss.

She looked at the mallard.

"This isn't my responsibility," Gadriel said darkly. "So a few girls are going to get expelled—so what? I didn't *make* them do anything; I just tempted them. They'll learn a lesson and move on

---

61   Like most millennials, Gadriel finds the idea of actually *talking* to someone on the phone to be utterly repulsive. In Gadriel's case, of course, 'millennial' refers to a different turn of a different millennium—but the point still stands.

with their lives. There are worse things."

The duck quacked angrily. Likely, it suspected that Gadriel was hiding a whole loaf of bread inside her knitted vest. But the fallen angel couldn't help hearing a note of condemnation in the sound.

"Well obviously, it's going to escalate!" Gadriel snapped. "Wormwood doesn't play for half-points and kittens."

Quack, said the duck.

"No one asked you," Gadriel muttered sulkily.

She stormed over to the wooden bench in front of the pond and sat down heavily, pulling her stolen chocolate bar from her pocket.

"Half-melted," Gadriel mumbled. "Just my luck." She pried open the wrapper on the chocolate bar regardless, stuffing it into her mouth with sticky fingers.

The duck waddled off in a huff, leaving her alone and forlorn.

Suddenly, there came a *ding* from Gadriel's pocket. She dropped the chocolate bar with a curse, fumbling to pull out her phone again. Smudges lingered on the screen as she unlocked it.

Holly: You're not allergic to peanut butter, are you? Asking for a friend.

Gadriel stared down at the phone with a growing sense of deep and terrible guilt. She was briefly assaulted by the mad impulse to toss her phone into the lake. But she restrained the impulse—and after a second, she typed her reply into the phone morosely.

Gadriel: My only allergy is sacramental wine.

The phone *dinged* one more time.

Holly: Excellent. I think I'll pick up some baking supplies tomorrow. Watch this space.

Gadriel buried her face in her hands. "I'm a modern-day Judas," she moaned. "I'm going to betray a pretty girl and her niece with a peanut butter-chocolate kiss."

Somewhere at her feet, there came another *quack*. She glanced up and saw the mallard nosing at the fallen chocolate. It soon raised its head to give her a reproachful look, as though to say: *this is not bread, either.*

"Fine!" Gadriel snapped. "Have it your way!" She shoved to her feet, kicking the chocolate bar aside. "I don't have to defeat Wormwood. I just have to… *inconvenience* her." She nodded her head at the revelation, suddenly far more confident. "That's right. I can do that much. Why, I'm an ace at bothering people."

Quack, said the duck.

"Case in point," Gadriel said. She straightened out her knitted vest and took in a deep breath. "I'll have to get to planning," she muttered. "But I can do this. Yes." She turned away from the pond with a determined stride. "If I do it right, then she'll never even know that it was me."

The mallard stared after her sceptically. But Gadriel didn't need anyone else's approval. She was more than petty enough to pull this off all on her own.

Chapter Sixteen

CUMULATIVE SIN METRIC (HOLLY HARKER): -912.5
CUMULATIVE SIN METRIC (ELLA HARKER): +217.1

It was Tuesday morning maths class, and something was very *off*.

Ella stared down at her maths test, furrowing her brow.

> A mediocre chocolate bar costs £1. Good chocolate costs far more. A miserable fridge thief has now stolen £10 worth of chocolate, one per day over four days. How much was the good chocolate worth?

Ella glanced up at Ms Schmidt's desk. The maths teacher was wearing daisies today—but for once, she had discovered a mood other than *very excited* or *very concerned*. Today, her lips were set in a flat, unfriendly line, and her eyes flashed with a deep, pent-up frustration. She typed away at the laptop in front of her with an uncharacteristic, barely leashed violence.

Ella scanned the rest of the test. Ms Schmidt's cats were nowhere to be found. Instead, every last question seemed to be fixated on *chocolate*.

At the bottom of the test was a bonus question.

How would you stop a fridge thief from taking your chocolate? Be creative.

Ella raised her hand slowly.

"*Yes*, Miss Harker?" Ms Schmidt snapped, over the top of her laptop.

Ella rocked back into her seat with a blink. "Er," she said carefully. "Ms Schmidt? I'm not sure I understand the bonus question."

Ms Schmidt straightened in her chair. "I thought it was fairly self-explanatory," she said, with a patience which Ella now suspected was actually a fragile veneer. "What confuses you about it?"

Ella glanced down at her paper again, just to be sure. "It's just… I don't think it's a maths question, is it?" she asked weakly.

Ms Schmidt narrowed her eyes. "Anything can be a maths question," she said in a low voice. "We use maths every day without even noticing it." Ms Schmidt had said such things before— but for some reason, the words held a particularly ominous tone today.

"Yes, Ms Schmidt," Ella said in a meek voice.

Jasper raised his hand.

"What is it, Mr O'Neill?" Ms Schmidt asked dangerously. There was a threatening glint in her eyes which suggested this question had better be a good one.

Jasper cleared his throat uncomfortably. "Er," he said. "I just wanted to make sure I'm thinking in the right direction for the bonus question. Could I *poison* the chocolate?"

"I'm not trying to get arrested for murder, Mr O'Neill," Ms Schmidt responded in a frosty tone. "Much as some might deserve it," she added under her breath.

Jasper leaned back minutely in his seat, as though trying to wriggle away from the ice in Ms Schmidt's voice. But he was, at the end of the day, an infuriating overachiever, and he couldn't seem to leave the matter alone. "Well... what if it was something that wouldn't kill the thief?" he asked. "Would *that* work?"

Ms Schmidt fixed him with a sudden look of keen interest. "Go on," she said.

Jasper swallowed. "My da loves chilli peppers," he said. "He has this ghost pepper powder he puts on his food. I imagine it'd be enough to make a fridge thief cry."

Ms Schmidt smiled. It was a pleasant smile—but it was somehow still fearful in its intensity. "Come and speak with me after class, Mr O'Neill," she said. "I may have an assignment for you. We'll call it extra *extra* credit."

No one else dared to speak again, after that.

After class, as Ella started packing up her things, she caught sight of Beatrix slinking towards her desk out of the corner of her eye. There was something wary about the other girl's manner that Ella had never seen before, and she frowned as she turned to greet her.

"Beatrix," Ella said, "why do you look like you're about to stick your arm in a lion's mouth?"

Beatrix winced, taking a step back. "I... I just wanted to ask you something," she said. "About band practice today."

Ella raised her eyebrows slowly. "Are you cancelling?" she asked. "That's not the end of the world, Bee."

Beatrix shook her head. "I'll be there," she assured Ella hastily, shifting on her feet. "It's just... someone else wants to join the band."

Ella blinked. "They do?" she asked. "Well, what do they play? Are they any good?"

Beatrix scuffed her foot against the wooden floor, now staring at her toes. "Millie wants to sing for us," she said.

Ella's mouth dropped open. "*Millie?*" she demanded. "You want *Millie* to join the band?" Ella glanced swiftly around the room for the girl in question—but Millie had wisely disappeared, leaving Beatrix to do her dirty work for her.

"She's a good singer!" Beatrix said defensively. "She's had years and years of choir."

"No!" Ella sputtered. "Absolutely not!" She grabbed her pencil case, stuffing it violently into her bag. "What is it with you and Millie, all of a sudden? First you're… *helping* her with history, and now you want her in our band? You do remember how awful she's been to you all year?"

Beatrix wilted. "Millie's been really nice ever since history," she said. "I just thought… if she joins the band, then she might *stay* nice." She grabbed pleadingly at Ella's arm. "Millie's on the disco committee. She said if we let her sing, then we can play a few songs on Friday. It'd be our first real gig, Ella."

Ella groaned, collapsing back into her chair. "I hate it," she said. "All of it." But she couldn't hide the hint of grudging interest that had come into her face at the idea of playing a real gig in front of an actual crowd—and she knew that Beatrix had seen it.

Beatrix released Ella's arm and clasped her hands together beneath her chin in a gesture of supplication. "Please?" she said. "Please, please, please? We can try it out, just for *one* day. If she's awful, then we can kick her right out again!"

Ella sighed. "*Fine,*" she said reluctantly. "Millie can come to practice, just for today. But the first time she insults either one of us, I'm kicking her out of the music room and locking the door. You tell her that."[62]

Beatrix squealed with delight. "Yes!" she said. "I'll handle it all, I promise." She threw her arms around Ella, squeezing her tightly. "I'll see you after school, then!"

Beatrix extracted herself again, hitching up her bag and hurrying for the door. Ella grumbled and grabbed at her maths folder, tossing it into her bag with the rest of her things.

"Miss Harker?" Ms Schmidt said from her desk. She was looking down at one of the maths tests in front of her with an exasperated expression. "'Leave a vicious guard cat in the fridge'? Really?"

Ella shrugged and picked up her bag, heading for the hallway. "You said 'be creative'," she replied.

"Right," Ms Schmidt mumbled. She tucked the papers into a folder—and then, she stood and pointed at the desk just next to Ella's. "Mr O'Neill!" she said authoritatively. "I need to speak with you about some chilli peppers."

***

For once, Ella was not looking forward to band practice. When the last school bell finally rang, she found herself dragging her feet all the way to the music room, already contemplating ways in which she might escape.

---

62   +2 Points of Virtue (Ella Harker): Being the Bigger Person.

It was no surprise, therefore, that Millie had arrived before her. The blonde girl was sitting in a plastic chair just next to Beatrix's drum set, with her feet propped up on another chair. She had a booklet of sheet music open in her lap, which she read with interest while Beatrix stood behind her, looking on anxiously. The crutch that Millie had been using for the last few days was leaned against the back wall.

"Don't you two know anything more current?" Millie asked, as Ella headed in. She wrinkled her nose. "This stuff is so... *old*."

Ella scowled at her darkly. "You know where to find the door," she said.

Millie sighed theatrically, flipping the booklet closed. "Well, it's not like you could learn anything new before the end of the week," she said. "But if I'm going to stick around, then I want to do some Billie Eilish."

"Oh, we'll get right on that," Ella sneered. "Any other karaoke requests I should know about?"

"I like Billie Eilish," Beatrix offered hesitantly. "I'm sure we could figure out at least one of her songs."

Ella rolled her eyes. "Whatever," she said. "We'll talk about it once we get through Friday. Are you sure you can get us permission to play before then?"

"I already brought it up at our committee meeting yesterday," Millie said smugly. "It's fine as long as it's only a few songs. And we can't have any cursing in the lyrics, obviously."

Ella let out a frustrated breath. "At the meeting *yesterday?*" she said. "Before you'd even asked if you could sing with us?"

"That's right," said Millie. "The only reason everyone agreed to have the band was because I'm singing. No one would be interested in it otherwise." She twisted her lips into a grimace. "By the way, we're going to have to find a better band name. I can't even *say* 'The Dis'—er." Millie fumbled the word. 'The Disestablishment'—"

"It's 'The Disestablishmentarians'," Ella shot back. "And it doesn't surprise me that *you* can't say it." She clenched her hands, digging her fingers into her palms. "This isn't *your* band, Millie. You can't just walk in here and start changing everything."

"I'm just offering my advice," Millie said nonchalantly. "The name is dumb. It's going to hold us back."

"We are not changing the band name!" Ella declared. "That is *final!*" She narrowed her eyes at Millie. "Besides—we still don't even know if you can sing. If you're tone deaf, then we're kicking you to the curb."

Millie sniffed. "I sang the solo in *Ave Maria* last year," she said. "I can handle some oldies music." She gestured expectantly towards Beatrix. "Get my crutch, will you?"

"Didn't your mum teach you to say 'please', Millie—" Ella started.

But Beatrix had already fetched Millie's crutch before she could finish. Millie took it with an overly sweet smile at Beatrix. "*Thank you*, Beatrix," she said, in an exaggerated tone. She used the crutch to push herself up to her feet, settling the sheet music for *Jolene* onto a stand in front of her.

"I bet you don't even need that stupid crutch any more," Ella muttered.[63]

---

63   +1/2 Point of Sin (Ella Harker): A Mean-Spirited Comment. Also True.

Millie cleared her throat. "Get ready to eat your words, Harker," she said.

And then, she started singing.

She belted out the lyrics shamelessly, barely pausing for breath as she begged Jolene not to take her man. Even with no instruments behind her, she could have drawn a crowd. It was immediately clear that she'd had a private tutor at some point; she even did the stupid vibrato on the highest notes.

Millie stopped abruptly after only a few measures. Beatrix clapped excitedly from a chair. "That was *amazing!*" she gushed. "We're going to be a hit!"

"I hate you," Ella said shortly.

Millie leaned on her crutch, smirking. "How's that for tone-deaf?" she taunted.

"Oh, shut up," Ella said, as she headed for the cage where her guitar was currently locked up. "You might be a mess once we start playing behind you—"

"Aha!" an adult voice cut in. "I've found all three of you at once. Excellent."

Mr Sweet was standing in the doorway behind them. He still looked awfully bedraggled, and Ella had to wonder whether he'd slept at all the evening before.

"You're a man today?" she asked.

"Oh, I'm not risking being a woman at school," Mr Sweet said firmly. "It's not worth it. Ms Wood can be the only one here, absolutely."

"Er," said Ella. It had occurred to her that there were plenty of *other* women at the school, herself included—but this hardly seemed like the time to point that out. "Why were you looking for us, exactly?"

"I was—" Mr Sweet glanced suspiciously over his shoulder, as though wary of spies. "One moment."

He stepped fully into the music room, shutting the door behind him. He then started walking about the classroom, glancing into the instrument cages and nudging at chairs with his toe. "You haven't seen any snakes in here, have you?" he asked conversationally—as though this were a perfectly normal question to ask.

"No, Mr Sweet," Ella said slowly. "Should we be on the look-out for one?"

Beatrix went pale. Gradually, she picked her feet up off the floor, tucking them onto the chair beneath her.

Mr Sweet waved a hand. "No, not at all," he said. "I'm sure it's fine." He turned back towards the girls with a renewed smile. "Now then… I wanted to ask you all about Ms Wood's history tests. Do you know anyone who's passed one of them?"

Ella exchanged looks with Millie and Beatrix. One by one, they each shook their heads. "Not that I've ever heard of," Ella said. "No one's ever said so in front of me."

"If anyone could pass one of those tests, it would be Jasper," Millie added. "And you should have *seen* his face after the one on Monday."

Mr Sweet nodded to himself as they replied. "You know," he mused, "I was hoping you would say that." He tapped idly at one of the music stands. "Ms Wood said it herself—we've all been thinking too small. Cheating just one or two tests? A drop in the bucket. And she's bound to catch you at it eventually. No—I think we require a more permanent solution."

Beatrix raised her hand energetically. Mr Sweet blinked at her. "Er… yes, Miss Relish?" he asked. "You don't have to raise your hand. We're not in class."

Beatrix dropped her hand again. "Are you saying we should push Ms Wood down the stairs?" she asked.

"What?" Mr Sweet asked. "No! Dear Lucifer, thirteen-year-old girls are *bloodthirsty.*"

Beatrix frowned. "I'm *twelve* years old, Mr Sweet," she corrected him.

Mr Sweet rubbed at his face. "I do have a plan to get rid of Ms Wood," he said carefully. "But it does not involve pushing her down the stairs."

"Pity," Millie muttered.

"I'm going to have to swear you all to utmost secrecy," Mr Sweet said. "Once we start, you cannot mention that I am involved in this—not even if you think you're in private. Absolutely *no* snitching." He shot a meaningful look at Beatrix, who blushed with embarrassment.

"Understood," Ella told him. "Now get to the point."

Mr Sweet cleared his throat. "*None* of you are going to sit for any history tests tomorrow," he said. "In fact, no one is going to set foot in room 201 at all." He pointed at Beatrix. "You, young lady, are going to need to have a long, meaningful chat with your mother tonight."

Beatrix blinked. "Me?" she squeaked. "With my *mother?*"

"Yes indeed," said Mr Sweet. "In fact, she's key to the entire plan." He leaned forward, lowering his voice conspiratorially. "Now let me explain to you *exactly* how you're going to frame this for her…"

Chapter Seventeen

CUMULATIVE SIN METRIC (HOLLY HARKER): -912.5
CUMULATIVE SIN METRIC (ELLA HARKER): +216.6

It was a cool, overcast Wednesday morning, and Gadriel was stuck outside the school building. To be perfectly fair, he wasn't trying very hard to get inside.

A sizeable crowd of students had formed a barrier in front of the double doors. Makeshift posters circulated among a sea of navy uniforms, with slogans like 'DOWN WITH THE BIRCH' and 'MAKE MS WOOD HISTORY'. Despite the signage, there was a peppy sort of atmosphere; Gadriel had noted that nothing perked up students quite like the prospect of skipping school, regardless of the reason.

Though several other teachers were stuck outside with Gadriel, there was one particular adult figure at the eye of the storm who stuck out from the crowd. Mrs Relish was in rare form today; she had eschewed her usual chic look for an off-the-shoulder, paint-spattered red shirt and artfully shredded jeans. Her short black hair had been intentionally spiked and mussed with gel.

Beatrix, nearby, was wearing her usual school uniform—but her black hair was chalked with bright neon colours, in a nod to her mother's rainbow-spattered shirt. The younger Relish was currently holding a phone in her hands, pointing it up at her mother.

"—time to say 'enough is enough'!" Mrs Relish declared to the phone. "Our children have suffered for too long under this ridiculous tyranny—and if no one else is going to stand up against it, then *this* mama bear will! Hashtag: EndofHistory! Hashtag: AxeMsWood!" She paused dramatically, then added: "Don't forget to like and subscribe."

Several encouraging whistles went up from the crowd of students, while two boys jostled with one another behind Mrs Relish, throwing peace signs at the phone's camera.

"Bloody hell," Millie Wilson muttered nearby, looking down at her phone. "We're actually going viral." She paused. "I mean, mostly with stay-at-home mums and yoga schools—but still."

"Mrs Relish adores attention," Gadriel informed Millie. "She has therefore finely honed her talent for *getting* attention." He chewed idly at a custard doughnut, scanning the crowd. His gaze caught upon Jasper O'Neill, who had started trying to sneak his way to the front doors of the school.

Gadriel sighed and strolled towards the boy, bringing a hand down on his shoulder. Jasper startled, glancing back at him.

"No one likes a scab, Jasper," Gadriel said. He jerked his chin towards the table of doughnuts behind them. "Go have a lemon tart."

Jasper blinked once, then headed obediently for the table.

"Who brought the tarts and doughnuts?" Ella called over

the gathering. She was still handing out poster board and pens to enterprising students, at least one of whom had drawn a very crude picture on someone else's face.

"I dunno!" Millie called back. "They were already here when we showed up!"

Gadriel hid his satisfied smile behind another bite of his doughnut.[64]

Beatrix bounced over with visible glee, shoving her phone back into her bag and high-fiving Millie. The morning's events had instilled an uncommon energy within her. "I can't believe it's working!" she yelled. "Mum is on fire!"

"She sure pulled this together in a hurry!" Millie shouted back. "What did you *say* to her?"

Beatrix beamed broadly. "All I had to do was say the 'f' word!"

Millie goggled at her. "You said the 'f' word to your mum?" she asked incredulously.

Beatrix nodded emphatically. "I used the word *freedom!*" she specified.

"What does this have to do with freedom?" Millie asked with a choked laugh.

"I don't know," Beatrix admitted, "but it worked! Mum said it's our god-given right as Americans to rebel against British institutions!"

"Aren't you *half*-American?" Millie asked, squinting at Beatrix.

---

64   There is a universal law which dictates that crowds will form around two things: free snacks and free t-shirts. Given the choice between the two, Gadriel was obviously partial to sweets.

"I have citizenship!" Beatrix said defensively.

Ella forced her way through the crowd, still clinging to several poster boards which were nearly larger than she was. "Does anyone actually *know* Ms Wood's first name?" she demanded. "I need some new material! I'm running out of tree puns."[65]

"Surely not," said Gadriel. "You can *never* run out of tree puns." He held up his fingers one by one, starting up a list. "'Ms Wood is Unpoplar'. 'Ms Wood Needs to Leaf'. 'Drop the Deadwood'—"

"Mr Sweet!" The headmaster waded through students with great effort, straining to reach Gadriel. His face was bright red with anger and embarrassment. "You're the school counsellor, by god! Do something!"

Gadriel dropped his fingers, glancing at the three students. "Hm," he said speculatively, swallowing another bite of his doughnut. "Would you please stop this nonsense and go inside, girls?"

"Uh… no?" said Ella.

"Definitely not," said Millie.

"Not until our demands are met!" Beatrix declared, pumping her fist in the air.

Gadriel shrugged at Mr Parker. "I'm a school counsellor, headmaster, not a hostage negotiator," he said. "If you'd like my expert opinion on the matter, I'd advise you to engage with their concerns and come to a mutually agreeable solution."

---

65   +2 Points of Sin (Ella Harker): Skiving Off School. +1/10 Points of Sin (Ella Harker): For Several Terrible Puns. +5 Points of Virtue (Ella Harker): Sticking Up For Classmates.

"I am *not* going to negotiate with thirteen-year-olds!" the headmaster sputtered incredulously.

"Well, you could always negotiate with *her*," Gadriel suggested, pointing at Mrs Relish. The woman had now handed her phone off to Jasper, who looked very confused indeed to be holding a lemon tart in one hand and a smartphone in the other.

"You can call me a Boston revolutionary!" Mrs Relish proclaimed to the phone. "Because I'm here to *spill tea* about this awful woman! Hashtag: MsWoodHasNoClass."

Headmaster Parker turned back to the girls. "What is it you want?" he asked flatly.

"We want Ms Wood sacked," Ella informed him over the edge of her posters. "She's a menace. Everyone's failing her tests, and no one wants to set foot in her classroom any more."

"Now you're just being ridiculous," said the headmaster. "If I sacked a teacher every time the students complained about them, I'd have no teachers left!"

"Ms Wood is different," Ella retorted. "She *likes* making students upset, and we all know it. We're not putting up with her any more. If you want to keep her at the school, then you can have her—but you won't have a Year 9 if you do."

"Actually, we've got students out here from Year 8 and Year 10, too," Millie cut in. "I think they're mostly just eating the doughnuts, but they still count."

"Would you like a doughnut, actually?" Gadriel asked the headmaster. "There's plenty still left."

Mr Parker clenched his jaw. "This is beyond silly," he said. "So you know, girls, I've already called your parents. We'll see what they have to say when they get here—" He cut himself off abruptly, whirling upon Beatrix. "Are you *filming* me, Miss Relish?"

Beatrix had pointed her phone at the headmaster as he spoke. "You're live on social media!" she chirped. "I've got a public account now—I'm 'Baby Bear in London'. Mum already sent me thousands of followers!"

"Oof," said Millie, leaning on her crutch. "You're going to regret *that* name in a year or two."

Beatrix shrugged. "Mum says it's all about unified branding," she replied. "D'you know, I already had someone message and offer me a free handbag this morning?"

Millie raised her eyebrows. "How *nice* a handbag?" she asked.

The headmaster made a sound of deep, incoherent frustration.

"What is going *on* out here?"

Gadriel turned and saw that Holly had arrived. It was immediately clear that she'd had to sprint across town again—her face was flushed, and she was still wearing her apron from the café, over a black t-shirt and trousers. She threaded her way awkwardly through clumps of students, barely ducking in time to avoid a sign. Her eyes picked Ella out of the crowd, and she diverted her path towards them.

"Miss Harker!" the headmaster roared, gesticulating furiously in her direction. "There you are! It's time we had another talk!"

Holly came up short, blinking. Her brown eyes slid to Gadriel, plainly bewildered. "Gabe?" she said blankly. "Why are *you* here?"

"Oh, I work here," Gadriel said casually. He offered out a jam doughnut to Holly, who took it without thinking. She glanced down at the pastry in her hand with visible confusion. "On a tangential note," Gadriel added, "I don't suppose you brought any sweets with you? I believe you mentioned peanut butter."

The headmaster stormed towards Holly, thrusting a finger into her chest. "I insist that you remove your niece from the premises *immediately*," he demanded.

Holly stared down at his finger incredulously. "Do you mind?" she said. Her tone was mild—but any bystander could have translated the words into their *real* meaning, which was roughly: *If you, a grown man, do not remove your finger from my person, then I will shortly break it.*

The headmaster retracted his finger, curling it safely into his palm. He cleared his throat. "I regret to inform you, Miss Harker, that your niece is one of the prime instigators of this little riot," he said, in a somewhat less confrontational tone.

Holly glanced at Ella. "You are?" she asked. This idea did little to soothe the confusion in her features. "Are... are all of these people angry with you, Ella?"

Ella rolled her eyes. "No, Aunt Holly," she said, with exaggerated patience. "We're all protesting. Bee's mum is helping."

"I am suspending your niece for the rest of the week!" the headmaster blustered. "I want her gone *now*, Miss Harker."

Beatrix fumbled for her phone excitedly. "Ooh, can you say that again?" she asked. "You'll have to speak up a bit—it's loud out here."

Ella sighed heavily, handing off the poster boards to Millie, who struggled to hold them while balancing on her crutch. "Guess I'll see you next week," Ella muttered. "So much for playing at the disco."

Gadriel considered Holly carefully. Several conflicting

emotions had started fighting for prominence on her face. Holly Harker was not at all fond of conflict; obviously, she was even less fond of breaking rules.

But there was a different impulse buried somewhere beneath her hesitance. It was… an infuriated sense of unfairness. A suggestion of protectiveness. Something that one might even call a *mama bear's instinct*.

Gadriel turned his head and lifted his hand to cover his mouth.

"SCREW THE MAN," he said. "SUPPORT YOUR NIECE. WE BOTH KNOW YOU WANT TO."

To Gadriel's surprise, *this* temptation snapped into place almost immediately, in a way that no other temptation had done so far. Holly straightened her back and set her jaw.

"My niece is not going anywhere," Holly declared, gesturing emphatically with her jam doughnut. "And since you so kindly dragged me out of work in order to yell at me, Mr Parker, it turns out that I now have several hours of free time on my hands as well." Holly passed the doughnut off to Beatrix and snapped a hand out towards Ella. "Give me a poster."[66]

Ella stared at her aunt with her mouth agape.

"This is—" The headmaster floundered, suddenly at a loss for words. "You can't—"

Ella shoved one of the blank signs in her aunt's direction. Millie offered out a permanent pen. Holly took both brusquely, popping open the pen with her teeth. She paused suddenly,

---

66   +5 Points of Virtue (Holly Harker): Supporting a Child at Personal Cost.

staring down at the poster board. "…what are we protesting?" she asked.

"Our history teacher, Ms Wood," Ella said blankly.

Holly awkwardly wrote the words 'MS WOOD MUST GO' in big, blocky letters.

Mrs Relish whooped at her from across the crowd, clapping her hands in approval.

"I really think you ought to have a doughnut," Gadriel told the headmaster helpfully. "I expect we're going to be out here for a bit."

A dark shadow fell over Gadriel as he spoke these words. It was a cold, Stygian darkness—the sort of chill which most people would describe as someone walking over your grave. Gadriel had to work not to shudder as it engulfed him.

"Enjoying the show, Gadriel?" Wormwood asked silkily. The fallen angel was dressed in a crimson suit today; the outfit made her stand out against the students in their drab school uniforms like a garish splotch of blood. Just how such a tall, gaunt figure had sneaked up on Gadriel through that crowd (in heels, no less) was entirely beyond him.

None of the mortals present reacted to Wormwood's question—though all of them shivered visibly. Gadriel rubbed at his arms. "Brisk sort of weather we're having," he said distractedly. He shoved the rest of the custard doughnut into his mouth and swallowed quickly. "Oh, would you look at that?" he announced. "I'm getting a call. If you'll excuse me, everyone."

Gadriel backed away from the group, pulling out his phone and setting it obviously to his ear.

"It's more exciting out here, you must admit," Gadriel

managed breathlessly, as he strode away from the gathering. "I could sit alone in my office, I suppose—but the view there is awfully depressing." He spoke the words into the receiver, though he fixed his eyes on Wormwood while he talked.

Wormwood picked at her wickedly pointed nails as she fell into step next to Gadriel. Her flat green eyes were aflame with the sort of vexation which normally spelled the end of nations. "What do these children think they're *doing?*" she murmured.

"Rebelling, I think," Gadriel supplied helpfully. "They're at that age, you know." He forced a friendly smile. "Oh, come now—doesn't it remind you of old times, just a little bit?"

A Year 10 boy passed them by, nearly smacking Gadriel in the face with his sign, which read: 'WE WALNUT STAND FOR THIS'.

Wormwood narrowed her eyes at the sign. "I *hope* you're not comparing our glorious revolution to this... temper tantrum," she said.

"Oh, you know me," Gadriel replied modestly. "I enjoy small performances. I do know they're not for everyone, though." He arranged his features into a sympathetic expression. "I will admit, I was worried that something like this could happen, with all of that talk about going bigger. You're an apocalyptic fish in a small pond, after all. Sometimes, going too big too fast can trigger... things like this." He waved conclusively at the gathering around them.

The shadows around Wormwood darkened. Her green eyes glinted dangerously in the gloom. "I ought to poison the drinking fountains," she said in a low voice. "Or perhaps I could call down a plague—"

Gadriel nearly fumbled his phone; he caught it at the last possible second, securing it against his ear again. "Please, let's not!" he interjected hastily. "We're still doing all of the paperwork from your plague in China, remember? The Celestial Bureaucracy sent three messengers last century asking where to find you."[67]

Wormwood crossed her arms ominously. The temperature had now dropped even further in her vicinity, and the grass beneath her heels had shriveled.

Gadriel swallowed. "But really, you're above all this, aren't you?" he wheedled in a high tone. "I mean, this is basically drudge work. A cadre of children and their pushy parents are hardly going to appreciate an artist's touch."

"This was supposed to be my holiday," Wormwood complained darkly. "And it was going so well at first, too."

Gadriel reached out to pat her shoulder cautiously—though he didn't dare let the hand linger. He gathered up his resolve one last time, trying to shake the feeling that the shadows were *looking* at him. Finally, he forced out the words he'd been working up to. "AREN'T YOU IN THE MOOD TO MOVE ON TO SOMETHING NEW?" he suggested carefully.

Wormwood paused—and Gadriel held his breath. He'd done his best to keep his inside voice even more *inside* than usual, this time. But it was never precisely *safe* nudging a harbinger of the

---

67 The Celestial Bureaucracy is famous for its legal processes, many of which can take up to a thousand years. The Greek goddess Epona filed a suit with the Celestial Bureaucracy's courts in the year 101 BC over a conflict involving some horses. To this day, she is still working her way through the system.

apocalypse, no matter how delicately one tried to do so.

Wormwood turned those dead, serpentine eyes upon Gadriel. Finally, she said: "I think I'm in the mood to move on to something new." She gestured contemptuously at the children around her. "You can keep this little sandbox of yours."

Gadriel released his breath all at once. His head felt light and unsteady, as though it might float away at any moment. "Oh," he said faintly. "Well, that's… a shame. I'll be sorry to see you go; it would have been a real honour working with you."

"Keep at it, Gadriel," Wormwood told him idly. "Even chocolate adds up, after a few millennia."

She turned away from the protest with a sweep of shadowy wings. Where the shadows passed, signs drooped and people's voices died. But with every step the fallen angel took away from the gathering, the tension in Gadriel's shoulders loosened just a little more.

As Wormwood's form retreated past the edge of the school grounds, Gadriel called out: "Does this mean we're not on for lunch today?"

Wormwood did not respond.

A few seconds later—once Gadriel was utterly certain she was gone—he dared to mutter a tiny, victorious "yes!" He dropped his phone from his ear and pumped his fist once, as he headed back towards the others.

"Do *you* know what instrument Nero played as Rome burned?" Ella was asking Mr Parker. She'd pulled out a test now, reciting questions from it one by one as Beatrix trained her phone on the headmaster.

"Oh, for goodness' sake!" Mr Parker snapped. "Everyone

knows Nero played the fiddle, Miss Harker." He pushed the test away, now striding urgently towards the parking lot. "I am done entertaining this inappropriate display. All three of you are suspended for the week."

The headmaster grabbed at a doughnut as he passed the table of snacks, chewing at it with irritation.

Gadriel watched him go with a self-satisfied smile.

"He's not going to do anything about Ms Wood, is he?" Ella muttered crossly.

"Oh, he doesn't have to do anything," Gadriel told her. "Now that everyone's talking about Ms Wood out in the open, people have agreed that it's all right to stand up to her. The cat's been let out of the handbag, and Ms Wood knows that."

Holly blinked at Gadriel. "Isn't it normally 'let the cat out of the bag'?" she asked.

Gadriel cleared his throat. "I've heard it several ways," he said authoritatively. A moment later, though, he did a double-take, staring back at Holly.

Somewhere in the last ten minutes, she had *gained* five points of virtue.

"What happened?" Gadriel demanded. "I was so close! I barely looked away—"

He cut himself off abruptly, thinking back over the events of the morning. A groan escaped him, and he ran his fingers back through his hair in frustration.

Holly reached out gingerly to touch his arm. "Is everything all right?" she asked worriedly.

"I did it," Gadriel moaned. "It was *me*. I tempted someone into a *virtue*." He closed his eyes. "I can't let Barachiel find out.

He'll never let me hear the end of it."

"Get him a bit of chocolate," Ella advised her aunt. "He'll be fine in no time."

Holly squeezed sympathetically at Gadriel's arm. "I *do* have the ingredients for peanut butter chocolate biscuits at home," she told him. "I was going to make them this evening. You could… come back with us after we're done here, if you'd like some fresh from the oven?"

Gadriel slitted his eyes open hopefully at that. "That *does* sound lovely," he admitted. In fact, he thought, the promise of warm peanut butter chocolate biscuits was *nearly* worth the setback.

A very small, very quiet part of him suggested that the company would *also* be pleasant. But he did his best to ignore it.

Millie nudged Beatrix. "Ella's aunt is hitting on the school counsellor," she said in a stage whisper, loud enough for everyone to hear her perfectly.

Gadriel shot Millie a sceptical look. "I suppose we know who *isn't* getting any peanut butter chocolate biscuits," he told her stiffly. "Real shame, that. More for me."

He couldn't help but note very distantly, however, that Holly's cheeks had gone pink.

"Where's my baby bear?" Mrs Relish called out breathlessly. She dashed for the group, sweeping Beatrix up into her arms and spinning her around. "I'm so proud of you, darling! Look at all of these people who've come out to support you!"

Beatrix giggled, looking up at her mother through her technicolour fringe. "This isn't about me, Mum," she said. "It's about, um. *Freedom*."

Mrs Relish set her down again, nodding seriously. "Yes, it certainly is," she agreed. "Now... Mr Parker informed me that you've been suspended for the rest of the week. Do you know what that means, baby bear?"

Beatrix shook her head, wide-eyed.

"It means we're going to be out here *every day* this week!" Mrs Relish declared.

Gadriel choked on a laugh.

Holly's gaze shifted down towards Ella. Her hands tightened imperceptibly on her sign. "I'm... very proud of you too," she said in a small voice. "I hope that's all right."

Ella flushed and looked away. "It's all right," she mumbled sheepishly. She hunched her shoulders and cleared her throat, glancing around. "As long as it comes with peanut butter chocolate biscuits, anyway," she added more loudly.

"I think that can be arranged," Holly said warmly.

Chapter Eighteen

CUMULATIVE SIN METRIC (HOLLY HARKER): -917.5
CUMULATIVE SIN METRIC (ELLA HARKER): +214.4

Very little schooling happened that Wednesday at Battenberg Grammar. There were plenty of doughnuts, however, and at least one very long conga line in front of the building.

After school hours had finished, Holly gamely offered to cook dinner back at her flat for Gadriel and the three girls. Given that Millie's mother was far too busy working a hospital shift to come and upbraid her, and her usual after-school pursuits on the school grounds were currently forbidden, she agreed to come along with only a single roll of her eyes. Though Beatrix was also sorely tempted, her mother swept her away for further bonding before she could plead her case.

Gadriel expected that the atmosphere between Ella and Millie would be tense—but there was a glow of hard-won satisfaction between all parties which temporarily softened existing animosities. Conversation over chicken curry centred mostly on speculation about Ms Wood, who never had shown up to react to the protest.

"Ms Wood sure can dish it out," Millie said contemptuously, "but she can't *take* it, can she?" She speared triumphantly at her curry with a fork.

"D'you remember when she told Hannah she was doomed to repeat history?" Ella asked.[68]

"I don't," Millie mused. "But I *do* remember when she threw a history book at Jonesy."

"She did *what?*" Holly said in astonishment. "Why didn't anyone say something?"

"Oh, we did," Ella assured her matter-of-factly.

"You think adults listen to us?" Millie scoffed. "They always assume we're exaggerating."

Holly, who had opted to eat her curry with a spoon, now stared at the two of them with a heapful of chicken and rice halfway to her mouth. Her expression was appropriately horrified.

"We *said* she was a birch," Ella told her with a shrug.

"Either way, I suspect we've seen the last of Ms Wood," Gadriel reassured them. "It's a shame that you all got suspended for your efforts, but... well, authority figures rarely react well to rebellion."

Ella squared her shoulders. "If she *does* come back, then we'll all just walk out again," she said flatly. "I can't wait to enjoy the rest of the school year without her."

---

68   Wormwood was speaking of actual history when she said this, of course, and not of Year 9 history class. But all of the students had rightly understood the *spirit* of the comment, which was very nasty indeed.

"Hear, hear," Millie said in a lofty tone. She lifted her glass of ginger ale. "To the end of Ms Wood!" she proposed.

Ella lifted her glass in return, clinking it against Millie's. "And to Mr Sweet," she added graciously, with a sideways glance at the fallen angel. "For absolutely unrelated reasons, of course."

Holly shot Gadriel a curious look. "Unrelated reasons?" she asked.

"They're probably talking about the chocolate," Gadriel replied innocently.

"Do we get peanut butter chocolate biscuits now?" Ella asked. "I finished all of my dinner, see?" She lifted up her empty bowl, displaying it to her aunt.

"Yes, I will make us all some biscuits," Holly said. "It's going to take a bit, mind you."

"Can I watch?" Millie asked with interest. "Mum's always too busy to bake. It'd be nice to learn a recipe."

Holly smiled at that, in a way that made the apples of her cheeks bloom. It was a lovely smile, unburdened by the shadow that had lurked at the edges of her expression for so long. Gadriel stared at her raptly.

"I wouldn't say no to a bit of help," said Holly.

Ella hopped up from her chair. "I'll start on the dishes, then," she said briskly. "You're on drying duty, Mr Sweet."

"I'm what?" Gadriel said, jerking his eyes away from Holly. "When was that decided?"

"Remember the story about the ant and the grasshopper and stuff?" Ella asked him imperiously. She tapped her dirty fork meaningfully against the sink. "If you're too lazy, you don't get any sweets."[69]

Gadriel considered this seriously, weighing his instinctive laziness against his insatiable sweet tooth.

"You don't have to," Holly assured him. "You're a guest, after all."

"Well now you've done it," Gadriel mumbled. "Using reverse psychology on me, are you?" He shoved to his feet and headed over to join Ella. "Where *are* the towels, anyway?"

In truth, the entire scene felt... warm, and homey. It was comfortably cosy—rather like his knitted vest. Gadriel couldn't help basking in the sheer normalcy of it all. His mind drifted inevitably back to the early days. Things hadn't always been rosy for him as a guardian angel, of course—but it was easier just now to remember the good parts, with families all gathered up around the hearth and children chasing each other around.

Why, he wondered, were there so many Rules concerned with collecting virtue and so few concerned with collecting moments like this one?

"You should ask her to dinner," Ella mumbled next to him.

The words jolted Gadriel from his thoughts. He glanced sharply at her. "I don't know what you mean," he said—though his eyes flickered instinctively back to Holly as he spoke. She and Millie were already deep into the process of mixing the dough; a single smear of peanut butter lingered on the peak of her large,

---

69   Gadriel had never been a child at all, and had therefore never been subjected to any of Aesop's Fables, including *The Ant and the Grasshopper*. But if Gadriel had been an animal in said story, then he probably would have simply *stolen* the sweets—er, the food.

proud nose.

"She's nice enough," Ella said sensibly. "Hard working, too. And you'll always have lots of biscuits."

"You sound like you're selling me a fridge," Gadriel said. "What's with the sudden sales pitch?"

Ella heaved an exasperated sigh. "She's less uptight with you around," she admitted. "It's a relief, honestly."

Gadriel cleared his throat. "Well, I... that's not precisely how I..." He threw his towel over his shoulder. "This is a temporary job," he said finally.

"Right," Ella murmured. "You're off again as soon as Mrs Lisbon comes back." It was difficult to tell... but Gadriel *thought* he might have detected a tinge of disappointment in the words.

"Yes, that is... definitely what I meant," Gadriel lied. "No getting around that, is there?"

"Oh, please," Ella scoffed. "After all of the bribes and the poker and the skiving off work, it's *now* you just can't do anything?" She narrowed her eyes at him. "You're scared she'll say no, aren't you?"

"I am *not*," Gadriel protested.

"Oh, sh—um, *snickerdoodle!*" Holly cursed, over at the kitchen table. "Ella! Could you whack up the oven? I put it at the wrong temperature, but my hands are all peanut buttery now!"

Ella raised her eyebrows at Gadriel one last time, before turning away for the oven. This, unfortunately, left Gadriel entirely alone with his thoughts.

There wasn't technically anything *wrong* with the idea, was there? It wasn't unheard of for fallen angels to tempt mortals into, well... 'relationships' was probably a strong word, but it

OLIVIA ATWATER

happened. But the concept made Gadriel squirm for some reason—and he was not, as a rule, very fond of examining uncomfortable feelings.

It's because you have a squishy nougat centre and you know it. The thought rose unbidden to the surface of Gadriel's mind, and he cringed at its accuracy.

Gadriel didn't *want* to get attached. His days of following around a single mortal at a time were over and done with. By Lucifer, he was a free agent now!

"The biscuits are in!" Holly announced, as she wiped down her hands. "All done but the waiting."

Ella glanced at Millie. "I've got Chainsaw Truckers 4 in my room," she said. "Bet I'd crush you head-to-head."

"Bet you wouldn't," Millie replied smoothly.

Ella sprinted for the hall, while Millie followed primly in her footsteps.

"Just don't kill each other, girls!" Holly called after them. "I mean—not in *real* life."

A door slammed just down the hallway... leaving Holly and Gadriel together in the kitchen. Entirely alone.

Probably, Gadriel reflected, Ella had intended just that—though he couldn't entirely discount the possibility that she was looking forward to violently annihilating some pixilated stand-in for Millie Wilson.

Hm, he thought. *Why not both? She's a go-getter, after all.*

Holly sneaked a surreptitious glance at Gadriel. "I could put on some tea?" she suggested. "Or... perhaps some cocoa?"

"Or—counteroffer—you could... sit down and do nothing," Gadriel replied reasonably. "I'm not sure I've seen you do that before. It could be novel."

Holly reached absently for the towel over his shoulder, tugging it away. The movement brought her close enough to give him a fresh whiff of that soap and coffee scent she carried with her. Her eyes drifted nervously to the floor as she tucked the towel through the handle of the oven door.

"I do find 'nothing' to be very agreeable as a *concept*," Holly said. "Only, the execution—"

"You start by sitting down," Gadriel repeated helpfully. He reached past her to pull out a chair, gesturing towards it meaningfully.

Holly sighed ruefully, and sat down in the chair.

"Excellent first step," said Gadriel. He straightened his knitted vest in a businesslike manner and settled into the chair just next to her. "Now—I need to start making up for lost ground. You have been *far* too virtuous today. What temptations might I offer you, Miss Harker?"

Holly chuckled wearily. "I can't get smashed with you tonight," she said. "I'm running out of sick days. But..." She smiled shyly at him. "I do enjoy your company. So you might tempt me with that."

"I really don't think that's worth any points," Gadriel muttered to himself. But he found the words absurdly pleasing, nevertheless.

Holly leaned forward, folding her arms atop the table. "Incidentally," she said, "I now have hard proof that you *are* good with children. Ella likes you? I nearly died of shock."

Gadriel shook his head. "I only bribed her," he said. "I'm quite sure I explained that part."

"No," Holly stopped him, holding up a finger. "You *listened* to her. And I've been rubbish at that, haven't I?"

Gadriel sighed, leaning back in his chair. "She'd need to *talk* to you in order for you to listen," he said. "But you're in charge of her life, and that's complicated. It's simple for her to talk to me—I'm relatively unimportant. And I brought chocolate, obviously."

"And you care," Holly said softly. "It's written all over your face, you know."

Gadriel glanced up at her sharply. "I do *not*—" He paused significantly. "Denying that doesn't sound very good either, does it?"

"It does not," Holly confirmed. Her tone was bursting with amusement.

Gadriel stared sulkily at the table. "I don't... *want* to care," he amended himself. "Caring makes things very difficult."

Holly settled her chin into her arms, looking up at him. "You said you don't fall in love with people any more," she murmured. "When did you decide that was a bad thing?"

Gadriel was silent for a long moment. There was, for once, a yearning within him to be honest. Likely, he thought, it had something to do with the scent of fresh peanut butter chocolate biscuits wafting on the air.

"It always ends badly," he said finally. "Back when I had more... *exclusive* clients, it was a given. Either I fail, and... well, that's *awful*. Or else I succeed and..." He trailed off uncertainly. "I outlast people."[70]

---

70   For a guardian angel, a job well done means that their charge

Holly's face softened. "You're lonely then," she said.

Gadriel shrugged uncomfortably. "You can't be lonely if you don't get attached in the first place," he said.

"Of course you can," Holly said gently. "It's in the word. *Alone*." She studied Gadriel worriedly. "You're even fighting with your brother, come to think of it. Do you have anyone to take care of you when *you're* upset?"

Gadriel cleared his throat. "What do I have to be upset about?" he asked flippantly. "There are biscuits in the oven."

"Hm," said Holly.

Gadriel narrowed his eyes at her. "Not you too," he complained. "You sound *exactly* like Barachiel."

Holly smiled at him from the cradle of her arms. "I don't mind sounding like Barry," she said. "I like him very much. But I promise I won't ever ask you to follow any silly rules, Gadriel."

There was, again, that warm sense of cosiness between them. It was impossible to shake, in fact. Much to Gadriel's horror, he felt his heart softening as he considered that dreamy smile.

He reached out, very slowly, to swipe the peanut butter from the end of Holly's nose.

She blinked. "Oh. That's a strange place for peanut butter to end up, isn't it?"

"I think I've figured out why it's so difficult to tempt you, Miss Harker," Gadriel said quietly.

Holly glanced up at him in confusion. "Because I remember

---

lives well and passes on peacefully, surrounded by loved ones—at which point, the angel is then assigned a new human being to watch over. All guardian angels, therefore, are fated to say endless goodbyes.

the *last* hangover?" she asked.

"Because you have someone who desperately depends upon you," Gadriel said softly. "Every time you think about doing something a little bit *wrong*, you remember Ella, don't you?"

Holly's smile faded into a wistful expression. "I do," she said. "I may not know how to talk to her, but... that just means I have to work extra hard at everything else."

"And who takes care of you when *you're* upset, Miss Harker?" Gadriel asked meaningfully.

Holly's eyes turned misty. "Lately," she said, "I think *you* do."

Gadriel stared at her, thunderstruck.

Oh no, he thought. *I've stumbled right back into old habits. When did that happen?*

Holly's phone trilled from the counter, interrupting his thoughts. She pushed back to her feet and padded over to pick it up. "I'll just take this in the other room," she said. "Give me a moment."

There commenced a brief conversation in the living room, to which Gadriel was only halfway paying attention. Holly was using her obliging voice, which meant that it was probably someone in authority.

When she finally returned, she was smiling tiredly again.

"That was Mrs Applebee," Holly said. "Ms Wood cleaned out her desk today, and no one can get hold of her. The girls are going to be allowed back at school, as long as they don't cause any more trouble."

Gadriel relaxed with relief. "Well, that's one less thing to worry about," he said. "Though... to be honest, I was looking forward to seeing what Mrs Relish had on the docket for

SMALL MIRACLES

tomorrow's protest."

Holly considered him speculatively. "Are you... chaperoning the school disco this Friday?"

Gadriel blinked. "No one has asked me to," he said. "Though... I suppose no one would stop me if I showed up to do so, either."

Holly leaned against the door frame. "If Ella's allowed back at school, then she'll be playing her first concert that evening," she said. "I'd like to be there, if I can. Maybe you could use a plus one."

Gadriel hesitated. But the thought came to him that he still had 5.5 points of sin to account for—and further time with Holly could only help with that endeavour.

"I will... do my best to arrange it," Gadriel promised.

The oven's timer sounded, recalling Ella and Millie from their bout of automobile carnage. The fresh biscuits soothed Gadriel's unease—and for just a bit longer, everything was perfect.

Chapter Nineteen

CUMULATIVE SIN METRIC (HOLLY HARKER): -917.5
CUMULATIVE SIN METRIC (ELLA HARKER): +214.4

It was Thursday morning, and something was very wrong indeed.

Ella stared down at her empty folder in consternation.

"Miss Harker?" Ms Schmidt prompted her, as she reached Ella's desk. "Your homework?" The teacher had already gone halfway around the classroom collecting homework from the rest of the students.

"I had it," Ella said dimly. "It was right here in my maths folder."

"I'm afraid I can't give points for forgotten homework, Miss Harker," said the teacher sympathetically. "Check more carefully next time before you leave home."

Ella stared at the back of Ms Schmidt's pink and white magnolia blouse as she continued on, picking up papers from the students at the front of the room.

"Did your dog eat your homework?" Millie asked flippantly.

"No!" Ella hissed at her. "I really did do it. I finished it first thing after band practice on Tuesday."

Millie shrugged. "I set up all of my homework deadlines on this app on my phone," she said helpfully. "I can show you if you want—"

"For the last time, I'm *not* lying!" Ella gritted out. "And I did put it in my folder. Someone must have taken it out again."

Millie shot her a sceptical look, and Ella flushed with embarrassment. Even she knew how ridiculous the words sounded.

"Right," said Millie. "Whatever you like. I'll just shut up, then."

She turned her attention back to the front of the room and promptly went back to ignoring Ella.

WHAT A FOOLISH MISTAKE THAT WAS, said a voice in Ella's head. AND NOW YOU SOUND FOOLISH AS WELL.

Ella stared down at her desk, pressing her lips together.

YOU HAVE ONLY YOURSELF TO BLAME, the voice added smoothly.

It was a depressingly familiar voice. For months, it had been there, pointing out her every little mistake. 'You have only yourself to blame' was one of its favourite, most awful refrains.

"I *did* pack my homework today," Ella said to herself uncertainly. "Didn't I?"

Suddenly, she wasn't quite so certain.

"Perhaps set an alarm this time, Miss Harker?" Ms Schmidt suggested, as Ella headed for the door at the end of class.

SHE DOESN'T BELIEVE YOU EITHER, observed the voice in Ella's head.

Ella sucked in a tight breath. "I'm not *stupid*, Ms Schmidt," she said sharply. "It was just one bit of homework."[71]

Ms Schmidt blinked behind her horn-rimmed glasses. "There's no need for that sort of tone, Miss Harker," she said.

Ella clenched her jaw. "*Sorry*, Ms Schmidt," she said. It took every ounce of her willpower to grit out the words, insincere though they were.

She swept into the hall before the teacher could respond, storming angrily for her locker.

Beatrix and Millie fell into step next to her as she strode away from the classroom. Millie yawned broadly. "*So* much more homework already," she complained. "Is she trying to drown us in kittens?"

"I'm going to have to call up my tutor again," Beatrix said glumly. "I didn't understand half of what she said today."

You don't want to talk right now, the voice said to Ella.

"I don't want to talk right now," Ella muttered tightly.

"Is this about Chainsaw Truckers?" Millie asked dubiously. "I *warned* you I'd thrash you, but you insisted on playing anyway."

Ella turned the corner to her locker and dropped her bag at her feet. A distant ache had begun at the back of her eyes as she spun the padlock dial, searching through numbers. "You probably cheated," Ella said shortly.[72]

"You are *such* a sore loser," Millie groaned. "I'm never playing video games with you again."

Ella tugged at the padlock on her locker, trying to open it.

---

71   +1/4 Point of Sin (Ella Harker): Using a Raised Tone.

72   +1 Point of Sin (Ella Harker): A Mean-Spirited Comment.

The lock didn't budge.

"Hey, um… Ella?" Beatrix started in a small voice. "I was talking to Millie about band names—"

"Ugh, this bloody locker!" Ella seethed. "I swear I put in the right numbers!" She spun the dial on the padlock again several times, starting the combination over from the beginning.

"We were thinking something like 'Millie and the Marshals'," Millie added. "What do you think? It's catchy, right? It's got some nice alliteration. It even sounds a little like an oldies band—"

Ella whirled on her abruptly. "I *said* we weren't renaming the band!" she sputtered. "We are definitely not changing the name just to suit your giant ego! How do you even walk around with a head that stupidly big?"[73]

Millie jerked back sharply. Her face hardened. "God, you're being such a *birch* today," she said.

"Oh yeah?" Ella said. "I notice you don't have your crutch any more. Did you finally get tired of pretending I sprained your ankle? Because I could sprain it for real this time—"[74]

"Ella!" Beatrix gasped. "Oh my gosh, would you listen to yourself? You're being so awful!"

The words struck Ella with a brief uncertainty. She paused with her hand on the padlock, struggling to think through the flood of anger that climbed through her veins and pounded at her head.

---

73   +1 Point of Sin (Ella Harker): A Mean-Spirited Comment.

74   +1 Point of Sin (Ella Harker): A Mean-Spirited Comment. +5 Points of Sin (Ella Harker): A Threat of Violence. Adjustment note: mild, insincere.

WHAT A TRAITOR, whispered the voice in her head.

Ella sucked in a deep breath. "Why don't you go have lunch with your new best friend, Beatrix?" she said. "Just don't come crying to me when she gets bored and drops you again."[75]

She tugged one more time at the padlock... but it utterly refused to open.

Ella slammed her fist against the door and grabbed her bag, stalking for the school canteen. She wrenched the door open violently, trying to steady her breath—

—and promptly slammed directly into Jasper O'Neill and his fresh tray of lunch.

Ella bounced back smartly, tumbling to the floor. A dull pain jarred her elbow, and she let out a cry.

"Oh, bollocks!" Jasper swore. "I didn't mean to—I'm so *sorry!*"

Ella stared up at him from the floor, as something wet trickled down the front of her shirt. A whiff of sickly sweet chocolate drifted up to her nose.

"Oh my god," Ella rasped. "Is this... chocolate milk?"

"I think it looks good on you," Millie observed from behind her. There was a familiar chill back in her voice now that hadn't been there earlier.

YOU JUST CAN'T DO ANYTHING RIGHT TODAY, CAN YOU? said the voice in Ella's mind.

Jasper had offered out a hand—but Ella ignored it, shoving clumsily to her feet. A small crowd of students had gathered now to witness her embarrassment. She wiped once uselessly at the

---

75   +1 Point of Sin (Ella Harker): A Mean-Spirited Comment.

front of her uniform, fighting back a tightness in her throat. Her face was hot, and her eyes had started to sting.

She whirled away from the canteen, shoving through the people behind her.

How embarrassing, the voice murmured. Are you going to go and cry alone now?

Ella slowed her steps and swallowed. There was a spot beneath the dome in the playground where she knew she could go—it was where she'd always gone before, when something truly awful happened at school...

...but for some reason, the scent of chocolate milk interrupted that idea with a different one. Her steps turned towards the front of the school, winding hesitantly towards room 113.

Ella knocked uncertainly at the door—so softly that she wondered at first whether the person inside might even hear her.

"Come in!" called a voice from behind the door.

Ella creaked the door open, padding in miserably.

"I'm sorry, Mr Sweet," she said in a shaky voice. "I know it's lunch. I've just... I've had a really awful morning, and I could really use somewhere to hide—"

Mr Gadriel Sweet glanced up from his desk, blinking in surprise. For some reason, his eyes focused just past Ella's shoulder—and he blanched.

"What are *you* doing back here?" he whispered.

Ella swallowed self-consciously. "I didn't mean to bother you," she said. "I'll just go—"

"No, not you!" Mr Sweet said quickly. "I didn't mean *you*." He leapt to his feet, reaching out for Ella's shoulder. She had the oddest feeling, suddenly, that he had stepped between her and...

something *else*.

THIS WAS A TERRIBLE IDEA, the voice whispered sweetly. LOOK AT HIS FACE. YOU'RE NOTHING BUT TROUBLE.

"Perhaps we ought to talk," Mr Sweet said quietly. Ella wasn't entirely certain the words were meant for her.

PERHAPS WE SHOULD, the voice said.

Chapter Twenty

CUMULATIVE SIN METRIC (HOLLY HARKER): -917.5
CUMULATIVE SIN METRIC (ELLA HARKER): +223.65

"You can use the office," Gadriel mumbled at Ella. "I'll... be right back."

Ella nodded miserably. Though she'd kept her face carefully blank, there was a slight trembling in her lower lip that set off a strange panic in Gadriel's chest. He nudged her towards the nearest chair.

"I *will* be right back," he repeated in a low voice. "Don't go anywhere."

He turned to face the fallen angel in the doorway once again.

Now invisible to most of the mortal world, Wormwood had changed forms. Today, he was a tall, gaunt man in a white suit, with the same pale hair and flat green eyes. In this guise, it was immediately apparent that the red pigment Gadriel had once mistaken for lipstick was something far less wholesome and far more ominous.

Wormwood smiled grotesquely, showing off his painfully white teeth.

"I take it back, Gadriel," he said. "I liked you better as a woman." His voice was still faintly thready, but the effect on his male voice was softer. He sounded deceptively calm.

Gadriel moved precariously for the door, keenly aware of Wormwood's unrelenting gaze. He had to force himself to step within arm's length of the other fallen angel in order to close the door behind him—he couldn't help the instinctive worry that Wormwood was biding his time, preparing to strike like a serpent as soon as he was close enough.

Wormwood took Gadriel's arm again, every bit as casually as he had done the first time they had run into one another at the school. Gadriel flinched at his touch, despite himself.

"I will admit," Wormwood said, "you nearly had me fooled. I had no reason to suspect you, of course. You used your relative unimportance against me."

"I'm afraid I don't know what you're talking about," Gadriel said warily. "Perhaps there's been a misunderstanding?"

"Oh come now, Gadriel," Wormwood said, as he started down the hallway. "You were fortunate enough to fool me once, but surely you're not convinced that you can do it again." His flat eyes flickered sideways to fix upon Gadriel. "I started wondering yesterday, after I'd left, just what you were up to that someone had bothered to make you a real identity. Imagine my surprise when I did a bit of digging and discovered that there's no record of you being on a special job at all."

Gadriel swallowed. "Well, that's... I called in a favour," he lied. "I've built up a few in my time."

"Yes indeed," said Wormwood slowly. "You've got plenty of favours *and* debts, don't you, Gadriel?" He stopped walking as the main hallway of the school came into view, spread out before them in all of its glorious monotony. The posters seemed somehow even more drab and depressing beneath the long, out-stretched shadow of his wings.

Wormwood surveyed the school with a contemptuous gaze. "After second thoughts," he said, "I'm positive I've pieced to-gether this entire ridiculous scenario. Let me describe it for you: You, Gadriel, lost a game of whist to that hypocritical Angel of Crooked Cards. She called in her debt and asked you to do your old job guarding some sad little girl and her painfully pedestrian school." His grotesque smile reappeared. "But she omitted a few key facts, didn't she? You weren't expecting to see me here. You're far too aware of your own limitations to face me voluntarily."

Gadriel remained carefully silent. Wormwood's observa-tions were largely accurate, if slightly off-target—none of which boded very well for him personally.

"The Chief of Gamblers has fed you to the wolves and dis-appeared," Wormwood said with a tsk. "That sort of behaviour isn't very becoming of an Angel of the Lord now, is it?" He leaned in towards Gadriel's ear and lowered his voice. "She didn't tell you, did she? That she tried to face me herself... and failed miserably."

Gadriel glanced at Wormwood sharply.

The fallen angel chuckled. "I thought not," he said. "The only thing I *can't* figure out is why the Chief of Guardian Angels would send a petty bottom-feeder to face someone she couldn't defeat herself. Truly, she must be desperate."

"I didn't mean to get in your way, of course," said Gadriel, who had a very keen sense of self-preservation and zero quibbles with lying for a good cause.

"Of course," Wormwood said soothingly. He closed his hand tightly on Gadriel's arm, and his cruel smile widened. "Obviously, I'm still going to make you rue the day you were created. I hear it's particularly frigid in Caina this time of year."[76]

A faint, high-pitched noise escaped Gadriel's throat. "Surely, that's not necessary—" he began.

Presently, however, the glass double doors of Battenberg Grammar opened. A tall Black man in a sharply pressed button-down and jeans entered the hallway. His eyes fixed grimly upon the two fallen angels.

"Wormwood," Barachiel said stiltedly, "I'm afraid you're obliged to remove your hands from my... employee."

Wormwood arched both eyebrows. "Your employee?" he repeated. "I know you're getting old and senile, Barachiel, but surely you haven't forgotten the small matter of Gadriel's Fall?"

Barachiel stopped a few metres away from the two of them, eyeing Wormwood warily. "Gadriel is technically subcontracting for Heaven right now," he said. "As far as the Rules are concerned, that makes him one of my employees. According to our earthly truce, there shall be no further direct combat between Heaven and Hell, with the exception of circumstances detailed under section twelve—"

Wormwood groaned. "Spare me the dissertation," he said. He shoved Gadriel roughly forwards.

---

76   Many of history's worst traitors are frozen alive in Caina. As such, the phrase "when Hell freezes over" is less useful than most people would like to believe.

Gadriel stumbled weakly for the wall. His knees were still trembling uncomfortably. "I hate to be the one to bring this up," he said hoarsely, "but isn't this awfully embarrassing, all of us wearing the same gender? Surely, at least one of us could put on something a bit more androgynous—"

"Do shut up, Gadriel," Wormwood drawled. He kept his eyes firmly upon Barachiel, however. "And lo! Speak of him and he shall appear. Have you yet finished licking your wounded pride, O Chief of Catastrophic Blunders?"

Barachiel took another careful step forward, pressing a hand to Gadriel's back to steady him. "I'm not here for the sake of my pride, Wormwood," he said. "I'm just here to remind you of the Rules. You can influence mortals all you like, and we'll do the same. But if you cause any harm to an agent of Heaven, then the cherubim might well get involved… and I think we can all agree we'd rather that not happen."[77]

Wormwood shot them both a scathing look. "It hardly matters," he said. "Once Gadriel has fulfilled his agreement with you—or failed miserably, more likely—he'll no longer fall under Heaven's jurisdiction." He narrowed his eyes at Gadriel. "And believe me, I will be ready to drag him home as soon as that occurs."

Gadriel rubbed uncomfortably at his arm, where Wormwood

---

[77] The Rococo art movement has convinced far too many people that the cherubim are harmless, baby-faced children with wings. In fact, they are powerful, eldritch angels whose genders involve far more wheels, eyes, and extra faces than even Ezekiel could accurately describe. As a rule, no one *ever* wants to involve the cherubim.

had clutched at it. "Aren't we all jumping to extremes?" he mumbled. "I'm sure we can come to some sort of, er… mutually beneficial compromise."

Wormwood laughed contemptuously. "Why should I compromise?" he asked. "I'm already winning." He strolled for the glass double doors, still chuckling as he passed the two of them. "Please, don't mind me any further, gentlemen. You clearly have much to discuss." He smiled narrowly at Gadriel. "I'll see you again tomorrow. I do hope you'll *try* to give me a run for my money."

The door closed sharply behind Wormwood… leaving Gadriel and Barachiel alone in the hallway.

Gadriel straightened slowly, still shivering with the awareness of how very close he'd come to an eternity in Hell's most famous blast chiller.

"What in the name of Lucifer have you dragged me into?" Gadriel demanded shrilly. "You have played some awful pranks before, Barachiel, but an eternity of torment is not my idea of a bit of playful ribbing!"

Barachiel looked away, suddenly worn and weary. "I did my very best to offer you a way out, Gadriel," he said quietly. "Our deal was that you would tempt Holly Harker into twenty points of sin. You could have done that without ever putting yourself into Wormwood's path. You could have walked away."

Gadriel shoved the angel emphatically, though he was barely strong enough to make Barachiel sway on his feet. "You tricked me into this!" he hissed. "What was I supposed to do—just turn my back and let Wormwood turn this school into a potter's field?"

Barachiel shook his head slowly. "It's not the school that

Wormwood's after, Gadriel," he said. "All he wants is one little girl. The rest is collateral damage."

Gadriel stared at Barachiel, as a horrible suspicion formed in his mind. After a moment, he pulled his phone from his pocket, flipping through his notes on Holly Harker until he reached one particular item on the list.

6. Ella Harker sins enough for both women combined.

"It was right in front of me," Gadriel whispered. "I knew there was something wrong with her Cumulative Sin Metric. It's far too high for a girl of her age."

"I hoped you'd take an interest," Barachiel said softly. "I've always believed that you had good intentions, Gadriel. I'm glad I was proven right."

Gadriel shoved him again. "You're utterly bonkers!" he said. "I can't save a little girl from the *Third Calamity*, Barachiel! Why would you put me in this position? I'm not even a guardian angel any more! You should have your most powerful angel on this—"

"—I *had* my most powerful angel on this!" Barachiel interrupted abruptly. An awful, wrenching grief shadowed his face as he spoke. "I tried to stop Wormwood myself, Gadriel. I broke the Rules. I'm not supposed to handle cases personally, but I *knew* that no one else stood a chance against him." He leaned his forehead against the wall. "And I still failed."

Gadriel absorbed this silently.

"You're talking about Ella's mother," he said in a quiet voice. "Wormwood killed her."

"Not directly," Barachiel whispered. "But she died of despair, all the same. I couldn't save her, no matter how I tried." His voice was laced with an old, familiar anguish that Gadriel knew far too well. Every guardian angel had felt it at least once in their career, no matter how powerful or talented they were.

No one—not even the Chief of Guardian Angels—could save everyone.

"He's going to take her daughter, too," Barachiel said dully. "Just to prove that he can. He knows I'm still watching."

Gadriel's heart twisted. "But why on earth would you think I could succeed where *you* failed?" he asked plaintively.

Barachiel reached into the front pocket of his button-down to produce a single gold-trimmed card. He offered it out to Gadriel mutely.

For once, Gadriel took the card without question.

Pictured on the card was a woman dressed in wheat-gold colours, armed with a spear and a shield. Her dress was oddly rumpled and *comfortable* looking, however, and Gadriel couldn't help but think that her shield looked vaguely edible.

"The Princess of Disks?" Gadriel asked.

"It's your card," said Barachiel. "I've always associated it with you."[78]

"Hang on a second," Gadriel said. "I thought I was the Princess of Wands?"

"Goodness no," Barachiel said. "The Princess of Wands is far too spiteful. That card belongs to Wormwood."

Gadriel narrowed his eyes. "I'm feeling very spiteful *now*," he said. "So your deck thinks I can outmanoeuvre Wormwood?

---

78   The Princess of Disks is associated with an appreciation for little everyday things. She is especially fond of snacks.

That's an awfully overconfident prediction."

"I don't know why," Barachiel admitted. "I just know that you're the best person for the job. You have something I lack, Gadriel. Whatever it is, it's the key to defeating the Third Calamity."

Gadriel groaned. "I guarantee you, Barachiel, I am *not* going to defeat Wormwood with a piece of chocolate," he said. "Other than that, I am entirely out of ideas—"

He cut himself off abruptly.

Barachiel leaned in, keenly interested. "Gadriel?" he said. "You've had a thought."

"I have," said Gadriel, bewildered. "I'm as surprised as you are." He straightened in place, readjusting his knitted vest. "It'll rely an awful lot on your paper pushing skills. And I'll definitely need to stall Wormwood for a bit, if we're going to pull it off."

"I'm willing to try anything," Barachiel said promptly.

Gadriel nodded as the plan came together in his head. "All right, Barachiel," he said. "I'm going to need you to take down a message…"

***

"Ah, good," Gadriel said, as he slipped back through the door of his office. "You're still here."

Ella looked up at him from the chair in front of the desk, wiping surreptitiously at her eyes. "You said not to go anywhere," she mumbled.

"Well yes," Gadriel said, "but neither of us always does what we're told, do we?" He started for the chair behind the desk… but he hesitated partway there, and sat down in the chair next to

219

Ella's instead. "You *have* had an awful day, haven't you?" he asked gently.

Ella sniffled once, squaring her shoulders. "I left my maths homework at home," she said. "And then my locker wouldn't open, and I yelled at Bee, and Jasper spilled milk all over me, and…" Her voice trailed off miserably. "I feel like I'm just getting in everyone's way today. I can't do anything right."

Gadriel didn't bother fighting the instinct this time—he leaned across the distance between them and pulled Ella into a hug.

Fresh sniffles started against his knitted vest.

"You're not in *my* way," he promised her. "Actually, you did me a favour showing up when you did. I wouldn't have known there was a… *problem*, otherwise."

"I just can't make anything w-work," Ella whimpered. "Now Millie's taking over the band, and Bee likes her more than me."

"Oh, I'm sure *that's* not true," Gadriel said, patting her back. "It's just the new friend smell. It always wears off after a bit." He paused. "It's not just today though, is it?" he asked. "It's been… a few *months* of things not going right, hasn't it?"

Ella swallowed. "This doesn't have to do with my mum," she mumbled hoarsely. "I wish people would stop saying that."

Gadriel winced. "Well," he said slowly. "It does, and it doesn't." He was fairly certain that mention of murderous fallen angels wouldn't help the situation though, and so he said: "You've had to deal with a lot of changes all at once. It makes sense you're still working out the kinks with everything. Things slip through the cracks more often when you're trying to get your routines sorted out again."

Ella went quiet for a second, and he thought she might actually be digesting the words.

"So you… you think it'll get better?" she asked hopefully.

"It's already getting better," Gadriel assured her. "No more Ms Wood, remember? And even if you are having a terrible day, you'll be going home to your own personal pastry chef tonight. I'm sure your aunt will be happy to bake you some comfort food if you ask her."

Ella took a deep, steadying breath. "I *could* do with some biscuits," she mumbled.

Gadriel searched his pockets briefly, before letting out a sharp sigh. "Ah, what a time to be out of chocolate," he muttered. "And it's after lunch, as well."

"What does lunch have to do with it?" Ella asked dimly.

Gadriel cleared his throat. "That's not important," he said. "What *is* important is that you're going to get through this day, one way or another. And tomorrow…" He trailed off worriedly as he remembered Wormwood's promise. "Well, I can't promise that tomorrow will be much fun, either. But any time you need to talk, you know where I am."

Ella nodded listlessly, and Gadriel squeezed her shoulder.

"One day at a time," he said. "*Un jour de plus.*"

Ella knit her brow. "Is that French?" she asked.

"Oh, yes," Gadriel said distractedly. "It's something your aunt says sometimes. It really just means the same thing."

Ella straightened with a shaky smile. "You're *both* dorks," she said fondly.

Gadriel shrugged. "I am a very *comfortable* dork," he replied. "There are worse things to be." He stood up from his chair and offered her a hand. "Now—shall we both get back to battle?"

Ella took his hand. "Yeah," she said. "For biscuits."

"For biscuits," Gadriel agreed seriously.

Chapter Twenty-One

CUMULATIVE SIN METRIC (HOLLY HARKER): -917
CUMULATIVE SIN METRIC (ELLA HARKER): +223.65

Gadriel spent much of Friday morning anxiously watching over Ella Harker. He prepared early on by snatching Ms Schmidt's latest chocolate bar—'STOP NOW, THIS IS YOUR LAST WARNING' said the sticky note on the chocolate—but by afternoon, he still hadn't had occasion to use it. The fact that Wormwood failed to appear did little to soothe Gadriel's apprehension; rather, like a parent with a toddler, he found himself wondering why things had suddenly gone so suspiciously *silent*.

When the schoolday ended without so much as a glimpse of pale hair or dead green eyes, Gadriel *knew* he was in deep trouble, even if he didn't yet know the form that it would take.

After school, several students and parent volunteers started setting up the school hall for the disco. Gadriel, being a chaperone, performed the very important job of overseeing this process from a chair against the wall. Ella, who had stopped by to lend a hand, was now dressed in grungy jeans, heavy black boots, an unhealthy application of black eyeliner, and a faux leather jacket festooned with pins; this had confused Gadriel at first, until he remembered that her idea of Disestablishmentarianism involved fewer knitted vests than his did.

Gadriel checked his phone nervously several times in between wary glances at Ella, hoping against hope to see a helpful text from Barachiel. Just as the volunteers finished standing up the tables and started setting out the lemonade, his phone *dinged*, and he scrambled to open his texts, holding his breath for good news.

Holly: Where are you? I've brought cupcakes.

Gadriel stared gloomily at the screen. Never in his life had he been so disappointed by an offer of sweets.

He typed out a reply, nevertheless.

Gadriel: School hall. Straight back, can't miss it.

A minute later, Holly headed into the hall, searching around curiously. Contrary to her usual style of dress, she was wearing a slim green dress and tights. As her eyes caught on Gadriel, he saw that she'd put on a hurried bit of makeup.

"This looks fun," Holly said, as she approached his chair. "In that, er... awkward secondary school sort of way." She waved at Ella, who was currently setting up bowls of crisps and stacks of paper plates. Ella cringed with embarrassment and quickly averted her eyes.

"Does it?" Gadriel said sceptically. He glanced up at the swivelling multicolour lights that now lit the area in front of the stage. "I suppose the company matters more than the scenery."

"Oh, I'm just excited to see Ella play!" Holly said. She offered out a foil-wrapped tray. "You should take one before they all go. They're red velvet—Ella's favourite."

Gadriel reached for the foil… but halfway there, he paused and looked back up at her curiously. "There's half a point extra on you," he mumbled. "Did you eat some chocolate?"

Holly flushed. "I tried a cupcake this morning, just to see. But it's just as I remember—I still hate chocolate."

Gadriel shook his head. "And that is just as much of a tragedy now as it was yesterday—" he started.

But an uncomfortable thought struck him belatedly, and he stopped.

Oh no, Gadriel thought with sudden horror. *I've only got five points of sin left before I finish Barachiel's job. Two seconds after that, I'll be a block of ice in Caina.*

Gadriel pulled his hand back from the foil, curling his fingers into his palm. "D'you know what?" he said. "I realise this may sound strange, but I feel like we should *both* avoid temptation this evening. Toe the line, so to speak." He laughed weakly. "Wouldn't want to ruin the concert, after all."

Holly blinked. "That *is* uncharacteristic," she said. "I never thought I'd see the day you turn down chocolate."

"You're right," Gadriel muttered. "Of all the things I've had to do for Barachiel in the last few days, this is by far the most egregious."

"Well, the cupcakes will be right on the table over there," Holly told him with amusement. "In case you change your mind." She strolled for the table where Ella was, setting the plate of cupcakes down next to her. For all of her teenage embarrassment,

Ella still cast her aunt a sideways glance and sneaked a cupcake out from underneath the foil.

It was just as Holly returned to Gadriel, newly bereft of cupcakes, that Mrs Relish swept into the school hall. Beatrix's mother was dressed somewhat... *strangely* for the affair, in a tan fringe jacket and jeans. Accenting the outfit were the least realistic aquamarine cowboy boots and ten-gallon hat that Gadriel had ever seen, all covered in colourful beads and sequins—a New Yorker's idea of what a cowgirl might wear, perhaps.

Mrs Relish paused several times on her way in to take pictures with her phone, smiling broadly as she tapped out hashtags. Eventually, however, she caught sight of Holly and let out a delighted noise. "Holly, darling!" she said. "I didn't realise you were chaperoning as well! Oh, you look adorable. Like Christmas in July."

Holly blinked and looked down at her green dress. "Oh," she said. "I suppose I do, a bit." She glanced back up at Mrs Relish. "You're very... dressed up yourself." Holly did her best to make this comment sound agreeable, though Gadriel could *hear* her searching for a way to make such a surplus of sequins sound charming.

"Oh, just supporting the girls," Mrs Relish said with a wave of her hand. "I always say, go big or go home. Besides, it will make for better pictures." She waved her phone at Holly. "Mind a photo for posterity? Mrs Wilson couldn't be here, but at least we've got *two* of our three band mamas."

Holly smiled. "I don't mind at all," she said. The suggestion that she was a 'band mama' and not a 'band aunt' was touching enough to dispel even her deep-seated sequin horror.

Mrs Relish thrust her phone wordlessly towards Gadriel, who took it with a blink, before throwing her arms around Holly. "Say yee haw!" she crowed.

"Er—yee haw," Holly mumbled with a flush.

Gadriel realised a moment later that he was expected to take a picture. His instinctive reaction to this was not at all charitable—but he remembered just in time that he was supposed to be *preventing* potentially sinful situations rather than instigating them, and he swallowed down his sequin sarcasm accordingly. "Yee haw," he muttered sourly.

He snapped a few pictures and shoved the phone back at Mrs Relish, who dropped her embrace in order to flip through the photos. "Ooh, no," she murmured. "No, that won't do. I'm not sure that any of these will work. Let's try again—bigger smiles, this time?"

Gadriel took a deep, steadying breath. "Perhaps it's the... *glare* on your outfit that's the problem," he said. It took every ounce of his willpower not to add: *Just go outside, and the satellite pictures will catch you from orbit.*

Holly shot him a sheepish look. "Maybe we can take more pictures later," she told Mrs Relish weakly. "It's barely evening, after all."

"Oh, I suppose so," Mrs Relish said. "The lighting in here is questionable, though. Ooh—wait, I haven't shown you the band page yet!" She tapped at her phone, then offered it to Holly. "I had a colleague do up a professional logo!"

Holly squinted at the phone, blinking. "Does that say 'Millie and the Marshals'?" she asked. "I'm almost positive that's not right."

"I know," Mrs Relish sighed. "I told Beatrix it should be *her* name on the band, but she assured me that she won other concessions in return. At least she knows how to negotiate."

Gadriel's sense of anxious doom ratcheted up. "Oh no," he said. "I know exactly what's going on here."

Holly glanced at him. "You do?" she asked, bewildered.

Gadriel didn't have the chance to respond. Millie and Beatrix chose that moment to enter the school hall, hauling pieces of Beatrix's drum set with them. Both girls were wearing matching outfits with sequined hats and boots, identical to Mrs Relish's accoutrements. Millie had entirely eschewed her crutch for the evening.

But it was the ominous sound of clattering spurs which heralded the arrival of the Third Calamity.

Wormwood strolled in behind the girls, whistling idly to himself. He, too, was wearing a ten-gallon hat and cowboy boots— but these looked so authentic that Gadriel suspected they were still covered in dust from the original Wild West. The fallen angel's spurs were stained with the same crimson colour as his lips; the bolo tie around his neck looked unsettlingly close to a noose. As Wormwood saw Gadriel, his lips turned up at the edges in an eminently self-satisfied smile.

"He went for the indirect approach," Gadriel cursed. "I should have guessed."

Ella, who'd only managed to eat half of a very sizeable red velvet cupcake, did a double-take at the two girls. Her mouth dropped open, and she wiped a smudge of white icing quickly from her nose. "What are you *wearing?*" she demanded.

Millie set a pair of cymbals carefully down onto the stage.

"Our costumes," she said. "Mrs Relish bought us all matching outfits. I can't say I'm a fan of the boots, but I s'ppose the woman with the credit card gets the final call."

Ella set her cupcake down on the table, still goggling. "What do cowboy boots have to do with *anything?*" she asked. "We're not a country group!"

Wormwood leaned in towards Beatrix with a low chuckle. "THERE SHE GOES, TELLING YOU WHAT YOU ARE AGAIN," he said in his thin, wavering voice.

Beatrix unloaded two tom-toms from either arm. "*Jolene* is technically country music," she said. There was an unusually firm, tetchy sound to her tiny voice which gave Gadriel a deep sense of foreboding.

He stepped quickly between the girls, holding up a hand. "Why don't we all calm down and have a cupcake?" he suggested carefully. "A BIT OF CHOCOLATE SOUNDS GOOD, DOESN'T IT?"

Ella's eyes darted back to her half-eaten cupcake… and for a moment, Gadriel thought he might have staved off disaster.

"YOU'VE TRIED BEING SO NICE TO BOTH OF THEM, TOO," Wormwood crooned at Ella. "AND THIS IS WHAT YOU GET FOR YOUR TROUBLE."

Ella snapped her gaze back to Beatrix and Millie, clenching her jaw. "I am *not* wearing any of that," she said, crossing her arms. "We're 'The Disestablishmentarians'. We're supposed to be punk."

Wormwood gave another mocking laugh. "Chocolate," he said witheringly. "Is that *really* all you've ever got to offer?"

"We are *not* 'The Disestablishmentarians'," Millie responded smartly. "We're 'Millie and the Marshals'. We voted."

"You *voted?*" Ella said incredulously. "Well, I didn't get to vote!"

"You weren't there," Beatrix said simply. "You were too busy being a horrid birch. We had the majority, anyway."

The words stunned Ella into silence.

"What is going *on* here?" Holly asked. She and Mrs Relish had both headed over now, looking concerned.

"Nothing's going on," Millie sniffed. "Ella's just upset she can't get her way all the time any more."

"YOU'VE JUST BEEN BOTHERING THEM, THIS ENTIRE TIME," Wormwood told Ella. "THEY ROLL THEIR EYES AT YOU WHENEVER YOU TURN YOUR BACK."

"That is *not* true," Gadriel said warningly—but several sets of eyes turned towards him at once, and he remembered belatedly that no one else could see or hear Wormwood.

"It *is* true," Millie said shortly. "But we all know you'd take *her* side, don't we? You're dating her aunt."

Gadriel blinked. "What?" he said. "I am not—"

"You *so* are," Beatrix said apologetically. "It's really obvious."

Holly worked her mouth soundlessly for a moment. Her face had turned so red, it looked like a tomato.

Mrs Relish held up her hands. "Girls," she said sternly. "This is not an argument we need to be having before your first concert. Now—let's all buck up, put on our hats and our smiles, and finish setting up."

"YOU DON'T WANT TO PUT ON THAT STUPID HAT," Wormwood told Ella.

"I don't *want* to put on that stupid hat!" Ella burst out. "We all know the only thing you care about is getting cutesy pictures for your followers and being able to say your daughter's in a band!"[79]

Mrs Relish narrowed her eyes. "Young lady—" she began warningly.

"Don't talk to my mum that way!" Beatrix yelled, balling up her fists.

"Oh, *please*," Ella scoffed. "Like you weren't thinking it yourself. How many times have you told me your mum loves her socials more than she loves you?"[80]

Beatrix gasped. Her face now flushed to match Holly's. "How could you say that in front of my mum?" she said. "I trusted you!"

Gadriel buried his face in his hands. The situation had clearly degenerated well past chocolate and little bribes. His toolkit was well-suited to causing situations like this, and not to *solving* them.

"I trusted *you!*" Ella shot back at Beatrix. "And here you are, in your little traitorous cowboy hat. I can't *believe* you agreed to let Millie name the band after herself."[81]

Beatrix scrunched up her face, flattening her lips into a line. "Millie *asked* me if I had any ideas," she said. "That's more than you've ever done—you've always made all the decisions about the band without ever asking my opinion." Beatrix tore off her cowboy hat, tossing it violently onto the stage. She had started blinking back tears. "And for your information—I was the one who wanted the *stupid hats*."

Ella stared at her.

---

79   +1 Point of Sin (Ella Harker): A Mean-Spirited Comment.

80   +3 Points of Sin (Ella Harker): Betraying a Confidence.

81   +1 Point of Sin (Ella Harker): A Mean-Spirited Comment.

"This is a mess," Gadriel groaned. "Let's all just take a step back and stop yelling, please. We can talk again once everyone's calmer—"

"YOU HAVE ONLY YOURSELF TO BLAME," Wormwood sighed at Ella.

Ella pushed past Beatrix with an awful, strangled noise—and fled for the door.

Chapter Twenty-Two

CUMULATIVE SIN METRIC (HOLLY HARKER): -917
CUMULATIVE SIN METRIC (ELLA HARKER): +228.65

"You need to go and handle your niece, Miss Harker," Mrs Relish said coolly, a few seconds after Ella's abrupt departure.

Holly raised her eyebrows at the other woman, still dimly stunned by the proceedings. "It's 'Miss Harker' now, is it?" she asked.

SHE HAS SOME NERVE, DOESN'T SHE? a voice murmured in her mind. SHE'S PARTIALLY TO BLAME FOR ALL OF THIS.

Holly clenched her fingers into her palms, opening her mouth to speak her mind—

"Don't," Gadriel said in a low voice. His hand closed gently on her arm. "It's not worth it. Ella's more important at the moment, isn't she?"

Holly sucked in a deep breath, fighting back the red haze of fury that threatened to overcome her. *He's right,* she thought tensely. *Ella comes first.*

She spun on her heel and stalked for the door.

See? Keeping your temper isn't so hard, the voice said. Now why can't Ella do the same? Nothing is ever simple with her.

"That is really starting to get under my skin," Gadriel said tightly. Holly glanced over her shoulder and saw that he had followed her.

"What, the walking pile of sequins back there?" Holly muttered at him.[82]

"Er… yes, that," Gadriel sighed. He curled a hand around her arm, squeezing it reassuringly. "This is all fixable. It's just… hormones, mostly. Now that everyone's stepped back for a second, we'll all just have some chocolate and work it out."

Holly managed a thin smile at him. "I thought you weren't going to have any chocolate," she observed.

Gadriel shook his head firmly, reaching into his pocket to retrieve a chocolate bar. "I've never had much self-discipline," he said, as he unwrapped the top.

On a hunch, Holly angled them down the hallway towards the girls' lavatory. The door was still nudged open by a crack; the sound of muffled sniffling trickled out from inside. "Shame you're not a woman right now," Holly murmured. "Just wait outside. I'll see if I can get her to come out."

Gadriel started saying something in return—but he cut himself off with a harsh cough, leaning against the wall. His eyes were wide and pained.

Holly stopped to stare at him. "Are you… all right?" she asked worriedly.

---

82   +1 Point of Sin (Holly Harker): A Mean-Spirited Comment.

Gadriel worked his mouth soundlessly. Tears had started streaming down his face. He tried again to answer her—but all that came out was a wheeze. He spat what looked like a half-melted piece of chocolate out onto the floor.

"Are you *choking?*" Holly asked urgently. "Please, just… say *anything.*"

Gadriel closed his eyes in agony. "Bad… chocolate," he choked out. "I'm… fine. *Go.*"

Holly hesitated, openly alarmed. But Gadriel shoved her bodily for the toilet door, and she relented reluctantly, pushing it open to head inside.

Instantly, she was struck by the *smallness* of everything in the room. The sinks and mirrors were three-quarters of her height, all situated for people who certainly were not *her*. The doors of the lavatory cubicles spanned nearly the entire length of the floor and ceiling, however, such that Holly had to listen closely in order to find the one that held her crying niece.

She knocked gently at the door.

"Ella?" she said.

The sniffling behind the door paused. Ella cleared her throat. "I don't want to talk," she rasped.

SHE NEVER WANTS TO TALK, DOES SHE? murmured the voice in Holly's head. ESPECIALLY NOT WHEN SHE'S MADE MISTAKES.

Holly pressed her lips together. "You're going to *have* to talk this time," she said. "I've been trying to give you space, Ella, but that clearly isn't working."

Ella remained silent, as though to prove her statement.

SHE DOESN'T CARE WHO SHE HURTS, the voice added. SHE'D RATHER JUST PRETEND THERE'S NOT A PROBLEM. AND DOESN'T

235

THAT REMIND YOU OF SOMEONE?

The idea stabbed directly for old injuries, so accurate that it stole Holly's breath. Bitter misery welled up inside of her, drowning all of the good intentions she'd originally walked in with under a smothering sense of helplessness.

YOU'RE BEING SHUT OUT AGAIN, the voice whispered. IT'S LIKE YOU DON'T EVEN EXIST.

Holly's throat closed up with panic. "Your mum was *exactly* like this," she choked out. "She never took responsibility for anything in her life. If you keep telling people to go away, Ella, they are eventually going to do it. Do you understand me? You'll want to walk it back someday, and by then it will be too late."[83]

Ella remained quiet.

"Fine," Holly rasped. "Stay in here and sulk."[84]

She whirled for the door. Her head was dizzy, and her mouth felt dry. Her pulse had started pounding in her ears, blotting out the rest of the world. It therefore came as a surprise when she stumbled back out into the hallway to discover that a different argument entirely had been happening behind her.

"—you and your lying knitwear!" Ms Schmidt was yelling. Ella's maths teacher loomed over Gadriel, who was currently doing his best to drown himself in a water fountain. The sleeves of Ms Schmidt's daffodil blouse had been rolled up in a way that clearly meant business. She prodded him emphatically in the

---

83   +1 Point of Sin (Holly Harker): Speaking Ill of the Dead. +1 Point of Sin (Holly Harker): A Mean-Spirited Comment. +1 Point of Sin (Holly Harker): An Emotional Threat.

84   +1 Point of Sin (Holly Harker): A Mean-Spirited Comment.

shoulder. "That was *good* chocolate, you miserable fridge thief!"

Gadriel came up for air, but he still wheezed helplessly. "…
tempt you… with a… cupcake?" he squeaked. The water had
clearly done nothing to help.

"You may *not* tempt me with a cupcake!" Ms Schmidt
snapped. "You don't even feel bad for what you've done, do you?
You're just sorry you got caught!"

Gadriel stared at her with growing horror. "No," he whimpered. "*Atheist.*"[85]

"Are you implying you took my chocolate because I'm an
atheist, Mr Sweet?" Ms Schmidt demanded. "Do you understand
how terrible that sounds?"

Holly swallowed down the knot in her throat, blinking quickly. "Wh-what seems to be the trouble?" she said hoarsely.

Ms Schmidt snapped her gaze to Holly. "This little weasel
has been stealing the chocolate right out of my lunch every
morning!" she seethed. "And now, his karma's finally caught up
to him!"

Gadriel groaned. "Not… karma…" he tried to say. But the
words were so garbled that Holly could barely understand them.[86]

---

85 No spirit, benevolent or otherwise, has any power over atheists. Atheists are therefore the bogeymen of the metaphysical world,
spoken of in hushed, terrified tones by divine beings everywhere.

86 Unlike most fallen angels, Gadriel had dabbled at least briefly
in comparative religion. He was therefore aware that the Hindu concept of karma does not technically come into play until one dies and is
reborn. Being an immortal fallen angel, he was therefore not subject to
karma.

He *was* subject to poetic justice, however—and especially to ghost

"I'm afraid I can entirely believe that," Holly mumbled to Ms Schmidt. She shoved down the aching wretchedness in her chest, trying to take in the situation. "You haven't hurt him, have you?"

Ms Schmidt planted her hands on her hips, narrowing her eyes at the school counsellor. "He's just had a taste of some ghost pepper is all," she said. "It ought to *start* getting better in anoth-er… fifteen minutes."

"*Fith-teen minutes?*" Gadriel whimpered clumsily.

"Don't you dare cry at *me!*" Ms Schmidt told him, with a hard prod in the chest. "Do you have any idea how *hard* the last few weeks have been for me? You wouldn't, would you, because you've only been thinking about yourself and your larcenous sweet tooth!" Her lower lip trembled. "You weren't thinking about what it's like to be dumped by your girlfriend—left alone with only your cats and your maths textbooks and your chocolate for company! I have only one bright spot left in my days, you walking fashion disaster, and you won't even allow me *that* much—"

Gadriel's eyes had glazed over with pepper-induced agony. But at this, he held up a hand between them, waving it urgently.

"You won't be stealing anyone else's chocolate anytime soon, now will you, Mr Sweet?" Ms Schmidt told him scornfully. "Learned your lesson, have you?"

Gadriel nodded emphatically. He put up one finger, as though to say 'wait a moment'.

Ms Schmidt knit her brow. "What?" she asked.

"First… name?" he croaked.

peppers.

The maths teacher blinked. "You want to know my first name?" she guessed in confusion.

Gadriel nodded again.

"It's… Janelle," the teacher said warily. "Why?"

Gadriel fumbled for the front pocket of his knitted vest—and produced a folded up playing card. He offered it out like a flag of truce. Very slowly, Ms Schmidt reached out to take it.

"Asthk for… Sara," he croaked. "She likes cats."

Holly raised her eyebrows. "Oh," she said.

Ms Schmidt looked down at the card, perplexed. But she shoved it into her handbag and shook her head. "Go and drink a glass of milk," she said shortly. "Don't ever let me find you near my lunch again."

She turned and marched away in a huff, stomping audibly as she went.

Holly offered Gadriel her shoulder. He sagged against her with another wretched little whimper.

"All right," she sighed heavily, helping him down the hall. "Let's find you some milk."

Holly settled him into a chair at the back of the school hall and went searching for some milk. When none easily presented itself, however, she returned with a red velvet cupcake and an apologetic expression.

"There's cream cheese icing on this," she said. "I haven't the first idea whether it will help or not."

Gadriel stuck his tongue out and dragged the cupcake across it. He worked the icing through his mouth for a few seconds, waiting hopefully… then heaved a hopeless sigh. "Now my mouth justh thastes like burning icing," he mumbled.[87]

Holly shook her head. "I don't feel *entirely* bad for you," she admitted. "You have only yourself to blame, after all."

For some reason, this phrase made Gadriel look up sharply. His brown eyes flickered with that odd ember light. "Wormwood," he rasped. "Where is Wormwood?"

Holly blinked. "I don't know who you're talking about," she said.

Gadriel focused even more intently upon her... and then, he swallowed visibly. "Five points," he whispered, widening his eyes. "What did you *do?*"

"You're not making any sense," Holly said. "Can too much pepper make someone delirious?"

Gadriel shoved abruptly to his feet—and sprinted back for the hallway.

***

By the time Gadriel had changed into a woman and ducked into the girls' lavatory, there was absolutely no sign left of Ella Harker.

Gadriel's mouth was still burning like the fires of Hell—but that was the absolute *least* of her troubles. Somehow, in the space of only five minutes, Holly Harker had sinned her last five points *and* Gadriel had managed to lose track of both Wormwood and his quarry.

"Doomed," Gadriel mumbled thickly. "I'm doomed."

At least, she thought, Caina would probably chill the taste of

---

87   God may show mercy, but capsaicin does not.

ghost peppers from her mouth.

Holly stared at Gadriel as she came out of the lavatory. "Ella's not in there?" she asked. A mixture of guilt and terror had overcome her, and Gadriel frowned warily.

"What'd you say to her?" she asked awkwardly.

Holly closed her eyes. "Awful things," she confessed. "I can't believe... oh god, *why* did I say those things?"

Gadriel's face softened. "Not your fault," she mumbled.

Holly shook her head. "It *is* my fault," she said brokenly. "I shoved all of my problems with Ivy onto Ella—after I *swore* to myself I wouldn't do just that." Her expression crumpled. "She was right, Gabe. I really am the worst."

Gadriel sighed heavily. "Bad night," she said. "We'll... find her."

Just what Gadriel was going to *do* once she found Ella was questionable, of course. If Wormwood figured out that Gadriel was no longer on the clock, there wouldn't be much salvaging the situation. But there wasn't really any choice, was there? Gadriel needed to keep Wormwood firmly in her sights if her plan was going to work... and she certainly wasn't going to leave the Third Calamity alone with an upset teenager.

"Phone?" Gadriel prompted.

It took Holly a moment to understand what Gadriel was getting at—but she nodded after a second and pulled out her phone to call Ella's number.

The line rang several times, before going to voice mail.

"Ideas?" Gadriel asked.

Holly bit her lip. "I don't know," she said. "I didn't see her in the hall."

Gadriel thought furiously. "Music room?" she suggested.

Holly nodded quickly. "I'll go and check," she said breathlessly.

They split up to search the school between them, checking both floors. But as minutes ticked by with no sign of Ella, a low-grade panic began to settle in. By the time Gadriel met Holly at the glass double doors, she looked ready to cry.

"There's no sign of her anywhere," she said. "Oh, god. I hope she just went home. I've left her a dozen messages asking her to call me—"

An idea *did* occur to Gadriel then. She swallowed a few times, trying to work through the remainder of the pepper in her mouth. "Can you *find* Ella's phone?" she asked. "Does it have a location service on it?"

Holly slapped her forehead. "Yes, of course," she said. "I'm so *stupid*." She pulled out her smartphone and started typing.

Gadriel looked over her shoulder at the map of London that had appeared on her screen. A little red dot was moving across the map; in fact, it had nearly reached the edge of the borough.

"That is... not good at all," Gadriel mumbled. "Is she leaving London?"

Holly let out a small breath. "No," she said quietly. "I don't think so. I think I *do* know where she's going." She zoomed in the map on a little patch of land labelled 'Blue Ridge Cemetery'.

"Ah," said Gadriel. "I see." She rubbed at her face with a sigh. "All right—we'll just have to go after her."

Holly started for the front doors—but her face was gloomy and uncertain. "The bus doesn't run that often here during the evenings," she said. "It's going to take... longer than I'd like."

Gadriel paused with her fingers still pinched at the bridge of her nose. Gradually, she looked back up at Holly.

It's not like I've got anything left to lose, she thought.

Gadriel closed the distance between them. Very slowly, she reached up to cup her palms against Holly's face—then leaned down to press her lips against her forehead.

In that moment, time stilled. Silence flooded in as Gadriel reached tentatively for the world around her—for all of the beautiful, confusing chaos there, jumbled together like snagged thread.

Her facility with miracles was rusty, to say the least. But as she opened her awareness up to creation, she remembered the soft thrum of its heartbeat and the comforting way that it all connected up to... *Something.*

That Something regarded Gadriel back—both utterly distant and incomprehensibly personal, all at once.

"Oh, don't look at me like that," Gadriel mumbled to it self-consciously. "I'm just visiting. This won't be a habit."

The Something waited patiently. It had all of the time in the world, after all.

Gadriel reached out carefully for one of the threads of chaos, tugging at it gently. Several connected threads straightened themselves out, unknotting slightly from the tangle. Gadriel squinted at the new pattern, trying to gauge her work.

"That's... not half bad," she admitted. "I'm still all right with the little things, aren't I?"

The Something smiled fondly.

"Ooh, *stop* that," Gadriel warned it. "Don't you smile at me. I'm still upset with you, just so you know. This is a onetime thing."

The strands closest to Gadriel shivered with approval. The

sensation was something like being patted on the head—if one's head were one's soul and the one doing the patting was the whole of creation itself.

Gadriel grumbled and released the strands. But the gesture had left behind a tiny, wistful warmth in her heart that she couldn't quite scrub away, no matter how she tried.

Time resumed—and Holly Harker blinked up at her. A faint flush had overcome the apples of her cheeks, where Gadriel held her face.

"Go wait for the bus," Gadriel murmured to her. "It would only take a *small* miracle for it to arrive so soon, you know."

Holly blinked several times more. "You're not coming with me?" she asked, with a sudden note of panic.

Gadriel shook her head. "I need to fetch something before I go," she said. "And besides… I'm going to take a shortcut. Maybe I'll manage to get there sooner." *Either way, I can't fly you there with me,* Gadriel thought.

Holly hesitated visibly. Gadriel dropped her palms from her cheeks and squeezed her hands.

"Your bus is outside, Holly Harker," she said softly. "Go and catch it. I'll meet you there—I promise."

Chapter Twenty-Three

CUMULATIVE SIN METRIC (HOLLY HARKER): -912
CUMULATIVE SIN METRIC (ELLA HARKER): +228.65

B lue Ridge Cemetery had a single large gate. Behind it, endless rows of gravestones were closely packed, all doing their best to tread on one another's toes.

The last bit of light in the sky was nearly gone by the time Gadriel found Ella Harker, tucked right between the graves for Ian Gilmore and Lara Burton. She'd settled herself on the ground before a gravestone marked 'Ivy Harker', with her knees pulled up to her chest. An evening chill had started creeping in at the edges, and her faux leather jacket seemed inadequate to the job of staving it off, if her shivers were anything to go by.

Wormwood stood calmly behind her, surveying the grave with a contented smile on his red-stained lips. Back-lit by the last rays of the setting sun, it was easier to see all four of his shadowy wings spread out before him, casting their darkness upon the girl and the grave.

The sight sparked an old, weary sadness in Gadriel's chest. *There's enough misery out here already,* she thought. *What sort of creature takes pleasure in adding to it?*

She tucked the thought away, along with the remnants of her two ragged wings, and made herself quietly visible.

"You probably should have brought a blanket," Gadriel said, as she approached Ella. "Mind you... I probably should have brought a blanket. I'm just realising that."

Ella snapped her head around, staring at Gadriel. "How did you *find* me?" she asked incredulously.

Gadriel smiled wryly. "I used my magical powers," she said. "Those, and a mediocre understanding of modern technology."

Wormwood shook his head with a sigh. "You're like a mosquito, Gadriel," he said. "You just won't stop buzzing until you get swatted."

Gadriel ignored him, padding over to stand next to Ella. The cold shadow of Wormwood's wings closed over Gadriel, and she shivered violently. "I did say you could come and talk with me," she continued, as casually as she could manage. "It would have been a bit warmer in the office. But that's all right—I'm here to annoy you, regardless."

Wormwood leaned forward. "She thinks she knows what's best for you," he said. "She's going to drag you back and force you to be a good girl."

Ella tightened her arms around her legs. "I don't want any chocolate," she said flatly. "And I definitely don't want any lectures."

Gadriel sat down beside her. "You're sure?" she said. "Absolutely positive? Because I've got a *fantastic* lecture about the Greek Cynics. Puts people to sleep in ten minutes flat. And on top of that..."

She offered out a crumpled bit of foil, several times the size of her fist.

Ella knit her brow. "What is *that?*" she asked.

"A BRIBE," Wormwood murmured. "MORE CHOCOLATE, PROBABLY."

Gadriel unwrapped the foil to reveal a single, very wretched-looking red velvet cupcake.

"It *is* technically chocolate," she admitted. "But I hear it's your favourite."

Ella stared at the cupcake.

"YOU DON'T WANT A BLOODY CUPCAKE," Wormwood hissed. "A CUPCAKE ISN'T GOING TO FIX ANY OF THIS."

His voice this time was harsh and overwhelming. It fell upon the world around them like a yawning void, dragging down everything in its path. It was a statement of horrible finality—a promise that terrible things were just around the corner, and nothing in the universe would ever be able to stop them.

Gadriel swallowed thickly. "You only get half," she added in a small voice. "It's the last cupcake, and I didn't get to try any. But I owe you for the half a biscuit, so this makes us square."

The shadows shivered around them. The messy cupcake looked terribly pathetic, in comparison to the colourless world around it.

But somehow—very slowly—Ella reached out with trembling fingers to pinch off a bit of cake and icing.

She stuffed the bite into her mouth, licking the icing off her fingers with a fresh sniffle.

Wormwood stared at her. "You didn't even tempt her," he whispered incredulously. "What is going on?"

Gadriel slid an arm around Ella's shoulders, tugging her against her side. "I've lost a lot of people, you know," she said softly. "I know how it feels, more than anyone."

Ella's jaw trembled. She took a deep breath and opened her mouth—but Gadriel cut her off.

"You're sitting in the dark in the middle of a graveyard," she pointed out reasonably. "Are you *really* going to tell me this has nothing to do with your mum?"

Ella closed her mouth again.

Gadriel sighed. "I've been avoiding it too," she said. "I'm a champion avoider at this point. I use the small pleasures as distractions, to help me forget all of the things I miss." Her eyes welled up with tears. "It mostly works, you know. But only when I don't look too closely."

Ella swallowed a soft whimper, leaning into Gadriel's side. Her makeup left black, winding tears down her cheeks. "I keep... *thinking* I'm all right," she said in a tight voice. "I'm so convinced that I am. And then it's suddenly not true, and I *need* her."

Wormwood's shadows tightened around them.

"SHE'S NEVER COMING BACK," he said. "YOU CAN'T HAVE HER."

Gadriel took a shuddering breath. "You can't have her," she agreed softly. "And she... she can't help you. I'm sure she'd *want* to, if she knew you needed it. But she's... asleep. She's in the next room over, dreaming."

She set the cupcake on the ground in front of them, and settled both her arms more fully around Ella.

"She'll wake up someday," Gadriel whispered. "And when she does... she's going to want to hear all about what you were up to while she was sleeping."

Ella buried her face in Gadriel's knitted vest with a hiccuping cry.

Gadriel held her close, in the shadow of Wormwood's wings. She gathered up every last scrawny bit of her power, shoving it into her inside voice. And when she spoke, she reached for the little things in Ella's mind: for six months of awkward tray bakes and attempted conversations and tentative hugs. For the knowledge that every last red velvet cupcake really belonged to *her*, because her aunt (who hated chocolate herself) knew that Ella loved red velvet cupcakes. For the simple day-to-day certainty that although Holly Harker was very bad at this indeed, she would always, *always* show up.

And what Gadriel said was: "YOU ARE LOVED, ELLA HARKER. AND YOU ARE NOT ALONE."

The statement burrowed deeply into Ella's heart. It joined with the awful, wrenching grief that had taken residence there, nestling itself firmly against the chill fear of loneliness and death which now would never leave. It was not a victory—not by any means. But it was a fond little candle against the darkness—and no matter how Wormwood clawed for it, Gadriel knew that it would never fully go out.

"Oh thank *god!*" Holly's voice carried across the graveyard, echoing against the tombstones. She crossed the final distance to Ella and Gadriel, sprinting breathlessly. Her hair was loose and hopelessly tangled; her modest attempt at eyeliner was smudged from crying. She fell to her knees next to them both, snatching Ella from Gadriel's grasp and hugging her tightly.

"I'm so s-sorry," Holly sobbed. "I said all of those awful

things, and I—I don't know how to undo any of it. I didn't mean it, Ella, I *promise*. I'm not going to leave you behind, not ever."[88]

"She's lying," Wormwood hissed frantically. "She'll lose her temper again, as soon as something else happens."

But Ella hugged her aunt back every bit as tightly, ignoring her misgivings.

"I n-never know what to say to you," Holly choked out. "I always get it wrong. That's not your fault, any of it. I just get so scared that I can't help you, and everything will just keep getting worse because I don't know what to do—"

Ella shook her head. "It's okay, Aunt Holly," she rasped. "I say awful things to you all the time. And I… I want to take those things back too." She closed her eyes. "I've been horrible, and I know it. I just… don't know how to stop."[89]

Holly nodded mutely, forcing herself to breathe. "We'll figure it out, okay?" she said softly. "All of it. One step at a time."

Ella gave a watery smile. "One day at a time," she mumbled. "Or… however you say it in French."

Gadriel rose unsteadily back to her feet. Wormwood had fallen silent—but she could *feel* his fury pressing in upon her like a vice. The shadows that made up his wings twisted violently around him; his flat, serpentine eyes glittered with barely suppressed malevolence.

Gadriel pressed a hand to Holly's shoulder and squeezed. Holly glanced up at her, blinking away tears.

"I have come to a decision," Gadriel told her quietly. "I have

---

88   +1 Point of Virtue (Holly Harker): A Heartfelt Apology.

89   +1 Point of Virtue (Ella Harker): A Heartfelt Apology.

decided... that I am going to fall in love with both of you. Right now, actually." She offered Holly a worried smile. "I have to go take care of something, because of that. But I won't be far."

Holly wiped at her eyes one-handed. "Oh," she breathed. "That's... very lovely." And though Gadriel hadn't used her inside voice at all, she rather thought that a little candle had lit itself in Holly Harker's heart as well. "I think I'll fall in love with you too," Holly said shyly. "If you don't mind, that is."

Gadriel shook her head. Despite the dark, looming figure behind her, she couldn't help the small smile that crept across her lips. "Please," she said. "Go right ahead."

She released Holly's shoulder, and headed away from the two women, into the deepening darkness. Within a few steps, she allowed her visibility to fall away, so that she and Wormwood could face one another directly.

"You haven't won anything, you little divine smudge stain," Wormwood said simply. "I have endless time. I'll stay with them both like a lead anchor. Eventually, I'll weigh them down."

Gadriel nodded reasonably. "I know," she said. "Even if I stay and fight and win against you every day, they'll both eventually end up in the ground here—or somewhere like it."

Wormwood closed the distance between them. He reached out to grasp Gadriel's chin, resting pointed nails against the skin of her cheeks. His dead green eyes bored into hers.

"You will lose everything you love," he whispered. "I will make sure of it."

Gadriel felt the words deep in her bones. They were awful words, because they were so very true.

But she had struggled with them now for more than a

thousand years… and finally, she had an answer for them.

"I'm sure you think it *ought* to matter that everything will end eventually," Gadriel said. "You have to think that. It's your job." She summoned up her courage and met Wormwood's dreadful gaze.

"Someday, the whole world will end," she told him. "On that day, you'll streak across the sky like a comet, and everyone will look at you and despair." She reached up to close her hand around Wormwood's wrist, pulling his hand from her face. "But creation wasn't made *just* to despair, Wormwood. There's an awful lot that's still going to happen between now and that last, dreadful moment. There are small lives being lived, and small triumphs being had, and small people enjoying their favourite red velvet cupcakes. And all of those small things still have meaning, even if they someday have to end."

Gadriel smiled at the Third Calamity. "Those small things all belong to *me*. I have decided to fall in love with them again—and you can't have them."

Wormwood smiled back coldly. "*That* is still up for debate," he said. "You can't own much of anything if you're buried six feet deep in the glaciers of Caina." He paused. "I don't think the cherubim are going to move themselves for one tiny, foolish fallen angel, whatever Barachiel might claim. I think I'm willing to take *that* particular gamble, Gadriel."

Gadriel pressed her lips together. *That,* she thought, *is a very good gamble.*

Technically, her dubious contract with Heaven was complete. Wormwood could drag her to Caina with perfect impunity, and no one with the power to do anything would so much as twitch their fingers.

As Gadriel worked to digest this thought, her phone *dinged* softly. She pulled it from her pocket and glanced at the screen.

Bookie: Nearly there. Everything is in order.

Four shadowy wings had started closing in upon Gadriel. She glanced up at Wormwood with her heart pounding in her chest.

"Wait!" said Gadriel quickly, holding up her hand. "If I'm going away for eternity, then it's only fair I get a last bite to eat. A last supper, if you will."

Wormwood paused heavily. His serpentine eyes narrowed. "We are *not* stopping off for burgers on the way to Caina," he said shortly.

"No need," Gadriel assured him. "I've always got some snacks on me." She rummaged hurriedly in her pockets—and produced a single, partially eaten chocolate bar.

Gadriel snapped off a piece... then raised an eyebrow at Wormwood.

She offered out the chocolate.

"To the victor goes the spoils, I suppose," she said. "WOULDN'T YOU LIKE A PIECE OF CHOCOLATE?"

The Third Calamity stared down at the piece of chocolate, ruminating heavily. But Gadriel had spent hundreds of years now tempting people into *just one more piece of chocolate*. In fact, one might go so far as to call her the Leonardo DaVinci of chocolate tempters... and Wormwood, unlike Holly Harker, was at least passingly fond of chocolate.

Very slowly, Wormwood reached out to take the piece of chocolate.

"I'm not letting you off in return for a bit of chocolate," Wormwood said suspiciously. "You're still going to freeze for all of eternity."

Gadriel shrugged. "Alas," she said. "It was worth a try."

Wormwood popped the piece of chocolate into his mouth.

The fallen angel choked almost instantly on the chocolate, spitting it onto the ground. His shadowy wings lurched with a painful spasm, flapping wildly against the gravestones. His poisonous green eyes flashed with panic, and he stumbled to his knees, clawing helplessly at his throat.

Gadriel sidestepped him neatly, tucking the chocolate bar back into her pocket.

"Whash *is* thith?" the Third Calamity demanded in a horrified gurgle.

"*That* is the terrifying vengeance of a very angry lesbian atheist," Gadriel said. A minor note of sympathy infected her tone, in spite of everything. "Give it, ah… fifteen minutes or so," she added helpfully.

Wormwood couldn't respond. The fallen angel had curled up on the ground, writhing in helpless agony.

Gadriel opened her phone's texts again and typed in a reply to Barachiel.

Gadriel: New address. You've got fifteen minutes.

Chapter Twenty-Four

CUMULATIVE SIN METRIC (HOLLY HARKER): -913
CUMULATIVE SIN METRIC (ELLA HARKER): +227.65

I mmortal beings do not always use the door. In fact, they especially avoid using such banal things as doorways when they are in the mood to make a statement.

As such, Gadriel was not at all surprised ten minutes later, when an enormous cloud of golden mist spread throughout the graveyard, choking all metaphysical sight in a wet morass of twinkling lights.

The golden soup soon settled into a thin fog upon the ground, though it didn't fully disappear. As it did, Gadriel became aware that she and Wormwood were now fully surrounded by an impressive array of stern clay soldiers in ancient Chinese armour.

At the front of the clay soldiers stood a small, weathered woman of Chinese descent. Her hair was piled atop her head in a neat, officious manner, and she wore a gentle, encouraging smile on her ageless features—but her uniform was clearly that of a high-ranking military general, and she carried a sword and a bow on her person, both of which looked to have seen regular use.

Barachiel stood politely behind her. In typical fashion, the Chief of Guardian Angels had decided to be a woman at the very same time that Gadriel had done. Her white, high-collared suit had clearly been chosen to impress—and all four of her white, feathery wings stood out magnificently behind her.

The woman at the front of the soldiers tilted her head, looking down at the fallen angel who still whimpered on the ground, curled up in pain.

"Oh," she said. "Our deepest apologies for the unfortunate timing." Her gentle smile remained firmly in place as she spoke.

"No!" said Gadriel quickly. "No, no. Your timing is perfect, in fact."

The woman inclined her head in acknowledgement. "Please, allow me to introduce myself," she said. "I am Lady Xian, humble servant of the Jade Emperor. I come with the greetings of his court, and I carry with me the stated will of the Celestial Bureaucracy."[90]

Gadriel smiled. "Oh, what an *honour* it is to meet you!" she said enthusiastically. "Well, I myself am just a minor, humble fallen angel. I doubt you will have heard of me. But *this*—" She gestured expansively at Wormwood, who looked up from the ground with bleary poisonous eyes. "—this is the great Third Calamity. May I present to you, Lady Xian, the fallen angel known

---

90   In life, the incorruptible Lady Xian was a famous general of the Xian tribe who became known for her unswerving loyalty to three emperors and for her facility at putting down rebellion. Since her ascension to immortality, Lady Xian has served the Jade Emperor with equal zeal. She is particularly famous among divine beings for phrasing her dire threats as very polite requests.

as Wormwood."

Lady Xian cleared her throat delicately. "What a pleasant co-incidence," she said. "The Celestial Bureaucracy has been very eager to speak with the great Third Calamity for some time now, on the matter of a worldwide plague which may have violated our authority. In fact, I carry with me a request for Wormwood's presence before the court. Several of our couriers have tried to deliver it before, but it seems that they have had trouble finding its recipient until now."

Barachiel met Gadriel's eyes with a silent, jovial expression.

Wormwood struggled raggedly to his feet, looking around. His eyes were still watery, and it took every ounce of his strength to gather up the remaining shreds of his dignity.

"I have... nothing to say... to the Celestial Bureaucracy," Wormwood rasped unsteadily.

Lady Xian bowed her head. "Of course," she said obligingly. "There has surely been some mistake. We will clear up the matter at court, and you will be free to go as soon as it is settled."

Wormwood eyed the woman hatefully. "I am not... going *anywhere*... with you," he choked out.

Lady Xian blinked. "Oh," she said. "That will not do. The Jade Emperor requires your presence. I am but his humble servant, and I cannot disobey his court." She considered Wormwood and his tattered, shadowy wings with a warm smile. "You might choose to fly away, of course. It has been said that you are swift and terrible, like a comet in the sky."

Wormwood narrowed his eyes. He had already started gathering up his wings, as though to do just that.

"Incidentally," Lady Xian continued pleasantly, "I have

brought with me one of my many gifts from the Jade Emperor. Might I show you this beautiful bow?" She pulled the bow down from her back, displaying it before her. "This is the bow of the glorious Hou Yi, who shot nine blazing suns down from the sky. It is one of the honours which have been bestowed upon me in return for my loyal service."[91]

Wormwood's wings wilted abruptly at the statement, curling back down towards the ground.

"But you are probably not interested in an old woman's embarrassing boasts," Lady Xian added. "Please accept my apologies for the digression."

Gadriel cackled with laughter.

"*You*," Wormwood choked at her. "I will… *torment*… a hundred thousand years!"

Gadriel wiped a tear from her eye. "Oh, I fully believe you," she said. "I'll see you after your court date, Wormwood."

Barachiel cleared her throat. "It may be some time before then," she said. "I was told the queue is currently about a thousand years long."

Wormwood made a strangled noise of rage, deep within his throat.

"What did you *do* to him, by the way?" Barachiel asked Gadriel curiously.

Gadriel's smile was now so wide and self-satisfied that her

---

91   Lady Xian is also well known for bragging about all of the imperial gifts she has earned. After several centuries of cornered water-cooler conversations, most of the Celestial Bureaucracy can recite her possessions from memory.

cheeks had started to hurt. "You're never going to believe this, Barachiel," she said gleefully. "As it turns out—I *did* defeat the Third Calamity with a piece of chocolate."

Barachiel shook her head in amazement. "You'll have to tell me all about it," she said.

Lady Xian gestured with one hand. The golden mist that had dispersed around their feet slithered its way towards Wormwood, solidifying around him. She inclined her head at Barachiel.

"Your cooperation in this matter has been most appreciated, O Chief of Guardian Angels," she said. "We shall send you a fruit basket."

Barachiel chuckled. "I must decline," she said. "Virtue is its own reward, Lady Xian. Especially in this… particular case."

Lady Xian smiled once more, as the golden cloud gathered itself up…

…and then, she and Wormwood and all of the stern clay soldiers were gone.

Gadriel collapsed to the ground with an overwhelming sigh of relief. Barachiel's footsteps padded over towards her.

"I'm afraid I've broken the Rules again, Gadriel," Barachiel said casually. "I skipped the entire official extradition process. Oops."

A mad giggle trickled from Gadriel's throat. "A thousand years in court!" she gasped. "Endless legal paperwork! In *triplicate!*"

"A terrible fate," Barachiel agreed. "And entirely fitting." She offered Gadriel a hand up from the ground. "I'm glad I was able to sort it out in time. I was worried I might end up in the general waiting room for a century or so."

Gadriel took Barachiel's hand with a shake of her head. "You are the most boring bureaucrat I have ever met, Barachiel," she said. "I had full faith in you."

Barachiel glanced behind them at Ivy Harker's gravestone, where Holly and Ella still huddled together obliviously, speaking quietly to one another. The joy in the angel's expression faded, and she sighed heavily.

Gadriel squeezed her arm gently. "No one wins them all, Barachiel," she said softly. "But we won *this* time."

Barachiel nodded minutely. "I suppose the cards were right," she said quietly. "You *were* the right person for the job. Chocolate saved the day, Gadriel."

Gadriel shook her head slowly. "It wasn't really chocolate," she said. "Or... well. It wasn't *just* chocolate."

Barachiel furrowed her brow. "What do you mean?" she asked.

Gadriel nudged her chin towards the two mortals. "It was Holly Harker," she said. "She really was the key to the entire thing, after all." She smiled fondly. "I can't out-tempt the Third Calamity—not on my own. But Holly Harker got up every day for six months and decided to love her niece. Even if neither of them believed it was working, it *was*. Every last tray bake was a little bit more proof that someone cared. Six whole months of *that*, all stacked up together, is what really took down Wormwood. I just... had to jog Ella's memory a bit."

Barachiel ruminated on that. "I thought the cards said you were going to need one of your old miracles," she said.

"Oh, I *did*," Gadriel assured her. "I used a small miracle to get Holly Harker here. And I delivered a cupcake in record time."

Barachiel spread her hands. "I'm duly impressed," she said. "You're still a fine guardian angel, Gadriel." Her eyes crinkled at the edges. "It's just a shame you won't come back."

Gadriel rubbed at her chin. "Well…" She drew out the word slowly.

Barachiel raised an eyebrow. "You're actually considering it?" she asked.

Gadriel held up a hand. "I'm not interested in working for the boss again," she said warningly. "But… I'm willing to work for *you*. Subcontracting, so to speak."

Barachiel blinked. "That's quite a change of heart," she said. "And what brings this on?"

Gadriel nudged her shoulder against Barachiel's. "You did," she said. "I always had reservations before, no matter how much we get along. I guess I was worried deep down that you'd always choose the Rules, even if it was between that and doing the right thing." She smiled warmly at the angel. "But you *did* break the Rules. Even just a little bit."

Barachiel pursed her lips. "I don't intend to make a habit of it, Gadriel," she warned.

"Of course not," Gadriel said. "You're still a stick in the mud—and that's absolutely fine. I just… needed to know that you *did* care that much." She considered the angel seriously. "You asked if there was anything you could offer me to get me to come back. And, well… I might have something in mind."

Barachiel smiled back. "Well then," she said. "Let's discuss the details, shall we?"

***

Gadriel smoothed back down her knitted vest as she walked back towards Ella and Holly, whistling softly to herself as she went.

"Ladies," she said, "it is absolutely frigid out here. Given that I just *avoided* an eternity in the freezer, I was thinking we might want to relocate somewhere more comfortable."

Holly helped Ella up to her feet. Both of them were shivering now, though there was a weary relief in the air between them.

Gadriel slipped her arm neatly through Holly's, jerking her chin towards the gate. "I have a feeling we could still make it back to the disco before it's done, if we really wanted to," she said in a leading tone. She glanced questioningly at Ella, who was still wiping at her eyes.

Ella was silent for a moment. "I don't think anyone wants me back there," she said quietly.

Gadriel rubbed at the side of her face. "Oh, you definitely put your foot in it," she agreed. "But that's not going to go away all on its own." She paused meaningfully. "I can help you sort that out if you want, though. I have thoughts."

Ella looked up at her hopefully. "You think so?" she asked.

"Oh yes," Gadriel said. "I'm about ninety per cent certain I can. You won't *like* it, mind you—but I'm sure it will work."

Ella nodded slowly. "All right," she said. "Just tell me what to do."

Gadriel filled her in over the course of their bus ride back to the school. Predictably, Ella was less than thrilled with the idea— but to her credit, she sucked up her displeasure and walked back into Battenberg Grammar with her shoulders squared.

The disco was in full swing by the time they walked into the school hall—though 'full swing' is a relative term when one is discussing school discos. The swivelling lights highlighted an empty, yawning gap between tables where no one dared to dance. Top 50 pop songs drifted over the room, loud enough to drown out most attempted conversations.

Millie and Beatrix stood out instantly among the awkwardly divided students on either side of the hall. They had settled themselves in the corner near the stage with plastic cups of lemonade, looking somehow even more miserable in their sequin-covered cowboy boots.

Ella swallowed once as she saw them. She straightened again, though, and marched directly for the stage with a determined expression.

Holly stopped in the doorway, biting her lip. "Should we go with her?" she asked worriedly.

"No, definitely not," Gadriel said. She cleared her throat. "If you'll excuse me for a moment, though, I think I'll just… go and make a call." She fell back for the hallway and promptly disappeared, as Holly glanced around in bewilderment.

Gadriel caught up to Ella shortly thereafter, as she reached the two girls at the base of the stage.

Ella's reception was predictably chilly. Beatrix looked away pointedly, while Millie rolled her eyes and stood up. "I'm going to get more lemonade," she muttered.

"Wait," Ella said sharply.

Millie raised her eyebrows incredulously.

Ella hesitated. "I…" She crossed her arms uncomfortably. "I've been awful and I know it," she said. "And I'm really sorry for it. That's not the whole of it, but it's the least you deserve. I know I'll owe you both a proper apology later."[92]

"*And* my mum," Beatrix added flatly.

"And your mum," Ella muttered reluctantly. She sighed heavily. "I'll sort out another apology for *all* of you, as soon as I can. But… I'd rather not end the night by letting you down again." She sneaked a glance up at the other two girls. "We've still got time to play a song or two, if you want. And… I'll wear the hat."[93]

Millie leaned back against the stage, considering her back. "The *whole* costume," she countered. "Boots and hat and everything."

Beatrix looked at Ella expectantly.

Ella cringed. "I… *fine*," she mumbled. "The whole costume."[94]

Millie pursed her lips, digesting the offer. After a few more strained moments, however, she nodded. "All right," she said. "I'm in."

Beatrix smiled hesitantly. "Okay," she said softly. She got to her feet and started clearing off the edge of the stage, stacking up the rubbish that had accumulated there over the course of the disco. As Ella stepped up to help, though, Beatrix turned around and hugged her.

"I want things to be all right," Beatrix said in a small voice. "I don't *like* us being angry at each other."

Ella looked down at Beatrix with surprise. For a second, her eyes filled up with tears again. But she wiped at her face and hugged the other girl back tightly.

---

92   +1 Point of Virtue (Ella Harker): A Heartfelt Apology.

93   +2 Points of Virtue (Ella Harker): Being the Bigger Person.

94   +2 Points of Virtue (Ella Harker): Being the Bigger Person.

"I want that too," Ella whispered. "I'm going to be better from now on. I promise."

Gadriel strolled back for the door with a pleased little bounce in her step.

She returned to Holly's side, fully visible, just as the girls took to the stage.

"Ella's so painfully adorable in that outfit," Holly said in a low voice. "I have to tell you, so I don't tell *her*."

Gadriel grinned. "Get plenty of pictures while she's wearing it," she said. "We may never get another chance."

Holly leaned into Gadriel's shoulder with a tired smile. "I still feel like everything's a mess," she admitted. "But... this is nice, isn't it? Just for now."

Gadriel looped an arm around her waist, drawing her in closer. Holly looked up at her, with her cheeks stained faintly pink in the darkness.

"Just for now," Gadriel said, "everything is... excellent."

She leaned down then, and pressed the very lightest kiss to Holly's lips.

It was just as she had expected—Holly Harker tasted like coffee.

Holly smiled against the kiss. She returned it for only a split second, though, before pulling back. "We're chaperones," she said in a low voice. "I believe there's a rule against public displays of affection."

Gadriel snorted. "I'm a terrible chaperone," she said. "I can't believe anyone let me through the door."

Holly grinned. "You said we were going to be on our best behaviour tonight," she pointed out.

Gadriel sighed. "Oh, all right," she said. "I guess I'm going to have to get used to toeing the line at least a *little* bit, if I'm going to stick around."

Holly tilted her head. "Stick around?" she repeated carefully.

Gadriel nodded seriously. "I've taken on a permanent position," she said. "You'd best get used to seeing plenty of me."

Holly's eyes flashed with pleasure. "I'm sure I'll suffer through it somehow," she said.

Millie walked up to a microphone on the stage then, clearing her throat. "Hullo?" she said. "Uh, yes. We are… Millie and the Marshals. And we're going to be rocking your socks off tonight."

Ella groaned softly, off to her right. But she kept her mouth shut and readjusted her bright red guitar.

Gadriel tugged Holly back against her, wrapping her arms around her waist as they settled in to watch the girls play.

Epilogue

CUMULATIVE SIN METRIC (HOLLY HARKER): -1013
CUMULATIVE SIN METRIC (ELLA HARKER): +22

It was five years later on a Sunday morning when the Chief of Guardian Angels walked into a neat little café near the foot of Montmartre in Paris.

As usual, Barachiel couldn't help but stand out from the crowd, with her striking posture and her white linen suit. She had never been one for *trying* to blend in, of course—she rather believed that putting on a human guise was more than concession enough.

"*Bonjour, madame,*" greeted a waitresses. "*Juste pour vous?*"

"Ah, no table necessary," Barachiel said with a smile. "I'm meeting someone here, thank you." She headed past the waitress towards the back of the dining area, where the person she was searching for had already sat down.

Gadriel looked up as she approached, and her face lit up. "Aha!" she said. "Barachiel! *Bienvenue à Paris!*" As Barachiel came closer, however, Gadriel's pleased expression melted into weary resignation. "Of course. You're a woman. Again."

Barachiel slid into the chair across from Gadriel with a rueful smile. "I'll admit it," she said. "I do it on purpose."

Gadriel threw up her hands. "Of course you're doing it on purpose!" she said. "I never doubted you were doing it on *purpose*. I'm just utterly perplexed as to *why* you do it."

Barachiel leaned back in her chair. "I know it's tacky," she admitted, "but I rather like it when we match. It makes us feel more like siblings. You know—wearing the same thing."

Gadriel groaned and covered her face. "This is exactly why I pretend I don't know you sometimes," she said.

"Oh, Barry! How lovely to see you!" Holly dropped by the table breathlessly, juggling a tray full of drinks. She was wearing a white button-down shirt and a black waistcoat today, with her hair pulled tightly back out of the way. "I didn't even know you were in town," she added, as she deposited a hot chocolate in front of Gadriel. "Are you staying for long?"

Barachiel shook her head. "I'm afraid I'm only here for a while," she said. "There's always plenty more work to be done."

Gadriel stopped Holly before she could go too far, leaning out of her chair and snapping her arm around the other woman's waist. "*Je ne veux pas que tu partes,*" Gadriel complained, "*pas sans un baiser!*"

Holly spun around with a wry smile. She leaned down to drop a brief kiss on Gadriel's lips. "I have to *work*," she reminded the fallen angel fondly. "I can't spend all morning canoodling with you—much as I might want to."

Gadriel sighed. "Oh, all right," she said with a long-suffering sigh. "I want it known that I'll be utterly inconsolable until you come back, though."

Holly shook her head. "I'm sure Barry will keep you company until I'm off shift," she said dryly. She glanced at Barachiel. "While I'm here—can I get you a coffee?"

Barachiel smiled broadly. "I'd like a hot chocolate, actually," she said. "If that's not too much trouble."

Holly beamed at her. "I'll get one out as soon as Gadriel stops detaining me," she assured Barachiel.

Gadriel let go of Holly with a confused blink. She turned her gaze upon Barachiel as Holly took the opportunity to dart away. "A hot chocolate?" she repeated. "And I didn't even tempt you. What is the world coming to, Barachiel?"

Barachiel crossed her arms over her chest, smiling with satisfaction. "You'd be shocked," she said. "Actually—I came here to let you know the good news."

Gadriel narrowed her eyes at Barachiel over her hot chocolate. "I'm *definitely* not interested in the Good News," she warned. "And I'm never quite sure whether your regular 'good news' is actually good."

Barachiel pressed a hand to her chest. "I'm wounded, Gadriel," she said. "And after I went to so much trouble, as well."

Gadriel frowned suspiciously. "Spit it out," she said.

Barachiel leaned her elbows onto the table in front of her, resting her chin on her hands. "I sent off a memo after one of your chocolate tirades, about a hundred years ago," she said. "I just got word back that it reached the right set of wheels and eyes. And—as it turns out—you *were* right. Chocolate *isn't* meant to be a sin."

Gadriel blinked. "What?" she said. "You can't mean—"

"The Rules have been updated!" Barachiel said cheerfully.

"Chocolate is no longer on the list of sins. Not inherently, in any case."

Gadriel stared at Barachiel, utterly thunderstruck.

"Saint Peter is *not* happy with me, by the way," Barachiel said. "He's got to go back through his records and make millions of adjustments now."

"He would have to, wouldn't he?" Gadriel said dimly.

Barachiel chuckled. "It's a good thing you aren't in the temptation business anymore, isn't it?" she said. "All of those hard-won half-points—just magically gone overnight." She glanced idly around the café. "Speaking of your current job… have you got an eye on your *other* mortal charge?"

Gadriel blinked several times, trying to refocus. "I—oh, Ella?" she said. "She's a late sleeper; she'll be by in a bit. Her and Baby Bear in Paris went partying at a club last night. Er... don't tell Holly."

Barachiel smiled. "Your old job suits you, Gadriel," she said softly. "You look… happy."

Gadriel sipped thoughtfully at her hot chocolate. "I *am* happy," she agreed. "It's all right—you can say you told me so. I'll let it pass just this once, given the change in chocolate policy."

Barachiel raised her eyebrows. "I would never say something like that," she assured Gadriel. "…not out loud, in any case."

Gadriel scoffed.

Barachiel's face softened. "I do worry… what you'll do when this particular job is done," she admitted.

Gadriel's eyes went distant. "I haven't the first idea what I'll do when it's over with this time," she said. "I know it'll be difficult. But…" She glanced towards Holly, who'd paused to take orders at another table. "I'm happy for now," she said softly. "And *just* for now… I think this is my little slice of Heaven."

Holly returned with another hot chocolate, setting it down in front of Barachiel. "You should come by for dinner, at least," she said. "I have *so* many biscuits to get rid of, Barry, it's ungodly. I have to practise a new recipe every time I get home from patisserie school."

Barachiel smiled at Gadriel. "I suppose I can make time for biscuits," she said.

Gadriel finished off her hot chocolate, setting the glass back down against the table with a soft rap. "My dear Barachiel," she said, "what else is time *for?*"

Afterword

I first had the idea for *Small Miracles* when I was sitting in a hospital, trying not to think about pending test results. For those who are fortunate enough never to have been in a hospital, it involves an *awful* lot of waiting, and I've always naturally filled such waiting time by making up new stories. This time, I ended up thinking a lot about all of the people who had rushed to support me while I dealt with my emergencies and about how much their presence meant to me. Having supportive friends and family can really make the difference when everything else is unstable—and I was fortunate enough to have *many* of these people at my side.

Obviously, *Small Miracles* draws a bit of inspiration from *Good Omens*—and I have added a sprinkling of hints and homages towards that book throughout the story. But at the end of the day, I wanted *Small Miracles* to be a story about tiny, personal disasters, rather than about giant, world-ending ones.

The test results that day were fine. Someday, they may *not* be fine—but if that day comes, I know that I will have several people sitting next to me until dawn, ready with a joke or a card

273

game to help ease my mind. And when we are all too weary to talk, they will simply sit there with me, letting me know that I am not alone. I'm not certain that there is anything more precious that I could ever ask for.

My husband always helps inordinately with my books, but I owe him a special thanks this time for providing several groan worthy puns. My alpha readers Laura Elizabeth and Julie Golick remained on guard against plot holes for this book, while Sophie Ricard continued her French nitpicking and Tamlin Thomas assisted with the genderfluid characters. Emma and my fantastic agent Christabel McKinley came through with several last-minute Londoner nitpicks when my usual go-to had to cut out, for which I am inordinately grateful. Ridiculous mathematical definitions were provided by Timmeh Chan (did I use them correctly, Tim, or have I now shamed you forever?). Lastly, several brave souls at my agency who shall not be named gamely provided embarrassing stories about their experiences in secondary school. You know who you are, and yes—you are the real MVPs.

About The Author

Olivia Atwater writes whimsical historical fantasy with a hint of satire. She lives in Montreal, Quebec with her fantastic, pro-seinspiring husband and her two cats. When she told her second-grade history teacher that she wanted to work with history someday, she is fairly certain this isn't what either party had in mind. She has been, at various times, a historical reenactor, a professional witch at a metaphysical supply store, a web eveloper, and a vending machine repairperson.

Want more whimsical comedy? I send out writing updates and eat historical facts in the Atwater Scandal Sheets. Subscribers also get early access to chapters from each book, before anyone else!

https://oliviaatwater.com
info@oliviaatwater.com

Also by Olivia Atwater

REGENCY FAERIE TALES
Half a Soul
Ten Thousand Stitches
Longshadow

TALES OF THE IRON ROSE
Echoes of the Imperium (Forthcoming — 2022)

STANDALONE
Small Miracles

NONFICTION
Better Blurb Writing for Authors

Made in United States
North Haven, CT
09 July 2024

54618509R00171